RENEGADES IN TIME

Books in the *After Cilmeri* Series:

Daughter of Time
Footsteps in Time
Winds of Time
Prince of Time
Crossroads in Time
Children of Time
Exiles in Time
Castaways in Time
Ashes of Time
Warden of Time
Guardians of Time
Masters of Time
Outpost in Time
Shades of Time
Champions of Time
Refuge in Time
Unbroken in Time
Outcasts in Time
Hidden in Time
Legacy of Time
Renegades in Time

This Small Corner of Time:
The After Cilmeri Series Companion

THE AFTER CILMERI SERIES

RENEGADES IN TIME

by

SARAH WOODBURY

To Brynne, Carew, Gareth, & Taran
My time travelers

Cast of Characters

David is the King of England, a time traveler, and married to **Lili**, who is also Ieuan's sister; they are parents of Arthur and Alexander.

Anna, along with her brother, David, first comes to Earth Two in *Footsteps in Time*. She is married to **Math**, and they are parents of Cadell, Bran, and Rhiannon.

Meg marries **Llywelyn, King of Wales** in *Daughter of Time*. They are parents of David, Anna, Gwenllian, Padrig, and Elisa.

Bronwen first appears in *Prince of Time* as an archaeology graduate student. She is married to **Ieuan,** who starts out as the captain of David's guard. They are parents of Catrin, Cadwaladr, and Gweneth.

Callum arrives in Earth Two on the heels (literally) of Meg, Llywelyn, and Goronwy in *Children of Time*. In *Exiles in Time*, he meets **Cassie**, another twenty-firster, who was stranded in the Middle Ages by Meg's plane in *Winds of Time*. They return to Avalon in *Castaways in Time* where Cassie joins MI-5. They are parents of Gareth.

Rachel arrives initially with Anna and Meg on the Cardiff Bus in *Ashes of Time*. She is a physician and married to **Darren**, who is a former MI-5 agent. They are parents of Esther.

Abraham is Rachel's father and a physician in David's court. He arrives in Earth Two in *Guardians of Time*.

Michael is David's bodyguard from *Champions of Time* and married to **Livia**, a former MI-5 agent. They arrive in Earth Two in *Refuge in Time* and are parents of Arya.

Christopher is David's cousin. He travels to Earth Two in his car in *Masters of Time*, after which he becomes known as the Hero of Westminster. The rest of his family comes to Earth Two in *Shades of Time*: **Ted, Elisa**, and **Elen**. He is married to **Isabelle**, daughter of **Matthew Norris**, the Master of the Paris Temple.

Huw is a boy when we first meet him in *Footsteps in Time* when David is abducted. He has been a loyal companion ever since.

William de Bohun is heir to the Earldom of Hereford and has been part of David's court since *Crossroads in Time*. He is famous for saying *you've got to be kidding me!* He meets his wife, Daisy, former Princess of England, in *Hidden in Time*.

Robbie in Avalon grows up to be Robert the Bruce, King of Scots. We first meet him in *Exiles in Time* as one of the Bruce men (all named Robert). At the time, Bronwen dubs him *Baby Bruce*.

Thomas Hartley was first encountered by Meg in *Winds of Time* at Hadrian's Wall. David meets him again at Carlisle Castle, and then again in *Masters of Time*, by which point he has become a Templar.

Henri – Templar, spy, and close confidant, Henri rides with David in his journey across France in *Masters of Time*.

Other companions

Aaron – Jewish physician first introduced in *Footsteps in Time*.

Jacob – Liaison with the Paris synagogue (from *Unbroken in Time*)

Boniface – The Pope

Amaury de Montfort – Master of the Templar commandery in Rouen

Philippe – King of France

Louis – Philippe's grandfather (deceased)

John "Primus" - Duke of Brabant, also known as *Johnny*

John "Secundus" – Count of Zeeland and Holland, also known as *Zee*
Guy (Gwijde in Flemish) – Count of Flanders; Johnny and Zee's grandfather
Robert – Guy's eldest son and heir
Ari – Mossad agent
Samantha (Sam) – Bangor Institute member, mechanic
Birdy – Bangor Institute member, historian and linguist

Avalonian Zeelanders
Marie
Jos
Paul
Arne

A Quick Recap of the Previous Book...

The previous book in the *After Cilmeri* series, *Legacy of Time,* opens at a martial tournament at Carew Castle. In the midst of the festivities, David has an allergic reaction to walnuts and travels with Lili to Avalon, where they encounter difficulties, to say the least, though they are also aided by many people along the way.

Ultimately, they are able to journey to Seattle, where David and Lili speak before the United Nations and the world. Chad Treadman's Bangor Institute is instrumental in facilitating their return to Earth Two. At the last moment, however, the helicopter in which they are traveling is hijacked by a rogue group of Zeelanders.

In short (very short!), *Zeeland,* spelled with two *ees,* sits on the west coast of Europe, part of a river delta system. Over time, its inhabitants reclaimed the land from the sea (thus, Zeeland/Sealand), building dykes that ultimately connected what had been separate islands. Politically, it was conquered by Danes around the time they sacked Paris in 845 AD. Zeeland then went back and forth between various foreign powers for centuries, until finally being incorporated into the Netherlands.

Since David was last in Avalon two years ago, knowledge of the changes he and his family and friends have made in Earth Two have been widely disseminated. In *Legacy of Time,* when David and Lili arrive in Avalon, they learn that dozens of rebel and splinter groups throughout the world have increased their activities and unrest because of it. For the Zeelanders, while they know changing

Earth Two's history won't change Avalon's, they want to do for "their" people in Earth Two what David has done for Wales.

Legacy of Time ends with the arrival of the helicopter back at the tournament grounds, right before the final archery contest is set to begin. Cassie kills the lead hijacker with an arrow, another turns out to be a Mossad agent who had infiltrated the hijackers' organization, and the rest of the hijackers are subdued.

David now has to deal with a new collection of Avalonians in Earth Two, many of whom he would definitely have preferred had stayed at home.

Even worse, it isn't only the modern Zeelanders causing trouble …

1

Lili was still recovering from yesterday. First had come the massive accident (that wasn't an accident) when a giant truck had smashed into their RV; she and Dafydd had then fled through the streets of Seattle; and finally, they'd both spoken at the arena in front of what Chad assured her was the entire world. It was all a bit much to process. Dafydd was doing a good job pretending he wasn't feeling it, but they'd been married long enough, and been through enough, for her to know he was hanging on by a thread too.

For that reason, she had left the arrangements for how they were going to travel from Avalon to Earth Two to Dafydd and Chad. Leaving in a helicopter seemed as reasonable a prospect as any, especially because Dafydd assured her it could be refueled in Earth Two. They were also carrying what her husband described as *a ton of cargo*.

All of a sudden, however, Lili wasn't so sure they shouldn't have taken matters into their own hands and simply jumped off the roof of their hotel. She had been looking out the window of the helicopter, waiting patiently, even though her heart wouldn't stop thumping uncontrollably at what was to come, when she saw a giant truck drive into the airport, right through the metal fence.

As she tugged on Dafydd's sleeve, trying to come up with something more coherent to say than *was that supposed to happen?* a second truck followed after the first, bumping right over the fence which was now lying flat on the ground. Then the airport's refueling truck pulled to a stop between the helicopter and the downed fence, blocking Lili's view. She leaned back in her seat, confused and deciding she had obviously misunderstood what was supposed to happen. It wouldn't be the first time since her arrival in Avalon.

Dafydd, meanwhile, had remained focused on the conversation in his headset, which Lili could hear too. Marie, the FBI helicopter pilot, had been explaining why they hadn't taken off yet.

"Do you hear that?" Dafydd leaned forward, frowning and intent.

"That isn't the blades." This was from Birdy. She and Samantha, the co-pilot, were coming with them as representatives of Chad's Bangor Institute. "Let's go! What are we waiting for?"

"This is an aircraft like any other." Marie's voice implied impatience. "I can't just take off without authorization."

Even as she spoke, Chad began shouting at them through their headsets, "Go! Go! Go!"

And then came a noise even Lili recognized as gunfire. The refueling truck disappeared in a whoosh of flames, and the two helicopters that were supposed to be accompanying them to Mount Rainier, both of which had been hovering above the ground, crashed back to earth.

"Give me a minute!" Marie kept pressing buttons and speaking urgently into her microphone, words Lili wasn't receiving.

Because Lili had returned to watching out the window, she saw the men in black coming towards them before they reached the helicopter and slid open the door. She had a brief hope these were Chad's people, since they were dressed very similarly to his, but then the first man to enter pointed his gun at Marie's head and ordered her to take off.

A second said to Dafydd, in a heavy accent Lili couldn't place, "At long last, you will do as you are told."

Lili had no idea what that meant. She was endeavoring to breathe without choking, less because she was so afraid of these men (which she was) than because she didn't want to distract Dafydd from negotiating. There was a time for her to speak, as she had done in the arena last night, and there was a time to be silent.

Marie finally put the helicopter in the air, following the same flight path Dafydd and Chad had worked out. The windows on the sides and front were large, so Lili could see the city laid out beneath them and the mountain up ahead.

"Are you okay?" Chad spoke softly into their ears.

Dafydd was the one to reply. "For now. Are you?"

Rather than answering the question, Chad said, "They came in force in two armored personnel carriers, right through the airport fence. I'm sorry; I let you down."

That was what Lili had seen. In the past, there had been heavy criticism of Dafydd because his traveling might rend the universe asunder. These men could have been at the airport to stop him from going to Earth Two by disabling the helicopter. If Lili had known more about the way things were supposed to have gone, maybe she could have found the words to give a warning. Not that it may have made any difference, since Marie hadn't been able to lift off soon enough anyway.

"You didn't," Dafydd said. "We'll be okay."

The leader of the hijackers finally noticed him talking and shoved his gun towards Dafydd's chest. "Who is that? What are you saying?"

"Why are you doing this?" Dafydd looked up at him, as calm as could be. Lili's hand was in his, so she could feel the tenseness in his grip, but he didn't let his fear show. He had been in dangerous situations before, though perhaps none more so than in this moment.

"You know why."

"I genuinely don't."

"You have abandoned our people to their fate."

"I don't know who your people are."

"We are Zeelanders."

Lili gaped at him, but Dafydd managed to say, "I'm the King of England, not the Duke of Flanders."

The man put his face right into Dafydd's. "You abandoned us! Why do your people get to be free, and ours don't?" He spoke like John Primus and John Secundus might have, as if the war against France had just happened instead of occurring seven hundred and twenty-eight years ago.

"If the people of Zeeland petitioned for help, I would always listen. But they did not."

"The men of Zeeland do not beg!"

"Coming up on the mountain now, sir," Marie said.

All five hijackers turned to look out the front window, and Dafydd took their moment of inattention to whisper to Lili. "Don't look at the mountain, *cariad*. Look at me."

"I want to see it."

This time, when the darkness came, that held breath of nothingness, Dafydd wrapped his arms around her. She barely remembered traveling the other way, when they'd gone *to* Avalon, since she'd been so terrified about Dafydd dying and had her arms wrapped around *him*. That journey had felt quicker and hadn't sucked the air from her lungs as this one did. The lights within the helicopter dimmed and, more tellingly, they could no longer hear Chad's voice.

They burst out of the darkness into a sunny afternoon in Wales, soaring over Carew Castle and the tournament grounds.

They were home!

Immediately, Dafydd brought her back to the urgency of the moment. "If they wanted to kill us, they would have done it already."

He meant to be reassuring, she knew, but sometimes her husband could be a little too practical.

Her own jaw felt tight in reply. "That doesn't mean they can't murder half the people in the stands if they oppose them."

"Their guns aren't the advantage they think they are."

The lead hijacker ordered Marie towards the grassy space in front of the archery targets, saying, "Many people are here. Good. You may land us now. They must see our power and that we have their king."

"You don't need your guns," Dafydd said softly. "Please put them away."

The lead hijacker looked at him with disdain. "Do you think me a fool?"

"If you come out with guns, my people will shoot you."

The man sneered his reply. "Arrows and swords are no match for our weapons."

"They have spears too. And, eventually, you are going to run out of bullets."

"We have enough for this."

The helicopter landed in the grass, and the leader motioned for the hijacker nearest the door to open it. Once he'd done so, that man pressed in close to Dafydd and Lili to allow the others to exit the helicopter in front of him.

Hardly three breaths later, the lead hijacker was killed by an arrow to the throat. A barrage of arrows followed. All of a sudden, the other hijackers were down too, their armor not protecting them the way they expected, and their weapons useless against so many. Dafydd's people converged on them from every direction.

Seeing it, the last hijacker pointed his gun at the back of Marie's head. "You too."

"Me?" Marie's voice went high. "I don't know what—"

The hijacker cut her off with a bark. "You're one of them, a Zeelander. I have no qualms about shooting a woman, so cooperate, or we're going to be cleaning your brains off the controls."

Marie's hands flew into the air. The co-pilot, Samantha, had her hands up too, and her eyes were wide. Birdy sat like a statue in her seat. Lili herself was barely breathing.

To Dafydd, the man said, "I have been embedded with the Zeelanders for nearly two years, ever since we first got wind of their plan to abduct you and force you to bring them here. We couldn't allow it, of course, not with what you have done for our people." Then he pulled out one of the confiscated guns he'd secreted in his gear and handed it hilt-first to Birdy. Indicating Marie with the barrel of his own gun, he said, "Shoot her if she moves. She may look pretty, but she's as bad as the rest of them."

The hijacker-turned-ally then removed his helmet, revealing a face as intent as Lili had ever seen in her life. "My apologies for any inconvenience this operation has caused you or your wife." He put a hand to his chest. "If I may introduce myself, I am Ari Cohen, Mossad."

Just like that, the threat was over. Within a few minutes, Lili was able to hold her sons. She cried as she hugged Bronwen, who'd looked after them like they were her own.

And then, at long last, in the quiet of their bedchamber, with their children asleep, she and Dafydd were finally able to hold each other properly.

"So that was Avalon, *cariad*." Dafydd rested his forehead against hers. "Fun, huh?"

He'd found exactly the right thing to say, as he so often did. Instead of the tears of earlier, at last Lili was able to laugh.

2

Carew Castle

22 September 1297

David

They'd put the four remaining hijackers in a tent on the north side of the River Carew, deliberately some distance from the castle and tournament grounds, with guards to prevent their escape. Two of them were wounded, one quite badly with an arrow to his upper thigh very close to his femoral artery. He wasn't going anywhere for a while. The helicopter was in the next field over, also guarded, though mostly to keep gawkers away.

David himself was still vibrating from the events of the day. He kept hearing Chad's *Go! Go! Go!* in his head. Lili had sought solace in tears, and then laughter. If only he could have done the same. He still might. But not yet.

"I'm going to let Ari take the lead." Callum spoke in an undertone to David. They were walking towards the prison tent, Ari and Livia just ahead. The beautiful day had turned into a cloud-covered night, and a few drops of rain had just fallen on their heads. "He knows their strengths and weaknesses. They won't be able to lie to him as easily as to me."

Not wanting Ari to overhear, David slowed his pace. "Are you sure? He's *Mossad!* You've told me stories—" He broke off, not quite sure how to continue the thought.

Over the course of fifteen years traveling back and forth between Avalon and Earth Two, David had accumulated a number of former spies as companions. Callum, Cassie, Darren, Livia, and Mark had all been MI-5 agents. He'd interacted with their bosses enough to feel at times he *knew* MI-5. He might even occasionally trust them. He'd never had a good run-in with the CIA, and, among the clandestine agencies, Mossad was known to be the most ruthless.

"He was pleased to be asked," Callum said.

David glanced ahead. Without his riot gear, Ari proved to be tall and slender, with dark eyes and dark curly hair cut close to his head. "If I were he, I would be too. I'm just not sure what to do with him, anymore than I know what to do with our prisoners. I shouldn't have suggested there was any chance they could have a role in forging an independent Zeeland. It was a mistake."

"You don't make very many of them, and, as mistakes go, it was pretty minor," Callum said. "Few heard you say it. The fight was already over. If anything, it was clever of you to imply there was still some hope of getting what they want. They might be more likely to talk if they think we could become their ally."

"It's true I'd love to put them to use rather than keeping them imprisoned. It feels like a waste, especially when self-determination for Zeeland is actually a laudable goal. At the same time, sic'ing the four of them on Europe is probably the worst idea possible."

With that, they arrived at the guard post outside the tent. Livia and Ari had paused to wait for them, and David put out a hand to Ari, not yet ready to set him loose. Though Ari claimed to be on his side, David still wasn't quite sure what that meant to him. "What more do we need to know about them before we begin? You were with them for two years. There must be something else you can tell us."

Ari spread his hands wide. "As I've said, they are true believers." Suddenly, his accent was identical to David's.

In the pause that followed, David barked a laugh. "So, you're American now?"

Ari wasn't the least bit apologetic. "I was born in the United States. Over the years, I split my time between there and Israel. My accent is adaptable, let's just say. I'm more comfortable speaking to you this way."

"Ooo-kay," David dragged out the word. Of all the things he needed to be concerned about in this moment, Ari's accent was at the bottom of the list. "Let's start with who they are."

"Marie, the pilot, you know. Otherwise, we have Jos, Paul, and Arne. Arne is the one with the most serious wound."

"Why did Mossad choose you for this mission?" Livia said.

Ari wet his lips, looking at each of them in turn.

Having spent so much time with spies, David understood his hesitancy. But while Ari's longstanding impulse might be to say as little as possible, David had no patience with it tonight. "We need to know what you know."

"Mossad monitors terrorist organizations around the world; I was on the European desk, with a particular focus on the Netherlands. I flagged the ZR's crusade early on, as soon as we began noting elevated chatter from them. But since we hadn't caught the expected conversations directed against Israel, at first the directive was to swipe left, so to speak."

"ZR?" David asked.

"The Zeelandic Revolution. It's what they call themselves."

ZR was almost as good a nickname as what Bronwen had dubbed them over dinner: *the AZs,* for *Avalonian Zeelanders.* By the time they'd adjourned for the night, everyone was using it, even John Primus and John Secundus.

At David's nod, Ari continued. "But then we realized what their code was about, namely you and Earth Two. Even at that early stage, a plot against you, sire, could not be ignored. I was sent to infiltrate their ranks."

"What's their funding?" Callum said.

"I never discovered it." For the first time, Ari looked uncertain, as if he couldn't believe he'd poured forth like that.

David reminded himself it could be an act. He was infiltrating David's court now instead of the ZR. "Go on."

Ari complied, even if against his better judgment. "Having always been good with accents, I set about working my way up their ranks. When I started, my Dutch, Flemish, and French were at native level. I added Zeelandic immediately. The ZR were desperate for expertise, and I had a rock-solid backstory. They were few in number to begin with, but they ramped up quickly. Mossad wanted their funder almost more than it wanted to stop them. I failed in that mission too. This is … all on me."

Livia gave a little tsk. "Surely not entirely."

Ari's eyes were back on David's. "A week ago, I was sitting in a café in Bruges, thinking it still might be possible to undermine the ZR in some real way. Then you and Lili arrived in Oregon, and the entire organization swung into action for real. By that time, I was fully embedded, with no ability to contact anyone on the outside. I had to choose between blowing my cover on the chance of stopping them, and likely being killed in the process, or sticking with them and hoping I could find a way to make them fail. In the end, all I could do was mitigate the damage. They were going to Earth Two, so I was going with them."

"What was their plan once they got here?" Livia asked. "They couldn't have thought they could free Zeeland simply by wishing it!"

"I was never told that part."

"Did they think their modern weapons were all they needed?" David said.

"You have to remember, what training they've had has been more of the insurgent or revolutionary kind rather than with a real military. Franc was the leader, but he's dead. Jos acts like he is a superb marksman, but in comparison he's a crap shot and a worse thinker. None of that would matter if he had his weapon trained on your wife and sons, sire. Regardless, they miscalculated."

"Okay," David said, accepting that Ari had told them what he could for now. "Let's see what they have to say for themselves."

The tent was twenty feet on a side, with a high enough ceiling to allow even the tallest of men to stand to his full height. It was certainly spacious enough to house the four surviving AZs and their guards, along with a few medical supplies.

Livia pulled up a chair next to Marie and Jos, who each sat upright on their separate beds, wrists chained to the posts and feet tied at the ankles. It had to be uncomfortable, but so would have been the other option: a stone cell in one of the castle tower basements, accessed by a trapdoor.

For his part, David leaned as casually as he could against a tent pole, while Callum stayed near the door, his arms folded across his chest.

Ari didn't begin with Marie. He'd said she was as tough as nails and wouldn't talk. He went instead to Arne, at whom David had been looking when he'd suggested they might find a use for the AZs.

"You're a traitor." Arne spoke before Ari could, indicating Ari might have been right in his choice to start with him.

"I'm Mossad, which means I am most certainly not a traitor." He gestured towards David. "They want to know why you hijacked the helicopter."

"They know why."

"They want to hear it again."

Arne sneered, but didn't answer.

Paul was the other injured man, wounded in his upper arm, and he spoke from the next bed. "Just tell them Arne. This is foolish stubbornness." And then, when Arne still didn't speak, he added, "We are here on behalf of the people of Zeeland."

"We understand that," Ari said. "What does that mean to you?"

"We're going to free them from their oppressors."

"Which are who? Right now Zeeland is ruled by the Count of Zeeland. His name's John and he's thirteen years old. And here, by the way."

Jos waved a hand. "He is nothing. France is the problem. Their defeat of Flanders was the beginning of the end for Zeeland."

That's what David had assumed, and it was good to have it confirmed. He had first mentioned the French to Arne when he'd been on the ground at the archery grounds. Franc himself had never specifically named his primary enemy. But then, from the start he'd assumed David knew what he was talking about.

"Again, how do you accomplish that practically?" Ari said. "There's four of you. What could you do against the entire French army?"

"We thought we had six." Jos spoke from his bed, unforgiving of Ari's betrayal and Franc's death.

"We didn't have to destroy the army." Arne appeared to have had enough with tip-toeing around the main issue. "All we have to do is kill one man, Philippe, the King of France."

David felt like heaving a great sigh. Given King Philippe's expansionist policies, he could see why the AZs had singled him out as their target. If they could stop him now, maybe the domino effect of conquest and dependence over the next several hundred years wouldn't happen. The entire history of Europe hinged on Philippe's actions. He was the big bad of this era.

"And how are you going to do that?" When neither Arne nor Paul answered, Ari prodded them a bit more. "Help yourself out here. Give me something."

But no amount of querying on Ari's part would get any of them to elaborate. Finally, he backed away and came over to where David was standing. "Sorry. They don't like me anymore."

It had to be nearly midnight by now, and David wasn't the only one who was exhausted. The shadows under Livia's eyes had merely grown larger as the evening had progressed. He didn't feel done yet, however. Instead of calling it a night, he pushed off from the pole and came closer to Paul's bed. "Let's say everything happened the way you hoped. You arrive in Earth Two. I'm your captive. What's next?"

The look on Paul's face indicated an internal struggle. He wanted to speak. David waited, hoping that instinct would win out. When none of Paul's companions told him to keep his mouth shut, he eventually opened it. "You would have joined us. You half-promised us aid already, even after we took over your helicopter!"

"That was after my people killed your leader and freed me. If all had gone well for you, I'd still be your captive."

"As would your wife." Arne spoke again, seemingly unable to restrain himself. "Either you joined us on your own accord, or you joined us because you wanted your family to live."

David had to work very hard to keep his expression bland. "And if I still refused?"

"You wouldn't have." This was from Marie, speaking for the first time and no longer maintaining even a thin guise of innocence. "Every one of your people would do as we demanded. Their sympathies—and yours—lie with Zeeland anyway. That's been obvious to everyone. Look how you've behaved since we got here. We took you captive, and still you suggested—what was the phrasing?—you could *find a use* for us? Nobody would have been surprised if you decided to ally with Count Guy of Flanders. We already know that King Edward did in Avalon."

She said Guy's name the Flemish way, which was *Gwijde*.

"He didn't win," David said.

"He gave up!" Paul shifted on his bed in his agitation. He, of all of them, still had hope that David could be convinced. "With you beside us, we would win. We can still win!"

Or not, David felt like saying, in mimicry of Ari, back in the field.

He stepped away, feeling more confident in his decision to deny the AZs their freedom. As Ari had said, they'd miscalculated. While David would prefer a free Zeeland and to curb Philippe's territorial ambitions, he could never condone the murder of a head of state.

The AZs weren't here to spark a revolution by providing the people with tools to throw off the yoke of oppression, as David had always worked to do. They intended to literally cut off the head of their enemy and hope the end result was the one they wanted.

3

23 September 1297

Johnny

(John Primus, Duke of Brabant)

Since midnight, Johnny's heart had been pounding out of his chest, starting from the moment he and Zee had made the decision to release the Avalonian prisoners, and continuing up to this very hour, the first murky light of dawn. *Zee* was the affectionate name for Johnny's cousin, to distinguish him from Johnny himself, since their given names were both John. *Zee* came from the fact that, even at thirteen years old, he was the Count of Zeeland.

It was also raining hard, the wind gusting so forcefully at times it was like it was raining upwards. Johnny had abandoned the idea of keeping a hood on his head, which meant he kept having to wipe rainwater from his eyes.

He also kept telling himself to settle down, that nothing good would come from having hands so sweaty that if he tried to hold his sword he would likely drop it. The rain was bad enough. He needed the sword. Or would in a moment.

"The new guards are on their way." Hans, Johnny's captain, who'd served Johnny's father before his death, crouched beside him behind the wall that demarcated this particular field. The prison tent was fifty yards away. They'd counted a total of eight guards: two in the field by the helicopter, two inside with the prisoners, and four set around the perimeter of the tent. By this point in their shift, those out in the elements were sleepy, hungry, and very, very wet. "We'll let them get settled, and then we'll go in."

"Where's the king?" Johnny asked, knowing that David had been among those interrogating the prisoners until midnight.

"He's awake again, but meeting with his family in a tent in the festival grounds. That puts him, Ieuan, and Math out of it. With the rain coming down this hard, they won't notice a thing."

It had been on Hans' advice that they had waited until dawn to free the prisoners instead of moving while it was still full dark. They had to see, and they couldn't risk torches. It was better not to rush. And this way, they could take advantage of the miserable state of the guards, using their lack of attention as a cover to move into place and make sure everything was set before they began.

Once the interrogators had retired for the night, Johnny had ordered his people to begin slipping out of their encampment. They were to leave behind all but the most necessary of their possessions and head to England as quickly as possible. With the tents intact, once dawn came, it would look to the casual observer as if all was quiet because everyone was still asleep. For the rest, between him and Zee, they had twenty soldiers in their company. Like Hans, these men were seasoned. Johnny and Zee had inherited them from their fathers along with their titles.

Voices came down the path from the castle. Before their replacements even came into view, the guards around the tent left their posts and the two inside the tent came out. As Hans had presumed, they were looking forward to their beds.

Two of the newly arrived guards, who appeared still to be buckling on their gear, disappeared inside the tent. Two more set out towards the helicopter, in the opposite direction from where Johnny crouched with his men. Zee's force was hidden in that direction, which meant Johnny had a count of ten, maybe less, before engagement.

During Johnny's last few breaths of preparation, the skies opened up even more, like the heavens were dumping buckets instead of raindrops on the earth. The new guards hunched their shoulders in their cloaks, hoods pulled down low over their eyes. It kept their faces dryer, but it also limited their field of vision.

That was a signal to move if there ever was one. Johnny stood up. Then, all around the perimeter of the field, his men began moving purposefully towards their prey. In the time it took for the guards to push back their hoods, wipe the rain from their eyes, register what they were seeing, and finally reach for their weapons, Johnny's men were upon them. Twenty-two to six (not including the men inside the tent) meant each guard faced at least three men and some four. About half were tackled to the ground before they realized what had hit them. Those who fought were soon convinced of the wisdom of surrender.

None were killed, as tempting as that might be to ensure continued silence and lack of resistance. Johnny had given strict orders. They were freeing the prisoners, not starting a war with England.

He and Zee had come to Carew Castle with high hopes—too high, in truth. While David had made it clear from the start that he sympathized with their cause, he was also not willing to send men across the English Channel on Flanders' behalf, much less lead them himself. Their decisive defeat by the French at Bruges showed him how fruitless their quest for freedom was. And really, could Johnny blame him?

Flanders was an important trading partner but, in recent years, England had started processing more of its own wool. They didn't need the workshops of Europe quite as much as they once had. David certainly didn't want to lose men and money in a war he didn't think he could win.

But without England, Flanders couldn't hope to get the best of France. They needed England's men, its expertise, and its weaponry. At the time, Johnny had been thinking in terms of the Welsh archers David could employ on Flanders' behalf.

He was thinking much bigger now.

The rain wasn't enough to completely mask all the activity, and one of the guards posted within the tent poked out his head to check what was happening in the field. He saw Johnny first and recognized him. "My lord—"

At which point Hans yanked him out of the doorway and put a knife to his throat.

"Call your companion to come out here," Johnny said in French, assuming a guard from Carew Castle would understand the language.

Johnny could see in the man's eyes that he didn't want to comply, but since all around him his friends were being gagged and tied—not killed—after a pause he did as he was bid. "Ralph." He projected his voice back into the tent. "I need your help with something."

Ralph was there almost immediately. "Help with what—"

Faced with a companion with a knife to his throat, Ralph had no choice but to submit too. Soon all the guards had their hands tied behind their backs and gags in their mouths.

Johnny ducked inside the tent to find the four Avalonian Zeelanders, or AZs as Bronwen had dubbed them, staring at him.

"I am Duke John of Brabant. My cousin, the Count of Zeeland, and I thought it was high time we were properly introduced."

4

23 September 1297

Samantha

(Sam)

A half-hour earlier ...

"**I**'m scared."

The moment Sam said those words out loud to the ceiling of her canvas tent, the view of which wasn't any more edifying now than it had been when she'd woken twenty minutes earlier, she felt better. She'd been raised to face hard truths and not shirk from what was right in front of her. She could hear her grandmother, even now, saying: "I'm sorry you're having a hard time, but this was your choice, so you'd be better off just getting on with it."

But what was *it,* exactly, in this instance?

Since it was still dark out, Sam had given herself thirty minutes to lie here, her brain and heart going a hundred miles an hour as they had for much of the night. They'd put Sam in her own tent, without even Birdy to share with her. Initially, Sam had seen the gesture as one of profound trust. She had come to Earth Two in good faith, and even with all that had happened at the airfield and then the tournament grounds, they weren't lumping her in with the AZs.

But then she remembered she had nowhere to go. *Back to Avalon?* Good luck with that.

Sam had spent a restless night repeatedly reliving their arrival the previous day, entirely unable to put aside the machine guns, the chaos, and the overall hijacking. To even compare it to losing the Iowa State softball final was laughable, except that she'd lain awake all night reliving that loss too, play-by-play. She was worried for her parents as well, particularly after that last video call she'd made to tell them she was going. They'd been supportive of her dreams, as they always had been, but she couldn't mistake the fear for her in their eyes.

Not that she could blame them. Or had, even then. They would have been watching Sam's departure in the helicopter, as all the world had done. They would know how dangerous it had turned out to be. She had told them she'd be fine. At the time, she hadn't known how profoundly she was lying.

As the youngest of four siblings, each of whom had established themselves in a professional career years before Sam had been old enough to drive, she had learned to be prepared for whatever life might throw her way. Because having one's teacher constantly rave about a brother's or sister's vast accomplishments was generally not a confidence-builder in a caboose baby, as Sam had been, she'd spent most of her life side-stepping their achievements, always doing things a bit differently and refusing to compete, since she couldn't really compete at all.

Her tangential thinking had paid off when Chad Treadman had made her one of his first hires at the Bangor Institute. She'd applied for a job as a technician, with her only degree from the community college closest to her family's farm. Even at twenty-two years old, as she'd been at the time, she'd had years of experience fixing everything from tractors to airplanes to computers, which was exactly what he'd wanted. The application process had even included a session building Legos.

In those first weeks, Chad had been involved with every hire, and he'd told her after he'd offered her the job that King David himself had left school at fourteen. He could see she was adept at thinking outside the box—and he needed more of that. From the start, he'd got her learning Welsh and French, both of which she'd dabbled in over the years, since she'd been an admirer of David since that interview where he'd been shot at and then time traveled in front of the eyes of the world. She'd already been a pilot, the one achievement the bright lights of her family couldn't diminish.

All in all, Sam had thought she was ready.

Telling herself in her grandmother's voice that time was a-wasting, she sat up on her cot and took in her surroundings. It had started raining again about an hour ago, the wind howling around the tent, a complement to her tortured thoughts.

She forced herself not to replay the hijacking for the fiftieth time. Or the five hundredth. It did no good; nobody could change the past.

Except, of course, when they could.

She was pushing to her feet, knowing her thirty minutes of dithering were up, when she heard the sound of the helicopter overhead.

In that split-second of realization, she shook off her fear and uncertainty. She had no time to be afraid or indecisive. Someone was flying that helicopter. If it wasn't Sam, it had to be Marie.

5

23 September 1297

David

Confused by the source of the sound he was hearing, David looked up at the ceiling of Anna and Math's pavilion, where they'd gathered this morning for a private reunion. "What—"

Sam entered through the flap that passed for a door. "They're gone! The AZs, I mean. That's the helicopter you're hearing."

Less than forty-eight hours ago—and seven hundred and twenty-eight years ago—David and Lili had stood with Chad Treadman in a massive arena in Seattle, and spoken to the world of a vision for Avalon, one with hope for the future. Not five minutes ago, David had accepted the mantle of King Arthur for the first time. It was quite a comedown to find himself throwing his cloak around his shoulders and heading into the wind and rain with Math and Ieuan, following after Sam to a new disaster. He was teetering on the edge of the laughter he couldn't find earlier at the way the universe constantly conspired to throw a wrench into his works.

Outside the tent, it was light enough to see without torches. David had gone hardly a dozen yards when Christopher appeared beside him. He and Isabelle had been sleeping in the encampment rather than at the castle. David's sons were safe there, along with Bronwen and Ieuan's three children. Like Math and Anna, the newlyweds had preferred to have their own pavilion rather than more cramped quarters at the castle.

Half the point of putting the AZs and the helicopter on the north side of the River Carew had been to separate them from the children. The other half had been to minimize the traffic near the helicopter. Long before this fraught moment, he'd worried about Avalonian technology contaminating everything it touched.

David himself had spent a restless, and far-too-short, night reliving the hijacking. Yesterday evening, his friends and family had been jubilant at his and Lili's return. But all David could still see was the gun of the dead Zeelander leader, Franc, being shoved into Lili's face over and over again. It was one thing to have someone shoot at David. He would time travel. But if one of the hijackers had shot Lili, she would have died, and there would have been nothing he could have done to stop it.

Once across the river, they didn't have to look hard to realize the helicopter was missing. Staring at the empty field did no good, so next they fetched up at the prison tent. Instead of the AZs, two of the cots were occupied by men in the livery of Carew Castle. The remaining six men were bound together, backs to the various poles that supported the tent. Sam went to one of the unconscious men. "He's alive. Breathing, anyway."

The hijackers, Arne and Paul, had been injured, punctured by the barrage of arrows that had greeted their arrival. David had assumed at least Arne would not be up and walking about any time soon, but all that was left of him were blood-stained rags in a heap on the ground next to one of the cots.

Math and David began ungagging the rest. The first man David released took a great, shuddering breath and looked up into his face. "My lord! We tried! There were so many of them. There was nothing we could do."

"Who was it—" Just as Ieuan asked the question, the door flap opened to reveal a whole bevy of twenty-firsters, including Livia, Callum, and Ari, the Mossad spy.

Robbie and Huw arrived on their heels. "The Johns are gone," Robbie said. "We took a moment to talk to those who pitched their tents closest to them. Nobody saw anything untoward in the night. Nobody heard anything either."

David looked down at the guard, who was among those struggling to sit up. "Was this the work of the Duke of Brabant?"

The man looked stricken. "Him and the other one, the one from Zeeland."

"The storm kept everyone inside." David allowed himself a single mocking laugh. "Including me. I assumed everything was fine. I was going to wander over here after breakfast."

"We stood together in this spot hardly six hours ago," Callum said. "This is not your fault."

"Then whose?" David said.

"Mine." Christopher's tone couldn't have been more apologetic. "It isn't like I went into detail, which I kind of didn't know anyway. It wasn't like I told them we were from the future! But I probably said something along the lines of *the AZs want to free Zeeland from the French*. I can see now it was like throwing oil on a fire."

"It never occurred to me that the Johns would betray us like this either," David said. "It isn't as if we were keeping the AZs a secret, even if that was even possible, which it wasn't. Bronwen started calling them the AZs at dinner. Two hours later, their nickname was all over the encampment."

"None of which makes their disappearance your fault," Callum said, matter-of-factly. "Arne was so wounded he was unable to walk on his own. Even so, we took precautions. We set eight guards. We were prepared for everything except being betrayed by our own allies."

"What about Birdy?" Sam said. "She would be the last of us unaccounted for."

"She spent the night throwing up," Livia said. "She's in the medical pavilion."

"Or is she?" Christopher said darkly.

"We will check." David motioned that the group of them should leave the prison tent again. The guards were helping each other now, and one had been well enough to run for a physician.

None of the twenty-firsters with David at the moment were doctors. Since David knew what had happened, at least in general, he didn't think there was much more to learn inside the tent, and he and his companions had plans to discuss.

Once outside, they gathered together a few yards away under a tree, beyond prying eyes and somewhat protected from the weather.

The wind was still blowing wildly, a match to David's mood. "The Johns are gone. The AZs are gone. Our helicopter is gone. We need to go after them. Let's talk about how we do that."

Callum was reliably ready with the kinds of answers David needed. "It's a little less than four hundred miles to Zeeland from here as a helicopter flies."

"The helicopter has a range of roughly that distance, provided it is completely fueled." Sam followed up with the next logical thought. "We left Seattle with a full tank of hydrogen. We used fifty miles of fuel to reach Mount Rainier. We refueled as best we could yesterday afternoon, but it takes approximately six hours of daylight to generate a hundred miles of range."

"Does how many people the helicopter carries affect that range?" David asked.

"Of course." Sam made a qualifying motion with her head. "The irony is that we could have packed more supplies into the cargo hold, but Chad was worried about exceeding the weight limitations of the helicopter. In the end, it carried the five extra men with weapons just fine."

"We had sun yesterday," Christopher said. "They aren't carrying five extra people now. Three hours might get close to topping it up. Maybe they could make it all the way to Flanders."

Sam waggled her head to imply uncertainty. "If I were Marie, I would want to refuel before crossing the English Channel."

David clasped his hands together before his lips, thinking and speaking at the same time. "It's been half an hour already. They might no longer even be in Wales. We have to assume they are going to reach Flanders by the end of today. As we learned last night, their goals are—"

"—to free Zeeland and to assassinate Philippe," Ari said immediately.

David ignored the way he'd just been interrupted. "How realistic is it to think they can succeed? As Livia pointed out last night, you don't win wars simply by showing up and wishing it."

Ari made a rueful face. "I don't know the Johns, as you call them, but I do know the AZs. They care nothing for their own lives. Only the mission. They are more ignorant than they should be about anybody's grievances but their own."

"And they have weapons," Callum said, "assuming they know about the stash in the floor."

Although the Avalonian weapons brought to Earth Two over the years had been put to substantial use, and at times had provided David's army with a significant advantage, David still saw two main problems with having them. First, they could never import enough weaponry to be sustainable long-term; and second, the danger of having the weapons fall into the wrong hands might be worse than not having them at all. As they could be about to find out.

Thus, the only *materiel* David had asked for this time from Chad were restocks of ammunition for weapons they already possessed, and a few components to aid in their repair and maintenance.

Except for the arsenal hidden behind a trap door.

Chad had told David about it when they'd refit the helicopter for their journey to Earth Two. David hadn't asked Chad to empty it. At the time, it was known only to a few. That was also why David had left it in the helicopter when they'd unloaded everything else.

"Marie has to know about it. I mean, I do, and I'm not with the FBI." Sam let out a little hiss. "Three Glocks, loaded, along with three extra magazines of fifteen rounds each. One MP5 sub-machine gun with four extra magazines of thirty rounds each; and three disposable shoulder rocket launchers: two AT4s and one called a SMAW."

"Three hundred rounds plus three rockets." David did the math in his head.

"Okay." Livia squared her shoulders. "I know that sounds bad at first blush, but it does mean their ammunition is limited, and what they can do with it is limited."

Ari spoke next. "I remind you again, these people are not particularly sophisticated. They got lucky at the airfield and again with the Johns. It can't continue."

"For them to be so focused might actually be good for us," Callum said.

"How can it be *good?*" Though having arrived with Robbie, Huw had remained silent up until now. Truly, to David's eyes, he seemed more mature with each passing day, and less like the boy David had encountered all those years ago. Of the four young men who formed an undaunted team, Huw was the eldest at twenty-four, followed by Robbie, at twenty-three; Christopher was a year younger, having turned twenty-two in June; and then came William de Bohun, who was just a few months younger.

"It means they're not going to hide or sit around somewhere," Callum said.

Livia nodded. "If they hunkered down and waited for an opportunity, we would never find them. But, as it is—"

"They are going to use it," Ari said. "I guarantee it. And, in so doing, they will overplay their hand."

"Our first priority, then, is to be there when that happens." David felt his chin go up. He had made many mistakes in his life, but this week's felt like the worst. The only recourse was to acknowledge them and move on. "Last night, I knew we had to come up with something better than what the AZs' planned for Flanders and France. I thought we had more time to consider what to do. I certainly hoped to be acting instead of reacting. Now, there's no help for it. The cards have been dealt. They have their hand, and we have ours. Our job now, in whatever time we have until we find them, is to stack the rest of the deck in our favor."

6

23 September 1297

Christopher

Christopher was left mumbling under his breath. "I *liked* them."

"They're young," Callum said, overhearing and understanding he was talking about the Johns. They were walking back to the castle, which would take them across the river and through the remains of the tournament grounds. "Boys can be reckless."

"They are noblemen. And knights." Robbie spoke as a nobleman himself and thus personally offended by their dishonesty.

"First off, we need someone in Flanders at the court of Count Guy." David tipped his head towards Huw. "Will you go as my ambassador?"

"Of course, my lord."

Then David looked at Robbie. "Scotland is a separate country, so in Paris you might not be seen as part of my court. That could serve us well when dealing with Philippe."

Robbie bent his head. "Whatever needs to be done, I will do it."

David's eyes went back to the ground, watching his feet as he walked. It meant he was thinking. Christopher found that comforting because it meant trouble for those who opposed them. "With Romeyn dancing attendance on the Pope, I have only Uncle Ted and Aunt Elisa in Paris right now. Philippe will assume they are partisan." He wrinkled his nose. "Likely, he will assume anyone I send is partisan, especially now that he is feeling so chuffed."

He was referring to the recent canonization of Philippe's grandfather, Louis. The Pope had made him officially a saint.

Philippe had been campaigning for the elevation for some time, as a symbol of the special place the French crown held in God's eyes and on this green earth. Thus, by extension, Philippe had been looking for confirmation of his own special place as a king among kings, steward of Sainte-Chapelle, the most beautiful and expensive chapel ever built, and keeper of the crown of thorns that had adorned Jesus's head at the crucifixion.

Christopher found it hard to get too worked up about any of this, but he didn't have the same religious feeling as most people in Earth Two, having grown up in modern Pennsylvania. Certainly, he had no allegiance to the Pope. Still, it would be a grave mistake to underestimate the importance of Louis' sainthood to his grandson and to the French people.

"Though Marie was FBI and I was from the Bangor Institute, we trained on the helicopter together," Sam said. "I thought we were friends. If we can find her, I might be able to get through to her. I should go as well, to Flanders or Paris, I don't care."

"Then she should come with me," Robbie said. "If the death of King Philippe is the AZs' ultimate goal, then Paris is where they will end up. I wouldn't trust Marie to fly for us under any circumstances. We need Sam to get the helicopter back home again."

"And that means I should go to Flanders with Huw," Ari said. "I speak the language. I spent two years with the AZs. I know how they think. I can help. Let me help."

Christopher ran his hand through his hair, disturbed his name hadn't yet come up. "What about me?"

"You can't—" Callum began.

"You have a wife—" Livia said.

David laughed, effectively cutting off the rest of the protests. They had reached Anna and Math's tent again. The rain had stopped, and the sky was clearing, though there was still a lot of movement to the air. "Christopher does have a wife, and as the daughter of the Master of the Paris Temple, Isabelle is uniquely positioned to help. Besides, if Sam is going to Paris, we need another woman to accompany her."

Christopher knew without asking that Isabelle would not object to being volunteered—or rather, volun-*told*—to go to France. "She knows the Johns, as well as their grandfather, Count Guy, from before, when they were all part of the French court."

"It may be that the Johns' initial decision to free the AZs and take the helicopter was impulsive," David said, "but they still followed through with it. At some point, cooler heads might prevail. For now, I don't expect it, and we can't plan on it. Certainly not before they arrive in Europe."

Ari cleared his throat. "I know I'm a newcomer, and I have no say in any of this, but we appear committed to keeping King Philippe alive. What if we weren't?"

This question was followed by a dead silence, and then Callum said, unexpectedly supporting Ari, "At some point, he won't be the only one asking that question."

David still didn't answer, simply watching the faces of everyone who'd gathered around him. Maybe it was good they were having this conversation outdoors, where their words could be blown away on the wind.

Then Christopher said tentatively, "The devil you know..." He felt his voice trail off.

David spread his hands wide. "The negative consequences of murdering the King of France with an Avalonian helicopter could far outweigh the momentary benefit we'd incur at his death."

Suddenly, the King of England was standing before them. It wasn't as if Christopher could ever forget who and what David was, but sometimes it was a bit too easy to call him *David* and fall into thinking of him as his cousin. He *was* Christopher's cousin, but he was also one of the most powerful men in the world. *This* was the right decision, he was declaring. *This* is the *right* thing to do. Everyone settled again, knowing the world was back on an even keel. Even Ari bowed his head and didn't argue.

David nodded to see it. "You'll ride for Pembroke and then sail. I'll arrange with Cardinal Francesco for his ship to take you to Portsmouth, where you can find ships to bring you across the Channel. Francesco owes us his life and will be happy to help. Then I need to call Aunt Elisa and Uncle Ted."

Communication within Britain was still in its infancy, despite the presence of Avalonian technology. They were limited, at a minimum, by their inability to manufacture new gadgets. Up until yesterday, they'd possessed just three shortwave radios: one based permanently in Dover, another in London, and a third with Christopher's parents in Paris.

Rather than needing line of sight like regular radio waves, short waves bounced off the ionosphere and allowed for communication across truly long distances—continents even, when the conditions were right. These three radios had been included in the cargo of Chad's plane years ago, though of course the plane itself was long gone. The radios had been instrumental in their last campaign against Philippe, during their rescue of the Jewish community of Paris. They'd taken their radio with them when they'd fled down the Seine, rather than leave it at the Paris Temple and risk its confiscation by French forces (even if they wouldn't have known what to do with it).

Sending it back with Christopher's parents had been a risk—and yet a calculated one. It was more important to know what was happening than to be left with reacting after the fact. As they were doing today.

They were now in possession of six more shortwave radios, five of which were currently in storage in Carew Castle's receiving room and one which had been used numerous times after David had returned to call both Paris and London. These new radios, far more than the first three that had been dragged out of a cellar somewhere and included in the plane's manifest at the last minute, were state-of-the-art, for an art that was over a hundred years old and had mostly fallen out of use in Avalon. Such were the advances in the last few years that these radios were smaller, more flexible and compact, with higher-capacity batteries. Each had even come with its own solar panel charger and was entirely portable. They were designed, for those who bought them in Avalon, to withstand the apocalypse.

These days, a wide variety of styles and brands were available for purchase, in addition to those Chad's company had started producing, for the sheer joy of it. Chad's corporation (as usual) was getting mileage out of the fact that David used them in Earth Two. Nobody for a moment begrudged him the publicity. Shortwave radios weren't quite the equivalent of mobile phones, but for Earth Two, they were the best they were going to get.

Robbie turned to Sam. "Do you know how to ride?" He had spent years with Christopher, so he knew skill in that department was in no way a given with a twenty-firster.

Sam made a dismissive motion with her head. "I grew up on a farm. I could ride by the time I was three."

Christopher laughed to hear it. Really, they should have expected anyone Chad sent would know about a whole lot of things. He was already feeling better. Between all of them, now that they knew better what they were dealing with, the AZs didn't stand a chance.

7

23 September 1297

Elisa

"**D**avid is on the radio." Ted put a hand on Elisa's shoulder. "You need to come now." His gaze went to Matthew Norris, the Master of the Paris Temple, with whom they'd been breakfasting. "He'd like you to be there too."

Elisa looked past her husband to the eager young man Ted had intercepted halfway across the floor. Having handed off his message, he was shifting from one foot to another in uncertainty or maybe impatient excitement. She and Ted couldn't sit next to the shortwave radio all the time, but they never left it unattended.

Matthew was complicit in their activities—and had been long before Christopher had married Isabelle. That made the three of them ... *what* did *you call the parents of children who'd married?* Nobody had ever properly elucidated what they were to each other. *In-laws?* Accurate, but not quite right.

If nothing else, these days she would call Matthew a *friend*.

Knowing her whole family was at Carew's tournament in Wales, Elisa had been surprised to hear her sister's voice, loud and clear, just the previous evening. Through their newly acquired radio, Meg had relayed the thrilling saga of David and Lili's departure to Avalon and subsequent return. Elisa expected to navigate some turbulent waters as long as she lived, whether in Avalon or in Earth Two, but it always seemed as if the things she worried about most were never what she actually faced.

David had also talked to Master Godfrid de Windsor, his regent in London (and Nicholas de Carew's half-brother). Nobody outside of the environs of Carew had known that David and Lili had gone to Avalon and returned. It was a rare instance when having no way to communicate was a good thing. Nobody had sent word to London of David and Lili's initial departure, in hopes they would return quickly. There was no sense in upsetting people unnecessarily, especially when there was nothing they could do about it.

Elisa could tell by Ted's tone that another call so soon after the first foretold something worrisome. David's initial request that they journey to Paris had come while he was still in London, before everyone had set out for Wales. She and Ted had been at the end of a series of negotiations regarding Normandy's constitution. That had been a difficult task as it was. Next, David needed them to speak for him to King Philippe about his treatment of Flanders, now that France had won the war.

Archbishop Romeyn, who had been a very capable ambassador for the last two years, had been called to Rome as part of his duties as the Archbishop of York. Romeyn had maintained King Philippe's trust all this time, despite being English. Between him and Matthew Norris, they daily tried to temper the worst of Philippe's excesses. Regardless, the court of France could not be left unattended at this trying time, which meant Ted and Elisa had done as their nephew wished. It had taken them a few days to wrap up things in Rouen, and then a few more to get here. They'd arrived only yesterday, just in time to take Meg's call.

When they'd used the Paris Temple as their base two years ago, even though Matthew knew about the miracle that was immediate radio communication, he had not been invited to use it. At the time, they had let very few into that inner circle. Ultimately, with Matthew a willing participant in the rescue of Paris's entire Jewish population, he had become a staunch ally, and a savvy one.

Entering the radio room behind Elisa and Ted, Matthew paused with one foot through the doorway. "The machine is smaller than I expected."

"Apparently, the radio by which David is speaking to us is even smaller and more portable." Ted made room for Matthew, and the three of them settled around the radio to listen while David laid out the disaster that was coming towards them.

Matthew leaned forward, prepared to speak like a veteran user instead of for the first time, and Ted directed the microphone towards him. "King Philippe is no less ambitious today than he was two years ago. Romeyn and I have been doing our best to maintain the truce, even if we failed spectacularly to stop the initial war between France and Flanders."

"I know you walk a fine line between advising Philippe and serving our interests." David was really the only one who could get away with calling Philippe by his given name. Everywhere, all the time, to everyone else, it had to be the whole thing: *King Philippe*. Or maybe even, *King Philippe of France*. The irony was that to much of the world, David was known only by his first name: *David*. As if there was only one. "You can't lose your position; you can't give Philippe any feeling, by word or deed, that we are as closely tied as we are. I have not experienced the danger you face every day, but I understand that you face it."

As David had openly acknowledged, Matthew had been required to pretend from the very beginning of his service to King Philippe that he wasn't David's ally. It kept him perpetually in a precarious position. King Philippe still didn't know David had based the Jewish evacuation out of the Paris Temple, with Matthew's full cooperation. He also didn't know that Templars throughout France had not only helped, but continued to be allied to this very day with David, rather than with Philippe. It was no less important that Philippe remain unaware of these facts today than it had been two years ago.

Ever since Christopher had married Isabelle, the young lovers' parental units had jointly walked a fine line in their outward interactions too. They'd waffled constantly between implied disdain and acknowledged filiality. Matthew had so successfully convinced King Philippe that he didn't like Ted and Elisa personally that it had been the king himself who'd told Matthew to ask them to stay with him at the Paris Temple instead of at Romeyn's now-vacant house. The king's idea, openly stated to Matthew, was to use him as an inside track into what the ambassadors from the court of the King of England were saying and doing.

Templars weren't supposed to lie. They were supposed to be upright and honorable in all things. Matthew held to his oaths with utter steadfastness, his loyalty to David a matter of neglecting to relay all information to the King of France rather than outright lies.

"Just another instance," Ted said, "of only being able to do what you can do."

Matthew, however, had begun to frown. "There is something about which I am still unclear, my lord. As you related your tale of these Avalonian Zeelanders, you spoke of their desire to change the course of history, as if they had some prior knowledge of its creation."

A silence fell among them. For all that Matthew was a close confidant, they still hadn't shared this one last truth with him.

Elisa could hear David breathing into the microphone as he thought. Finally, he said, "With the arrival of the AZs, the cat may well be out of the bag on this anyway. Ironically, it was only this morning I told Lili and the others that I would stop fighting the King Arthur mantle everyone wants to place on me. I am thinking now it doesn't matter if I fight it or not." And then, seemingly just to Elisa and Ted, he added, "Over the years, we have explained the whole truth of who we are to many, usually after we can no longer hide that truth. Matthew needs to know it all. It will allow him to make better decisions. It isn't fair for him not to know."

"You think the AZs have told the truth to the Johns?" Ted said.

"According to Ari, they don't have the sense not to," David said. "It would be a quick path to persuading them to do what they want."

Matthew had been looking from Ted to Elisa and back again. "What truth is this? What don't I know?"

David drew in an audible breath. "Matthew, the reason I didn't ally with Flanders as many wanted me to is because I feared the alliance would ultimately fail. We wouldn't actually defeat France and our participation would result in the loss of men and influence."

"Well, of course," Matthew said. "You explained that at the time."

"What I didn't explain is *why* I knew to fear it."

"We all feared it."

"Yes, but for you, there might still be some hope. For me, I knew events could play out as a worst case scenario because, in Avalon, they already had."

Matthew thought about that for a few seconds. "Please explain."

"You already know Avalon is a place beyond this world," David said. "You have never seen me disappear, but you have heard of it from others. What has never been explained as fully as perhaps it should have been is that this world, which, amongst ourselves, we

Avalonians call Earth Two, is a different universe altogether from the one in which Avalon resides. You are living in the year of our Lord 1297. When I traveled to Avalon this week, I went to a world identical to this one in every particular except that it has reached the year 2025."

Elisa had been watching Matthew's face carefully while David had been speaking, so she saw the moment full understanding dawned. "You have lived in the future? You're actually *from* the future."

"*A* future," David hastened to say. "Just one possible future. Earth Two's trajectory has diverged from Avalon's considerably in the last fifteen years."

"That would be because you arrived to change it." Matthew was smart enough to be looking for confirmation, rather than asking a question.

"Yes," David said.

"Because you've done things differently."

"Yes."

"This is what you told Jacques de Molay that made him trust you so profoundly?"

"Yes."

"What was the future of the Templar Order?"

David told him.

As David finished speaking, Matthew surged to his feet and began to pace. Elisa had to hold down the button on the microphone so David could hear him. "And what about our Jewish friends?"

Ted answered that one.

Then came a most urgent query: "Does Isabelle know?" Long gone was the first wide-eyed look Matthew had given Elisa about talking to David while he was hundreds of miles away. With Isabelle as a daughter, married to Christopher, a twenty-firster, it was inevitable he was brought into their inner, inner circle, and she was glad it had happened sooner rather than later.

Across the miles, David took in another full breath before answering: "Yes."

8

23 September 1297

Johnny

Johnny looked ahead from his position on the seat of the cart, his eyes straining to see the clearing where they'd left the helicopter, praying it would still be there; hoping against hope they hadn't risked everything for nothing.

"You worry needlessly, my lord," Marie said from behind him, in her strangely accented Flemish.

Johnny obviously hadn't been doing an adequate job hiding his anxiety. "Do I? You trust your man that much?"

He really should be thinking of her language as *Avalonian* Flemish, since she sounded the same as the others who'd come with her. Likely, her accent wasn't unusual in that future Avalonian Zeeland. Though it had been hard to credit at first, he no longer doubted their explanation of who they were. He was furious with King David for not telling him the truth from the start, even as he had to admit his anger was irrational. How would he have replied at any moment before this one if David had said, *by the way, Avalon is not actually the land of King Arthur. It's a world with a timeline running a thousand years ahead of us here.*

Johnny wouldn't have believed him. Possibly he would have walked away thinking he was either a madman or a saint.

But he knew the truth now: David was a man like any other. Like these newcomers here. Like Johnny himself. Nothing more.

To be fair, David had never actually claimed to be anything but an ordinary man. It was the people around him, including Johnny and Zee, who had elevated him to idol. A false one, as it turned out.

After their rescue, the AZs, a nickname Johnny couldn't help calling them, thanks to Bronwen, had explained in painful detail all that had happened in Avalon's past. King Edward had not died in that world, but had gone on to extend his will across all of Britain and much of France. He had conquered Wales; he had lost his war in Scotland this year, but his descendants had ultimately subjugated the Scots completely. And although he had initially intervened on the side of the Flemish, he had ultimately abandoned them, first to be conquered by France and then eventually by a new country called the Netherlands.

Johnny couldn't blame the Avalonians for being angry at their fate and for doing whatever they could to change it. He saw clearly now the best way to ensure Zeeland's future sovereignty was to prevent King Philippe of France from conquering Flanders and rending asunder everything they held dear. Zeeland's fate was entwined with

Johnny's. With King Philippe in the ascendancy, Johnny's family would lose their authority, and his entire line would die out.

In that future, Johnny and Zee's grandfather, Count Guy of Flanders, died in a French prison. Zee died of dysentery at the age of fifteen, though rumor had it he was murdered. Johnny himself tried to live a good life, even establishing a charter for Brabant that would be remembered for centuries. But during his reign he still allowed the subjugation of his people by France, at which point he died at the age of thirty-seven. Without any defenders, Zeeland would become a political pawn, such that even their language was not recognized as legitimate in the time of the AZs.

By not intervening in the war against France, King David had determined all their fates. Johnny could understand David's wish not to make the mistakes of his predecessor. But he could not forgive him.

"It would be no good going on without you." Marie was still speaking. "Your cousin knows that, and so does Jos. Neither he nor Lord Zee can fly the helicopter anyway."

With their initial leader dead on the archery field, Jos had assumed command of the AZs. The other two men who'd come with him, Paul and Arne, had both been wounded in the subsequent skirmish.

Arne was also Marie's *partner*, as she called him. They weren't married, but they shared their lives as if they were, perhaps even more closely than any married couple Johnny knew. He found the casual way she made it clear she was not to be questioned on the subject admirable, while also horrifying. She had given up her virtue to this man, who had made her no promises and had otherwise given her not-very-much as far as Johnny could tell: no land, no wealth, no security, no children, no future. Johnny couldn't figure out what would compel a woman to do that. Or why she claimed to love such an uncultured person.

Arne had also been badly injured on the archery field when an arrow had punctured his thigh very close to his life vein. He was alive because Marie had refused to fly more than ten miles from Carew Castle until they tended to his wound, which had opened again during their escape. Jos had protested, saying they had no chance of finding someone with the required skills to heal him. Marie had countered that all healers in Wales were trained at the university in Llangollen, and they would find one or die trying.

In the end, she'd had her way. Not that any of them could have stopped her, since (as she had rightfully pointed out) she was the only one of them who knew how to fly the helicopter.

Ariana, the healer in question, rode in the back of the cart with Arne and Marie, keeping an eye on Arne's wound. They'd been forced to bring her with them out of fear that traveling even this short distance would reinjure Arne. If that happened, she could patch him again before they took off.

Now, Ariana shot Marie a look of steel. "He shouldn't be riding anywhere. We shouldn't have moved him at all. How are you going to get him to where he needs to go?"

Johnny understood none of this, of course, since she spoke in Welsh. But Ariana had found a young girl from her village who had learned French, and she also sat in the back of the wagon, translating for them.

"We have a vehicle," Marie said shortly.

Ariana's eyes narrowed, and then almost instantly widened again, since they'd finally arrived in the clearing where Marie had *put down* the helicopter. In the intervening hours since they'd landed, the rain had stopped and the sun shone directly down on the vehicle, reflecting off the metal so brightly it was blinding if caught exactly right.

More luck, milling about the helicopter was Johnny's and Zee's entire company of men and horses that had ridden from Carew moments after they'd freed the captives and taken the helicopter. They had been prepared to make their way across Britain on their own. How Hans had unerringly navigated to this very spot Johnny couldn't guess, but he knew for certain that he deserved a rise in pay and would see to it once they arrived home in one piece.

Jos took charge the instant Ariana's brother-in-law halted the cart in the clearing. "We will go now. Load him up."

In his hands, he held one of the weapons they'd found stashed in the floor of the helicopter. Really, they could thank Arne's wound for that. When they'd lifted him into the passenger compartment, the blood pouring from his reopened wound had seeped onto the floor ... and then *into* it. Recognizing a trap door when he saw one, Johnny had pointed out what was happening, and Jos had ultimately found the trick to opening the compartment. At the sight of the modern weapons, the jubilation amongst his companions had been unrestrained.

With Arne sorted, Johnny glanced over at Zee, who might have aged a decade today. Johnny hoped what he'd learned, for the most part, was beneficial to his future. Given the way Jos was consumed by rage, he might not be a particularly good influence on the young man in the long term, but he was useful for now.

Even so, Johnny got down from the wagon seat in order to put a hand on the end of Jos's weapon and push it down so it pointed at the ground. "You don't need that here."

Just for an instant, Jos glared at him, and then he lowered his eyes to match the trajectory of the weapon. "My apologies, my lord. We have been very worried."

"Something I appreciate. I have been worried too. The sooner we are on our way, the better. Did we get enough sun to refuel?"

"Enough to get close to full range."

Marie had explained, as best she could, how the helicopter ran on water, of all things, which was turned into a fuel by a means that still wasn't clear to Johnny. He'd decided he didn't have to know exactly how it worked, only that the rain had stopped and the clouds had cleared enough while they were gone to make the refueling happen.

Then Jos said, "We should kill the healer and the other two with her," confirming everything Johnny had just been thinking about him. Thankfully, he spoke in Flemish and thus was not under-stood by the woman, her brother-in-law, or their translator.

"No." Johnny spoke flatly, without emphasis, as if Jos had asked a question.

"They will tell King David what they've witnessed."

"Of course they will, but by then we will be long gone, and it won't matter. It isn't as if David hasn't noticed his helicopter and prisoners are missing! In fact, that reminds me—" Johnny cast around for one of his guardsmen. "I will leave Hendrik here to speak to him when he arrives."

"You can't—" Jos broke off, not finishing the thought at the scalding look Johnny sent him.

"Can't I?"

Jos swallowed hard. "I mean to say, my lord, I think such a move unwise."

"You are free to think that, but you are not the Duke of Bra-bant nor grandson to the Count of Flanders. England is our most sig-nificant trading partner. Without it, we have no wool for our mills. I freed you because I believe you can help me win back my country, but don't think for an instant that you know me or your aims and mine are the same in all respects. You can go back to Avalon when you're done here. I have to stay and live with the consequences of our actions."

"You like him," Jos meant David, "even after what we told you?"

Johnny allowed all of the disdain he felt for these newcomers and their lack of honor to show. "Of course I like him. Truthfully, there is more to admire about him now that I know he is just a man like any other. He came to Wales at the age of fourteen, penniless and friendless, having grown up ignorant of the identity of his father. From those beginnings, he turned himself first into a prince of Wales, then the King of England, and now the High King of Britain. We do not want to make of him an enemy—" he made a qualifying motion with his head, "—not more than I already have."

"Don't you think it's too late to worry about that?" Jos just wouldn't let up.

"Peace can be forged out of any situation. You just have to decide to try." Johnny paused. "David taught me that."

Jos was looking particularly fierce again. The man had no notion when to keep his mouth shut. "When has David given up anything for peace?"

Johnny gazed at him, his fury at the English king not so much abating as being tempered by a cold dose of reality. "It comes to me, having learned the truth of his origins, that he may have given up more than we will ever know."

9

23 September 1297

Matthew

David had given Matthew the truth straightforwardly, but that didn't make his words any easier to accept.

Elisa put out a hand to Matthew, though she must have seen something in his eyes that gave her pause, since she didn't touch him. "She did not know about this before she left Paris two years ago, but she married our son with her eyes open."

"Are the events happening now different from what happened in Avalon?" Matthew found himself halting in front of the microphone, his fists clenching and unclenching.

"Not enough," David said. "Unlike King Edward, who didn't die in 1284 in Avalon, but lived another twenty-three years, I didn't bring an army to Flanders. By not coming in on the side of Count Guy, I basically ensured he'd lose. But since he lost anyway under Edward, who preferred peace with France, I haven't changed anything."

"Who is to say Guy wouldn't have won if you'd joined him. You aren't Edward."

"No, I am not, and I work very hard not to be. It's early days yet, though, and there's a lot more potential war to come. That's why my aunt and uncle came to Paris. That's why the arrival of this helicopter is so terrifying. We are in uncharted territory. It isn't just that we are changing history. We're introducing advanced technology. Who knows how much more different we will make this world. Some of it will hopefully be for the good. Some of it could very well be quite bad."

"What about Philippa?" Ted said. "That's another thing to think about."

"Who?" David asked. "Did you say Philippa, not Philippe?"

Elisa leaned in to take over the microphone. "In the aftermath of the Battle of Furnes, King Philippe captured Guy's twenty-two-year-old daughter, Philippa. He made her captive in Avalon too, though in that case it was to prevent her betrothal to Edward II, and I don't see you betrothing your Arthur to a woman three times his current age. Either way, she remains in the palace, hostage to her father's good behavior."

"King Philippe thinks that by imprisoning Philippa he can control Guy," Matthew said. "So far, it has been an effective strategy, but that may be more because Flanders was defeated so profoundly than because he loves her that much. If these Zeelanders arrive with a means to change the balance of power, Guy might choose victory for Flanders over his daughter's life."

"Would Philippe harm her if her father were to renew the war?" That this was David's chief concern reminded Matthew yet again who he was and why they would all, Matthew included, follow him to the ends of the earth—or, as it turned out, to any earth.

The Paris trio sat silent for a long moment, looking at each other. Taking hostages as part of a peace negotiation was commonplace in Matthew's world.

Elisa spoke slowly, "In 1165, King Henry II castrated and blinded Welsh hostages after he lost a campaign in Wales. The hostages had been handed over to Henry to guarantee their fathers' good behavior. The Welsh fought back anyway, and Henry followed through with his mutilations of both male and female hostages."

"That's a Norman example," Ted said, "but the French have maimed and killed hostages in the past too. For King Philippe to follow through with his own threat if Guy doesn't behave isn't without precedent. Remember about whom we are speaking. On top of what King Philippe did to Templars and Jews, in a few years he sends men to abduct and maybe murder Pope Boniface."

Matthew found himself stuttering. "He sends—he has the Pope—" He broke off, unable to continue.

"Abducted. Yes. He's held hostage for three days and later dies from the ordeal," David said. "I suppose, technically, Philippe doesn't have him murdered. Do you know where Philippa is being held?"

"In the palace on the Île de la Cité," Elisa said.

That was the island in the middle of the River Seine. Notre Dame Cathedral lay at the other end of the island. Together, it and the palace formed the heart of Paris.

Matthew cleared his throat, not dismissing what he was being told about the Pope but accepting for the moment that it wasn't the main point. "I have not seen her since she was brought in and haven't dared ask in which room she is being held. The not-so-secret passages, if they remain, have been reworked, at great expense, since you were last here. I have been unable to determine their exact layout myself, and I don't have Nogaret's nose for deceit to sneak around the palace when nobody is looking. The workmen who built them were brought in from outside the city and were sent away again when it was done."

"Is it in your mind to rescue her?" Ted leaned into the microphone, setting aside the question of whether King Philippe returned the workmen to their remote villages or had them killed.

"I could," David said. Someone else might have been incredulous that a single girl could be David's priority when so much was at stake outside the palace, but Matthew could see his point. As one girl went, so might a whole country. "Are we sure she's still alive?"

"The king has implied she is, as leverage over Guy." Matthew cleared his throat, all of a sudden feeling more tentative than was usual for him. But he had a question that needed answering. "What happened to her in Avalon?"

"She died in captivity," Elisa said, "which I know only because of my own deep dive into this period in France's history before we started our mission two years ago. That King Philippe took her hostage, even though David did not behave as King Edward did, is an example of how some pieces of history just seem to be inevitable, no matter how hard any of us works to change them."

Matthew could practically feel David nodding all the way from Wales. "That doesn't mean we aren't still going to try."

10

23 September 1297

David

Ari had a certain degree of wariness in his eyes as he entered Carew's private office, adjacent to the much larger receiving room. It was approaching twenty-four hours since he'd arrived in Earth Two, and Ari had looked wary a lot. To be fair, he'd had a great deal to be wary about. David wondered if he was having waking nightmares about yesterday, the same as David. Probably not, since he was an experienced Mossad agent. Days like yesterday were, for him, simply called *Monday*.

"You wanted to speak to me?" Ari said, confirming David's supposition about his degree of calm. Then again, like David, Ari might be excellent at faking it.

"We did."

Since David had last seen him, Ari had transformed himself into a medieval retainer. His gear was identical to that worn by members of the Carew Castle garrison. Although without a sword, he did have two knives, one on either side of his waist. Maybe at least one in his boot too. Once he opened his mouth, his accent would reveal him to be foreign. Until then, his appearance should allow him to blend in with the locals. And probably, with what he'd said about his facility with languages and accents, he'd have medieval English down by the end of the day.

As Ari walked farther into the room, he took in the faces of David's companions. David himself rested against the main table, his legs crossed at the ankles and his hands braced behind him on the tabletop. They'd been in here earlier looking at a map of Europe. Other papers scattered about represented the current state of life in Britain. David would have to see to them after he saw to this. Even the hijacking of the helicopter couldn't stop the wheels of government from turning.

The *we* in question were Abraham and Aaron, the former a doctor from the twenty-first century and the latter from Earth Two. Abraham had arrived years ago on the second journey of the Cardiff bus. Aaron was Meg's first real friend in Earth Two and had been a member of David's entourage almost from the start. The salient point for both of them in this moment was less that they were medical professionals or David's friends than they were both Jewish. As was Ari.

David began, "I'm letting you go on this expedition despite my reservations."

Ari was immediately offended. "I am perfectly cap—"

"Nobody is suggesting otherwise." Taking over from David, Abraham cut Ari off before he could protest further. "You *are* perfectly capable of a great many things, I'm sure. But you are a Jewish man, who is about to leave the safest place in Earth Two for our people and enter *the* most dangerous."

Ari put out a hand to David. "Sire—"

Abraham interrupted him again. "You aren't here at David's request, but at ours. We asked to speak to you. You think you have experienced the worst that life can throw at you, but you haven't lived in the Middle Ages before."

"I have faced antisemitism all my life," Ari pushed back. "My great-grandparents survived the Holocaust."

Abraham spread his hands wide. "While that was a horror perpetrated against our people on a scale as yet unsurpassed in this world or that one, every town in Earth Two is a hair's-breadth away every day from a massacre."

From the look on Ari's face, he needed more detail, and David was prepared to give it to him. This was bread and butter to the Avalonians. "A hundred and fifty Jews died in antisemitic riots in York in 1190, and that was after earlier rioting in Westminster, Norwich, Stanford, and Lincoln; just in Worcester, Simon de Montfort's followers murdered five hundred during his reign, followed in 1264 by another massacre led by Gilbert de Clare in Canterbury. And that's not to mention the two hundred Jewish merchants King Edward hanged in 1277 to pay for the war against Wales."

Abraham took up the tale again. "This is the reality the Jewish citizens of this world live with every day. You, as a Jewish man, can walk the streets of any major city in Avalon with your head held high and without fear. Sure, there might be an *incident*, or some people might look at you funny and say hateful things, but you do not en-dure the fear for your life and the lives of your children that we here experience every day. For Aaron, that dread and distrust is seared into his bones."

"Just as a reminder," David added, "if Edward had lived, he would have expelled all Jewish people from Britain in 1290. I have done my best here in Wales and England, but prejudice doesn't go away overnight, just because I declare it should. It remains always on the back burner, waiting to be lit by an unscrupulous rabble-rouser. Those who started with more but have achieved less become resent-ful. And the old prejudices rise again."

"I understand that history. I know what you're saying. Believe me, I do." Ari appeared to be struggling to be polite. "My lord, why do you think I saved your life yesterday?"

David didn't answer his question, since it was rhetorical any-way. "Philippe has already expelled the Jewish population from Paris in order to confiscate their wealth to pay his debts. Last I heard, just being Jewish there is a crime. I can't fix that; I can't stop King Philippe from doing what he will—to you or to anyone with whom you travel."

"Are you asking me to deny who I am?"

"I would never ask that of you," David said. "But if you leave here as one of my men, you're going to have to trust those around you with your life. You will need their protection. I get the sense you are not used to depending on anyone else."

David saw in Ari's face he had read him correctly. What David didn't say was the extent to which he was worried about his friends having to depend on Ari. Callum wasn't in the room because he thought his presence would do more harm than good, but he had confirmed to David that, in spy circles, Mossad was not known for playing well with others. Not that MI-5 or the CIA were team players either, but Ari seemed to be typical of his breed—a loner, someone who routinely ignored rules he didn't like or just flat-out believed they didn't apply to him.

David's court was very different from that of any other king. He actively discouraged individuals from pursuing their own wealth and power, rewarding those who focused instead on the greater good. Over the years, a few people had been poor team players, and they had either left the team or been persuaded to see the error of their ways. Some of them, like Gilbert de Clare, had died as a result of their own overreach. Others, like George, were back in the game.

Aaron had been keeping silent, allowing the twenty-firsters in the room to have their say, but now he moved closer to Ari and spoke quietly to him, in English, but not loud enough for David to hear.

Once Aaron finished speaking and stepped back, Ari bent his head to him. "I will be careful." Then he straightened and looked directly at David. "You can count on me, sire. I am the right man for the job. Please know that you can trust me one hundred percent."

Once Ari left the room, David and Abraham turned to Aaron with identical expectant looks on their faces.

Aaron allowed himself a small smile.

"I quoted Flavius Josephus." Aaron shrugged, as if just anyone should be able to call up a quote from a Roman-era Jewish general at will. "I told him God has given us this privilege, to die free men. I also gave him the name and address of our cell of Jewish militants in Bruges who've been resisting French rule and inciting unrest among the general populace. I may have implied you were reluctant to trust him with that information and what he does with it will be the making of him in your court."

Their liaison with the Paris synagogue had been a young man named Jacob, who'd come on the boats down the Seine with them to Rouen. A year ago he'd said he wanted to establish himself in Bruges, now that Normandy was free, and help his beleaguered brothers and sisters there. David had not demurred. Freedom was a bucking bronco. Once let loose, it couldn't be controlled, and he wasn't going to try.

"I am reluctant." He wanted to laugh again, less ironically than before. "Callum and I have discussed the possibility Ari could be a triple agent. He is Mossad, I'm sure, with a mandate to protect me, but Mossad could have been working with the Zeelandic Revolution from the start. The hatred for him I saw in the AZs eyes could reflect that additional level of betrayal. Or maybe, he hasn't betrayed them at all, and they are good actors. I could see Mossad wanting Philippe dead too. And Ari did already bring up the possibility of letting the AZs accomplish their mission."

Abraham looked uncomfortable with that thought. "But you're letting him go with Huw anyway?"

"He's right that we need him," David said. "I'd be a fool not to put him in the field. For now, I can let him have his secrets. Maybe it's just as well Aaron gave him one he might actually be able to use."

11

23 September 1297

Bronwen

"Excuse me, my lady. There's someone here to see you." A middle-aged servant with her hair pulled back so tightly it made Bronwen's own head hurt peered questioningly into the room.

"At this hour?" Bronwen slipped a precious tube of Chapstick into her pocket. David had brought her back a twenty-four pack, which was a true luxury of riches, but she still intended to nurse each one until every scrap was gone. It would have been better to wean herself off them, but it was one of the few pieces of Avalon she hadn't yet let go. "It's kind of late."

"It's a healer from Llandeg, a village to the northeast of us. She has come a long way."

Bronwen stopped halfway out the door. "Did she say why she wanted *me* in particular?"

"She said she was acquainted with Margaret de Clare, who spoke well of you."

Margaret was a friend, despite her family. She and Bronwen had met when Margaret had come to find her at Chepstow during the insurrection by William de Valence. Since then, the woman had been continually balanced on a knife edge, with her loyalty to David, as the King of England, on one side; and her loyalty to her family, on the other. Each of her brothers in turn, as well as her husband, had conspired to overthrow David—or simply kill him, as the case may be.

The most recent instance involved Almain, her husband, who had led a revolt against David and was still in prison in the Tower of London. Bogo de Clare, Almain's partner in crime, had escaped incarceration until the events of this week and was now a prisoner in one of Pembroke's dungeons, awaiting transport back to Rome and the judgement of the Pope for conspiring to assassinate Cardinal Francesco. By borrowing the cardinal's ship to take Christopher and the others to Portsmouth, they had delayed his departure, hopefully not forever.

Margaret had been implicated in none of these plots and had, in fact, quietly aided David when she could in such a way that her brothers and husband never realized she wasn't entirely their creature.

It wasn't Margaret here now, just a mutual friend, and Bronwen hurried to Carew's receiving room to greet her. Other than the healer, it was empty of people but not of possessions, as it was here that they'd brought the supplies from the helicopter so they could be catalogued and prepared for the journey to London.

"Thank you for seeing me so late, my lady. I am Ariana." The woman had planted herself in the center of the room as if she owned it. Once Bronwen appeared, she strode right up to her, talking as she came. She looked to be in her forties, taller than average, with brown eyes and something of a weathered face. "You will want to hear what I have to say."

"That is why I am here." It was close to ten in the evening. The children were long abed, even Bronwen's daughter, Gweneth, who fought sleep as if her life depended on it. She'd finally succumbed a half-hour before. Bronwen was not looking forward to getting her to sleep on the road to London. At the sedate pace they'd take, it meant a week at least of travel, staying at a different castle or guest house every night. Now that David had his own shortwave radio, he might make a longer journey of it and do a loop through England. Allowing the people to see him was a necessary part of being king.

Ariana's dark eyes studied Bronwen as if she could see right through her. She must have liked what she saw, or at least found Bronwen acceptable, because she nodded. "I was visited in the early hours of the morning by people I believe to be Avalonians. I did not know who they were at the time, but they did not seem—" she paused, fighting for the word, "—like you. They spoke a language I had never heard before."

Bronwen stepped closer, not hiding her extreme interest in this news. "Tell me everything."

"They came to my door, three men and a woman. Two of the men had the third hung between them. None of them spoke any Welsh, but we didn't need the same language to understand what was happening. The injured man had been pierced by an arrow in the thigh, and the wound was bleeding heavily, so much so I wasn't sure he would survive. I stitched the wound. Or, rather, restitched it and otherwise tended to him the best I could, as I was taught in Llangollen. He had a fever as well, as did one of the other men, who had a lesser wound to his upper arm, easily cleaned and bandaged again."

"And then what?" Bronwen was entirely riveted.

"They stayed with me for several hours, up to midday. I insisted on it and told them that if they left my home their friend would surely die. They understood what I was saying by then because one of the girls in the village has learned French, which their leader knew, and she translated for us. The most wounded man showed me his blade, as if threatening me would change what I did." She let out a snort. "Around noon, they demanded a cart by which to transport the wounded. I told them it was still unwise to move, but they insisted. My sister's husband drove us. We arrived at a clearing where a—" She stopped, for the first time at a loss for words.

"A vehicle was there? A flying one?"

Ariana nodded.

"It's called a helicopter," Bronwen said. "Go on."

Ariana had been so confident earlier, but just telling Bronwen what she'd seen was shaking her. "A host of cavalry were milling around by the *helicopter*." Ariana mimicked Bronwen's pronunciation with near perfection. "Then they ordered my brother-in-law and me away. I was sure they were going to kill us, but the young lord in charge stopped them. I didn't understand their actual speech, but could see there was conflict within their party over it. One of the men who had stayed with the helicopter challenged the authority of the one who'd come to see me."

Bronwen didn't for a moment doubt her story. The hijackers still had the helicopter, but it seemed they'd thrown away their head start to tend to Arne. "How did you know the one man was a lord?"

"He bore a sword and moved with a carriage that said he knew his worth. It was he who made the decisions about the injured man, even over the objections of those with him."

"Was he blond? Tall? In his early twenties?"

She nodded. "You know of him, then? He spoke French in addition to their strange language. Maybe a little English too. I don't speak anything but Welsh, so I wasn't much help to them."

"We know all of them. We just didn't know where they'd gone." Bronwen made to turn away, not wanting to wait another minute to share her news, but then turned back. "Could they still be in the clearing?"

Ariana lifted one shoulder in a half-shrug. "They were there when I left them. I kept looking back, but by the time we'd driven a half-mile from the clearing, the weather had come in again with a mighty squall. It seemed more important to come here than to watch them."

"Please wait in this room. Others will want to hear your story." Bronwen headed for the door. "May I offer you food and drink?"

"I ate on the road, my lady."

"Are you sure? It is no trouble." Bronwen looked back long enough to tip her head, as required by custom. "You won't be eating alone. It is the least we can do, given your news. We will provide food and a place to sleep tonight for your brother-in-law as well."

Ariana bent her head, giving way. This type of exchange was traditionally Welsh: a guest would refuse food the first time it was offered, but when it was offered again, as it always should be, it was expected for the guest to accept. Even with the urgency of the moment, Bronwen would not violate the forms.

She opened the door and gestured inside the servant waiting there with a tray, since Bronwen had known in advance the need for refreshment. She told him to wait with the healer while she collected Ieuan and David, and whoever else should hear Ariana's news.

It was a relief to learn John Primus was still commanding the party. She credited him with the fact that none of Carew's guards were dead, nor Ariana and her brother-in-law. In freeing the hijackers, he'd taken a risk. Once away from Carew, there was no guarantee the AZs would listen to anything he had to say.

War drew a fine line between rebel and patriot, depending on which side one was on. John's restraint wasn't enough to make up for the theft in the first place, and perhaps his honor could never be restored. But maybe, if Ariana's testimony was anything to go by, he was trying to make a start.

12

24 September 1297

David

Ieuan and Rhys appeared out of the fog. Rhys was a member of David's personal guard and one of the best trackers he knew, not that tracking was particularly required in this instance. David and several other companions had been waiting in a small wood on the edge of the clearing, in which Ariana and Einion, her brother-in-law, claimed the helicopter had been parked. They had left their horses fifty yards back, the better to scout the situation before they made themselves known. The fog was helping with the secrecy.

There had never been any question in David's mind that he was going to be among those riding out of Carew Castle in the pre-light of dawn in pursuit of the helicopter. He couldn't go all the way to France, but he could do this. Ariana's village was approximately fifteen miles from Carew Castle by road (though a third less by helicopter). The AZs could have been at this clearing literally ten minutes after they took off.

He had told himself a hundred times since meeting Ariana that they would find nothing here and the AZs had been gone since yesterday. Others had wondered if the helicopter had malfunctioned, stranding the Johns and the AZs in Wales. Thus, there had been some argument among David's people about leaving immediately last night, on the chance of catching them. But more heavy rain had blown through within the hour, and wiser heads had prevailed. Maybe Marie had risked flying through the storm again, but the weather was bad enough to keep David and his friends grounded.

Once David said he was going, there was no stopping the rest. Ieuan and Math wanted to be part of it, just like old times. Michael and Callum then refused to be left behind. If Christopher, Huw, and Robbie had still been in the castle, they would have insisted on being in the party too. William de Bohun, to his unending regret, was still suffering through a broken wrist. David had managed to limit the rest of their company to his personal guard, led by Venny, their captain.

They had pulled out a few modern weapons, so they could hold their own with the AZs if they opened fire. They could probably disable the helicopter—not David's first choice—because that was better than letting it remain in enemy hands. Without Sam, they didn't have anyone trained to fly it home, unless Michael or Callum had hidden talents David hadn't yet learned about. David himself had driven a car only a few times in his life, always under duress. He'd played flight simulator games fifteen years ago, but that could hardly suffice.

"The helicopter itself is gone," Ieuan said.

David tipped his head at the *itself*.

"There is something else you should see, though, my lord," Rhys said. "Someone has pitched a tent in the middle of the clearing."

"Someone?"

Ieuan spread his hands wide. "Given the flag of Brabant flying above the tent, the indication is that they represent John Primus."

So maybe there was hope after all. David was not shocked to learn the helicopter had flown away, but now he could still be glad they'd come. "Take me to them."

"They could have weapons," Michael said.

"It could be a trap to assassinate you as a final act of treachery," Venny put in.

"It could." David wouldn't deny it, though, in that event, he would time travel. Probably. And maybe that would be the point: David either died or was transported to Avalon. Either way, it would remove him for a while from the equation. "I can't see the AZs giving weapons to lowly soldiers."

"We should not underestimate them," Callum said. "We did that already, and we have paid the price."

David temporarily gave way, ending up crouching in the bushes, some yards from the two soldiers sitting with what appeared to be semi-unconcern around a campfire.

Ariana whispered low in David's ear. "I don't recognize either of them."

"I also wouldn't say they look like much of a threat," Michael said, also under his breath.

"And yet, they have set up their tent in such a way as to have an uninhibited line of sight of any approach within fifty yards." Callum laid out the general concern. "Or would have, if not for the fog."

"Honestly, if I didn't know better, I could still think of them as friendly." Math adjusted the quiver on his back. His great bow was at the ready.

"John Primus knows you," Ieuan said. "He should have known Ariana would come straight to you with her story. And still, he left her alive."

"So, our conclusion is they're here for us? For me?" David glanced at Ariana. "Did you know they were planning to leave men behind?"

"No!" Ariana's eyes went wide. "The nobleman paid me and sent us away. No amount of money could make me betray you, my lord. Never! We couldn't have made up a story like this on our own." Her voice had risen in her denial, which had Callum shushing her. Voices carried well in the fog, but the two men sitting around the fire still hadn't looked up.

David hadn't been concerned Ariana or her brother-in-law had somehow developed an attachment to the Flemish lords or Zeelandic mercenaries overnight. Yes, David was the King of England, but England was far less the enemy these days than it had been at any time in Welsh history. And he was also a prince of Wales. He had rarely needed to protect himself from his own people. The few exceptions had been some rebellious lords anyway, not common men and women.

"I believe you."

David's intent had been to reassure her. Nonetheless, a sudden resolve entered Ariana's face, and she straightened from her position behind the bush. "They should recognize me. And, as a woman, they'll see me as harmless."

Instantly, Rhys was on his feet to join her. "I doubt she's really all that harmless, but I should go too, if only to translate." He handed his bow to Callum and began to unbuckle the quiver at his back. "They won't know me, but I don't look like a member of your guard."

Since the sojourn in Paris, Rhys had taken it upon himself to grow a full mountain-man beard. David had no idea where the idea had come from. Nobody else in all of Wales deliberately looked like he did. Even the Jewish people of their acquaintance, among whom full beards were the standard rather than to be clean shaven or mustachioed, didn't look as wild. Rhys's wife loved it, however. As Lili had pointed out, she was the only one who mattered.

Ariana and Rhys made it all the way to the edge of the clearing before one of them stepped on a downed stick that cracked loud enough to prompt one of the soldiers to leap to his feet.

Hatless, the soldier had red hair and bore a long blade, which he pointed straight at Rhys. That answered the question of whether they had been left modern weapons. "Wie gaat daar?"

His words were the rough equivalent to *Who goes there?* English and Flemish, at their most basic, were not far apart, unsurprising considering from where the Saxons had originally come. So many words in both languages were short and to the point.

Rhys stopped where he was, his hands in the air, but Ariana walked two paces more. By now, David and his companions had snuck closer too so they could see better.

Ariana didn't understand the Flemish, but there could be only one reply regardless. "My name is Ariana, the healer who helped your friend yesterday. Do you recognize me?"

The red-headed soldier glared at her, not understanding her Welsh. The second soldier, who was older and stockier, had also risen to his feet, and now spoke in English. "I am Hendrik. Do you speak English?"

"She doesn't, but I do." Rhys walked forward enough to put himself just ahead of Ariana, whom he shielded a bit with his own body. "Ariana is the healer who helped Arne. Why are you here?"

David itched to be out there in Rhys's place, but of course the whole point was to ascertain the nature of the threat, if there was one, before he put himself anywhere near it. Knowing him well, Math kept a heavy hand on David's shoulder. If they were to enter the clearing, Math was going first.

"I was told to wait for the king."

Rhys eyed the soldier. "Why?"

"I have a message for him from the Duke of Brabant."

"I am a member of his guard. You can tell me."

Hendrik snorted. "I do not believe you."

David had heard enough. Brushing off Math's restraining hand, he strode out of the woods. The soldiers noticed him immediately, and while their first instinct might have been to brandish their weapons again, Hendrik lowered his.

"Sire." His eyes never leaving David's face, he crouched to put his weapon on the ground. "We are not here to cause trouble. We have a message for you from our lord."

"Why would that be? What does Duke John have to say to me?"

The red-headed soldier who didn't speak English still looked uncertain. He moved the point of his sword back and forth between David and Rhys in a jerky fashion, his eyes far too wide. David's men were filling the clearing, which perhaps was what had spooked him. Hendrik spoke to him abruptly in Flemish, and while David didn't know what he said that time, his words had the desired effect. The first soldier calmed enough to retreat a step towards the fire, though he still looked caught between fight and flight.

Hendrik cleared his throat and all of a sudden switched to French. "The Duke of Brabant says *I am aware of what I have done. I hope it does not cause you to make war on Flanders, but please understand I had no choice. I can't apologize. We must free our country, and this was the only way to do it.*"

The man's words came clearly, perfectly enunciated, but he spoke them without inflection as if he had no idea what they meant. Perhaps he didn't, and by leaving a messenger who didn't understand

French, but could perfectly recite his message nonetheless, like an opera singer with no Italian, John Primus was protecting himself.

David studied the man. "That's it?"

Hendrik switched back to English. "He instructed me to assure you he will return the flying vehicle, and the weapons too, when he is done with them."

13

24 September 1297

Johnny

"It seems to me you're having second thoughts about the mission." Jos was sitting opposite Johnny, his gun held loosely in his hand. He hadn't let go of it since they'd taken it from the stash in the floor, and for the last quarter of an hour he'd been eyeing Johnny with a look that implied suspicion. It was past noon by Johnny's guess, and they were in the middle of the sea, having finally reached a point where they could cross the English Channel. It was a relief, honestly, to no longer be able to see the upturned faces of people on the ground, staring up at them in shock or fear.

The helicopter had made far less progress from the time they left Carew than Johnny had expected. What had confirmed in him the idea to take it in the first place was something Christopher had told him: it could travel two hundred miles an hour at top speed. Four hundred miles to Flanders could be navigated in two hours! And yet, although they'd freed the AZs just before dawn yesterday, somehow, a full day later, they were just leaving Britain.

Jos had been furious at the delay. He'd shouted at Marie, first in the clearing, where they'd stayed for another three hours after the healer left, not because they didn't have enough fuel, but because of rain and high winds. While those same winds had blown away the clouds earlier, allowing the helicopter to refuel, they were strong enough to prevent the helicopter from launching.

Marie had defended herself with a will, saying, "Need I remind you this helicopter, for all that it is state-of-the-art, is exactly that! State-of-the-art! None of the navigation equipment works! Do you see a functioning GPS here? No, you don't! I don't know where I'm going. Without a map, in this wind and rain and endless cloud cover, I could run into a mountain and never know it until we are dead on the side. Lest you forget, none of us here can time travel!"

The words themselves didn't mean very much to Johnny, but he did understand the difficulty of not being able to see where they were going in the dark. Even more, it seemed a helicopter was subject to the weather far more than a ship or a cavalryman. For pilots, even more than for soldiers, inclement weather could be worse than the enemy. Even a novice traveler like Johnny had noticed the way the inclement weather tossed the helicopter around like it was a ship on the ocean in a storm.

Nonetheless, Jos kept up his shouting, castigating her for misleading them as to the helicopter's capabilities, and that long ago they should have chosen someone else to be the pilot.

Again, Marie's reply was adamant. "There *was* no other pilot, and you know it. Not there. Not here. You think Sam would have flown this morning in the middle of a storm? We are lucky to be alive as it is. I'm not risking everything because you can't wait a few hours. You have your weapons. We'll be in Flanders tomorrow."

And so it might prove to be. They had eventually flown from the clearing, the winds having gentled a bit, though by then it was growing dark. Before they put down for the night, Jos had hung himself out the helicopter door, trying to see the terrain beneath them. Fortunately, southern England was relatively flat, and the Thames River valley eminently recognizable. Last night, Marie had brought them to a point short of London.

Now, Johnny met Jos's gaze. "Of course I am not having second thoughts. We will defeat the King of France. We will free ourselves from his influence. My commitment to that mission is no less than it was yesterday when we rescued you."

"My apologies, my lord." Jos immediately made an effort to be respectful. Johnny had effectively forced it on him by reminding him who had freed whom from David's clutches. Johnny had noted numerous times during the tournament in Carew that many of the Avalonians struggled with honorifics. Eventually, if Jos lived long enough, he would have to overcome his plebeian instincts.

Meanwhile, Johnny had told a truth he believed to the very core of his being: he *was* utterly committed to their mutual endeavors.

At the same time, he had also told Jos a lie of omission in that he *was* having second thoughts ... just not about the mission. What he regretted was the way he'd gone about it.

When the helicopter had arrived, Johnny had understood what he was seeing, even if he'd scarcely believed it. Even more, he'd realized its potential to do what his father, his grandfather, and he had so far not—namely, defeat the King of France once and for all.

Zee too had been instantly enamored with the vehicle, climbing in and out a dozen times over the course of the afternoon. He'd helped unload the supplies, which had been carted into the castle. It was Zee, in fact, who'd first mused about the possibilities: "Wouldn't it be amazing if we could acquire a similar vehicle? Do you think that is something King David would be willing to discuss with us?"

At the time, Johnny had shaken his head. "He appears willing to discuss most anything, but he has made clear he is not going to ally with us against King Philippe. Why would he give us his most valuable asset?"

"Perhaps he would allow us to study it so we could build one of our own?"

"England has employed weapons in its own defense for years—weapons it has not shared with any other country. Why do you think David would start now?" Johnny had repeatedly answered a question with a question, not to ridicule Zee, but to make him think and find his own answers. He needed to understand why the answer was, and always would be, *no*.

Zee had been downcast. "I guess he wouldn't. You're right. Perhaps if my father were alive—"

"He isn't, Zee. We have to make our own decisions now. The weight of our lands is on our shoulders." Johnny had overridden him, more cruelly than perhaps he should have, since Zee's father had died only a month ago at the Battle of Furnes. According to the AZs, that hadn't been his fate in Avalon. There, in 1296, he had all of a sudden decided to betray Count Guy, his father-in-law, and been murdered by King Edward's men for abandoning their carefully constructed alliance against France. Either way, he was dead, and Zee was now the Count of Zeeland.

But even with Zee's youthful enthusiasm and his longing for a father he would never see again, it had not been he, in fact, who'd set the plan in motion. That had been Johnny, and it was still Johnny making the decisions and employing the authority to force the AZs to listen.

He could admit any number of regrets and recriminations, but he had to also face the truth: his second thoughts had not been enough to tell Marie to turn the helicopter around and go back to Wales.

The moment a man couldn't face the truth of who he was and what he'd done was the moment he put every future decision he made in jeopardy. In order to lead his men, Johnny needed to accept what was before him. To pretty up his actions with ideas of what was *right* and *fair* or *for the good of his country,* changed nothing. He *had* stolen the helicopter from the King of England.

That was bad enough, but there was more to Johnny's regret than making an enemy of King David. He had seen the anger in Jos's eyes when Johnny had forced him to lower his weapon in the clearing, as well as when Johnny had overruled Jos's stated desire to kill the healer and her brother-in-law. Johnny stood by his decision to keep them alive, but he had seen that kind of resentment in men's faces before. Jos was like an attack dog quivering on a lead, and Johnny was going to get his arm torn out of its socket if he wasn't careful. This man was not one to be ruled by others, regardless of their nobility. Johnny had seen the knowing looks the AZs exchanged when they thought he wasn't looking. They believed themselves superior to him.

They were also making assumptions about Johnny's intelligence and experience, based on his appearance, since all of them were older than Johnny and Zee. Johnny wasn't used to being judged and found wanting—especially by people as coarse as the AZs, who also knew nothing about him, his family, or his mind. Unlike David and his people, there was no wisdom in these Avalonians. No moderation. They behaved as if they would not have to live with the consequences of their actions. His regret was that he couldn't fly the helicopter without freeing them.

For now, the AZs' goals aligned with his, and they were entirely single-minded in their focus. This was the sole reason Jos had given way back in the clearing. They would have gone off on their own if they could have. But the only way they would have access to the Count of Flanders and the men who served him was through Johnny and Zee. And that meant treating them with at least a modicum of respect and pretending to listen to them.

Zee leaned forward in his seat. Like Johnny, he was wearing the ear protection that allowed them to speak to each other despite the noise of the helicopter. When the helicopter had soared over the tournament ground, the sound it emitted was the loudest thing Johnny had ever heard in his life. It was muffled inside the cabin, but not gone. "I've been meaning to ask, what did you do to that guard who tried to get away? You grabbed him from behind, and he collapsed."

Jos glanced at him. "Is that not something you've been taught?" And then he continued speaking, in a way that reminded Johnny once again that he had no respect for their station, even if he was willing to explain. "Did you think I choked him?" At Zee's nod, Jos put two fingers to the side of his neck. "I cut off the flow of blood to his brain."

"Can you teach me?"

Johnny found himself straightening in his seat. The last time he'd heard that particular tone in Zee's voice, he'd been talking about King David.

"Yes," Jos said, without even a glance in Johnny's direction to inquire if it was permissible.

"Zee." Johnny put all the weight of his nine more years of experience into his tone.

"What?" Zee looked genuinely bewildered to realize Johnny didn't approve. "To know would be useful!"

Johnny gave way, pretending he hadn't seen the look Jos sent him. It was for hardly a heartbeat, but it was definitely dismissive, and perhaps amused, as if Johnny was thirteen and inexperienced, rather than Zee. In point of fact, the technique they'd employed—

wrapping an arm around a man's neck and holding on until he fell unconscious—was not unknown to Johnny. He'd had enough training in the martial arts to understand that what Jos brought to the table was less in the way of superior skill than a willingness to be ruthless in pursuit of victory.

Jos was no man to emulate, however, and Johnny himself should have known better than to leave Zee in Jos's company in the clearing for the half a day it had taken to care for Arne.

To be fair to Zee, he was a count in his own right and had responsibilities in excess of his age. It was not his fault he was only thirteen and ripe for dark influences. Johnny was quite sure that's exactly what Jos was.

Back at Carew, the nonchalance with which Jos had subdued the guard in question hadn't given Johnny confidence. Instead, it had shaken him. Some men truly had the devil in them, and Johnny could almost see the horns rising up from the sides of Jos's head. Johnny could only pray his own behavior these last few days didn't mean he would soon be growing a pair of his own.

14

24 September 1297

Isabelle

By early afternoon yesterday, they had ridden from Carew to Pembroke, in order to board a ship for Portsmouth. From there, they could transfer to another ship that would take them to the coast of Europe. Before they left, Isabelle had actually volunteered for the journey.

In retrospect, that might have been a mistake.

"Where exactly is Zeeland, anyway, in comparison to Flanders? In all the fuss, I haven't ever had the wherewithal to ask." Sam settled herself beside Isabelle.

Huw and Christopher were nearby too, lounging about the boat because there was nothing else to do. For the moment, Isabelle didn't see Ari. He had a habit of keeping to himself.

Isabelle saw in Sam's face that she truly wanted to know, but she also thought she might have decided to distract her from her stomach, which wasn't taking the rocking of the boat very well. In fact, within an hour of leaving port, Isabelle was counting the minutes, if not seconds (a useful unit of time to which Christopher had introduced her) until they reached land, which she was assured would happen tomorrow.

"I'd never heard of it either before the Johns arrived," Huw spoke from his seat on a cask, "and I should have."

"To be honest, I had to ask Aunt Meg about it too," Christopher said. "There's New Zealand, of course, but I never questioned it had to be named for an *old* Zealand in order to be called *new*."

"From what I understand, it isn't even the same Zealand, though," Sam said. "That's an island in Denmark. The AZs' *Zeeland*, spelled with two *ees,* is part of what in Avalon is known as the Netherlands."

Isabelle nodded, finding herself genuinely distracted from her stomach. "Much of Zeeland has always lain below sea level, part of a river delta system. Over time, its inhabitants reclaimed the land from the sea, building dykes that ultimately connected what once were separate islands. Politically, it was conquered by Danes around the time they sacked Paris, before the French king gave them Normandy. It has even been known as Dutch Normandy."

Huw laughed. "The Normans, I know. All of a sudden, that explains a great deal."

Isabelle tried not to be offended. "I have Norman blood."

Huw put out a hand. "Forgive me. I know that. Sometimes I'm Welsh through and through."

Isabelle bent her head in acceptance. Really, she had been among the Welsh for long enough, and in David's court for long enough, to understand the long-standing grievances, and generations of pain, caused by her ancestors. With Wales's independence and David's ascension to the throne of England, many, including Huw, had been able to let go of it.

"They've resented being conquered ever since." Ari had arrived. From the grayness of his face, he was doing about as well with the seasickness as Isabelle.

Isabelle scooted over to make room for him, and he settled himself on the planks of the ship with what appeared to be relief.

"So ..." Isabelle's eyes were now on Ari, thinking to do for him as Sam had done for her, "we would like to know how you became involved in all this in the first place."

"What do you mean by *all this*?" Instantly, Ari put out a hand to her. "Sorry. In the past, with the proper application of seasickness medication, my current state could be avoided. One pill, and I could be fine for hours. How could I know we would be getting onto a boat within a day of our arrival? If I had, I would have packed a supply."

Isabelle wished he had brought those pills too because she could have taken one. He hadn't answered her question, though, so she tried again. "I mean with the Zeelander group. I could ask about Mossad too, but Christopher assures me you won't tell us the truth. When did you learn of them, and how were you chosen to infiltrate them?"

"You mean because I am obviously a total failure at being medieval?"

"I wouldn't—"

He brushed aside her protest. "I'm obviously not a good sailor, and I might as well tell you right now I didn't learn to ride a horse when I was three like Sam either. You might have noticed my ineptitude when we set out from Carew."

"Not everyone is good with horses," Christopher said. "I wasn't when I came."

"What I haven't actually said out loud, not even to David, and God knows why I'm telling you all, is that, while my intent had been to infiltrate the Zeeland group, I wasn't meant to come to Earth Two with them. I was, in a word, *unprepared*."

"Christopher has told me how hard it was for him at first, and David is his cousin." Isabelle had forgotten about her stomach enough to manage a laugh. "I wasn't prepared for what happened yesterday—and I have always lived here!"

"Not trying to one-up you, but I wasn't even selected for the original group of men to hijack the helicopter. I was an alternate, meant to ride in the first personnel carrier. When I finally learned the scope of the plan, I spent a sleepless night playing out all the possible scenarios in my head. By morning, I decided I had no choice but to give a drug to one of the men chosen ahead of me, to make it appear he had food poisoning. The hijackers then gave me the sick man's slot."

"That doesn't sound unprepared to me." Isabelle looked at him very seriously. "Honestly, that sounds brave."

Ari leaned back his head. "From now on, don't worry about asking me questions. Back at Carew, David brought me into his office to tell me I needed to learn to depend on all of you." He flapped a hand weakly to indicate the whole of the group. "I confess, I resented the very idea that he was right. Certainly, I thought he was naïve for suggesting it. But he wasn't wrong, as this first leg of the journey has proved. Pretty much nothing that has happened so far has gone the way I hoped or planned."

"Not for me either. I dreamed of coming here for so long, even before I started working for Chad." Sam looked at him curiously. "If your job wasn't to come to Earth Two, then what was it?"

"To stop them from coming. I know full well how spectacularly I failed." Ari managed a laugh too.

"You would think they would have bothered to really study David and how he thinks before they started any of this," Isabelle said, just as a larger than usual wave rocked the boat. She curled up against the side of the ship, feeling her own waves of nausea coming again.

Ari had assumed a similar posture. "I'm not sure what you mean. They did study him."

"And learned nothing! They look at him in the same way as do King Philippe and the Pope."

"And maybe the U.S. government too," Sam put in, clearly understanding before Ari.

"That's because he isn't going to hang the AZs and doesn't have the stomach to keep them in prison forever," Huw said, indicating why he was the leader of their little company. "They see him as weak. In point of fact, he's the exact opposite."

A look crossed Ari's face implying maybe he had misunderstood David too. Or maybe that was just another wave of nausea. "How do you all see things, then?"

Isabelle took up the explanation again. "David doesn't need anyone to think highly of him because he knows his own mind and his worth. He's pretty ordinary to look at. He dresses plainly. He doesn't go about with a crown and an attitude. They see him and think, *eh, you're not much.* In so doing, they've entirely misread the impact he has on everyone around him."

"She's right, you know." Sam shifted in her seat, again understanding before Ari. "Think of the sheer competence of Callum and Cassie, Michael and Livia. Abraham. The list goes on. And that isn't even to mention the way he has united the people of Earth Two."

Isabelle nodded. "What happened on that archery field yesterday was inevitable. If it hadn't been Cassie who shot Franc, it would have been Huw or Ieuan or Math or Constance or Cador—and then it was all of them anyway."

Sam leaned forward so she could see across Isabelle to Ari. "David leads because he can do nothing else, not because he wants to."

Ari was silent a moment. He really had to be ill to have allowed a look of surprise to cross his face. Truth be told, he had just done to Isabelle and her friends what they were saying everyone did to David. Finally, he said, "And we all follow."

"Yes," Isabelle said, noting his use of the word *we,* for the first time counting himself as one of them. "We do."

14

Gravensteen Castle

24 September 1297

Johnny

Johnny leaned against a pillar in Gravensteen's great hall and watched with a strange detachment as his grandfather made plans with the AZs on the next phase of the battle with France. Zee was all excitement, his enthusiasm for the coming days in no way diminished as a result of their travels. After an initial few quelling comments, Johnny had given up trying to rein him in and had done his best to hide his second thoughts.

With the AZs settled at a table, food piled in front of them, Johnny's grandfather rose to his feet. Having employed one of the many practiced excuses in his repertoire, he found his way to Johnny's side. It wasn't unusual for Guy not to occupy his chair for the whole of an evening. He had an issue with his left leg going numb if he sat for too long. Everyone was used to him pacing about, talking to all and sundry, even during a meal.

When they'd first arrived, Johnny's grandfather (like Zee) couldn't have been more jubilant to have acquired the most terrible weapon this world had ever seen. It meant his army's defeat at Furnes might soon become a distant memory. A month ago, he'd lost Male Castle in Bruges, his family's seat for generations, and seen it garrisoned by French forces.

That Guy, and maybe Zee and Johnny themselves, weren't in prison in Paris along with Philippa was a matter of luck. When the French had attacked, she'd been at Male, which her father had thought he could defend. His guilt at her loss was immense. They'd only retained Gravensteen because King Philippe hadn't deemed it worthy of his special attention. There was an arrogance in the French king that burned in Johnny's gut. Really, it was that very feeling that had led him down this reckless path in the first place.

His grandfather glanced at him out of the corner of his eye. "I hear you have commandeered ships to retrieve your people at Ramsgate, north of Dover. I have not countermanded the order, even though I think the journey wasted. Your men are dead. You must accept it."

Johnny blinked. "David won't kill them."

Count Guy picked at some lint on his sleeve and continued casually. "You're that sure of him?"

"I am. Do you know why I was able to free these mercenaries and steal the helicopter? Because it never occurred to David that he needed to protect himself against theft. And why? Because he himself couldn't imagine being as dishonorable as I have been."

At that moment, some of the more flamboyant of his grandfather's men sent up a cheer, standing on their chairs and toasting the

AZs. Nobody was looking at Johnny and Guy as his grandfather swung around to face him. "Will he raise an army?"

"Against us? I don't believe so. That too would not be in character."

"But you do expect some response." His grandfather resumed his inspection of the hall. Even at seventy, his back was straight, his eyes sharp, and his mind clear. Come to think on it, he was the same age, and bore a remarkable resemblance, to David's father, Llywelyn. Maybe there was a message in that.

"He will respond. I cannot predict in what fashion. He doesn't think like normal men." Johnny paused, recalling his earlier conclusion that David was a man like any other. It wasn't true, no matter how much he wanted it to be or how much he would like to bring David down to his level.

"I hear regret in your voice. Are you saying now that you wish you had never freed them?"

"I don't know."

"You are the Duke of Brabant and my grandson. You need to know. It is your responsibility to know."

"Would you rather I pretended all was well, or that I blundered onward, afraid of questioning my own decisions? You taught me better than that. I can admit my worries only to you. I can confess only to you my fear that I might have made a mistake, well aware it is a mistake that cannot be undone."

Count Guy grunted low in his chest. "You are right. If you and I cannot speak freely to each other, to whom can we speak? I don't want bravado from you. What do you fear the most?"

"That we have made of King David an enemy, even though I have done my best to mitigate the damage." And he told his grandfather of the message he'd left with his men in the clearing, assuming that the healer would seek David out. "We have lost our opportunity to convince him of the justice of our cause. He might have come around eventually. We may find him a far worse enemy than Philippe ever could be."

"You could have left a trap for him. That might have solved some of our problems."

Johnny hoped his grandfather was speaking theoretically, to urge him to really know his own mind. "And created others that might be far worse! Are you really suggesting I should have arranged for the death of the King of England? Philippe's death isn't enough?"

Guy shrugged. "Some might have."

"True." Johnny settled his shoulders, glad to have had this talk because he was seeing everything and everyone—even his grandfather—with clearer eyes. Zee's bloodthirst may have arisen from emulating Guy as much as Jos. Did Guy really view honor as a form of naïveté? What did that say about Guy's real opinion of Johnny? Or about Guy himself? "I am not that man."

"Sometimes what is required of us is difficult or distasteful. Our ability to make hard decisions is why we have been chosen by God to rule and not others."

That his grandfather would absolve Johnny of his dishonor did not improve his mood. All his life he'd looked up to Guy. "We should not underestimate David. King Philippe has done so in the past at his peril."

"That I recognize." Count Guy suddenly chortled. "Philippe gave up the most dedicated merchants and goldsmiths in his kingdom for an ephemeral infusion of their wealth. Our greatest ancestor, the first Count of Flanders, welcomed Jewish families into this country two hundred years ago. Your father's father tried to expel them in his will, and your father refused to follow his wishes. He was not a fool, and I am glad to see that his son isn't either." He looked upon Johnny with something of a proprietary air. Johnny felt a warmth inside, and had to acknowledge that he wanted his grandfather's approval. Still. Maybe forever. "I was never so happy as when my daughter married your father. It was a shame to have lost him so soon for no reason."

Johnny's father had died at the hands of one Pierre de Bausner, whom the family suspected was an agent for the French court but could never prove. At a wedding, Pierre impugned Johnny's father's honor, resulting in a duel, which Johnny's father had won—except Pierre had coated his dagger with poison. Johnny's father had died of his wound, which had been no more than a passing cut on his upper arm. The scoundrel had fled in the middle of the fight, and Johnny's father had let him go, not realizing what he'd done. Two days later, Johnny was the Duke of Brabant.

That event had taken place three years ago. Johnny had been nineteen. Now, at twenty-two, he at times felt decades older, never more so than this week. "I miss him every day."

"So what would your father do if he were here? How do we use this beast of the air?" Count Guy chewed on his lower lip. "Given everything you've told me, *can* we even use it?"

Johnny motioned towards the AZs. "They are thinking of a first strike, a trial run, if you will. I believe it is an idea we can work with." He studied his grandfather. "What you and I must also talk about is what happens once these Zeelanders have had their way and King Philippe is dead."

His grandfather waved a dismissive hand. "We'll find a way forward when the time comes. We always do."

Johnny chose not to counter his grandfather with the news that, in Avalon, they hadn't, in fact, found a way forward on their own. There, they'd lost everything, including their lives. It might even be that Johnny's own way forward, when the time came, would need to be different from his grandfather's.

Yes, Johnny was having second thoughts.

Again.

16

24 September 1297

Sam

"Whatever you think is happening here, or David thinks is happening, you're wrong," Ari said.

Sam froze on the other side of an elaborately stacked set of wine barrels. She didn't know if they were empty or full, but they were secured to the floor with netting, just about high enough to hide her position. This didn't sound like the same Ari from a few hours ago. This Ari was much more outspoken and sure of himself. Weirdly, his words were also coming out a bit slurred.

"Why do you say that? What do you think is happening here?" Christopher said.

She hadn't meant to eavesdrop. She'd come down the ladder into the hold simply to get out of the rain that was falling again. She'd basically been wet through since she mounted her horse yesterday. She could have sheltered with the others under a tarp on the deck, but the only seat left was next to Robbie, and she was still struggling with how to talk to the real, honest-to-goodness Robert the Bruce of legend.

"We are trying to play both sides against the middle," Ari said. "It isn't going to go well. You are all too young, and you have no clue what you're doing. I should be the one in charge."

"You wanted to let the AZs loose in Europe to do what they want."

Sam kept her head down, so she couldn't see either of their faces, but they had a lantern with them, and the shadow of Ari waving a hand in dismissal was visible on the floor and wall of the ship. "I did. I still do. But I won't argue about it again. He's your cousin."

Ari meant David, obviously.

"He is my cousin, but he's also my king. Weird concept, I know, but there it is. I live in Earth Two. I have to accept certain aspects of life here as it comes. David listens to everyone's opinion, and then he makes a decision, and we have to go with it."

"So you disagree with what we're doing too?"

"I didn't say that."

Sam was impressed with Christopher's ability to tread carefully with Ari. Then again, Christopher was a spy too, a member of *Y Ddraig Goch*, albeit with far less experience than Ari claimed to have, simply because of his age. Kind of like Ari had just pointed out. Regardless, what Sam really couldn't get behind was any plan that involved letting the AZs kill the King of France.

Ari scoffed. "What good is having advisers if he doesn't listen?"

"He heard every word you said, I assure you. He just disagreed."

Sam couldn't stay hidden. Either they were going to hear her breathing or discover her on their way out. She stood up and came around the barrels, speaking as she went: "The irony is that I think David is genuinely sympathetic to their cause."

Ari let out a short laugh to see her. "Spying is contagious, I see."

"I was just trying to get dry." Sam thought she managed to keep the defensiveness out of her tone.

"Our conversation wasn't a secret." Ari lifted a cup to her in something of a salute. "The captain had herbs for nausea."

Christopher looked at Sam, continuing the initial conversation rather than replying to Ari's latest *non sequitur*. "When we finally catch up to the AZs—and the Johns—we should remember that none of them actually want to harm David or England."

"Or Wales, so I hear." Ari took another swig of his drink. "I was just explaining to Christopher that our current plan is barely that, and it sucks anyway."

Sam finally realized Ari had drunk a bit more than just an herbal remedy. From the looks, he was well on his way to working through one of the wine barrels.

Christopher eyed Ari with concern too, and then turned back to Sam. "Ari says the AZs' organization was very compartmentalized. He hadn't even met Marie until they entered the helicopter. He knew only his small part of the plan."

Ari swung his cup around precariously, especially considering the continual rocking of the ship. "Being on the team, even as an alternate, meant no phones, no contact, never being out of sight of any of the rest. In truth, I thought there was no way they would succeed. Once we got in the helicopter, my job became to protect David."

"And what is it now?" Christopher said.

"Still doing it." Ari started to giggle. "Best in the world. I keep secrets. Everyone's secrets. Even yours."

"I don't have any secrets." Sam spoke automatically, believing what she said in the moment. But really everyone had secrets.

"You're worried about me. I see it in your eyes." Ari waved his cup at her again. "That's why I like you. You're smart. You're *nice*. You remind me of my little sister. I see you blaming yourself for what happened. You shouldn't. If it's anyone's fault it's mine. I already told David that." Suddenly, he leaned forward, his arms resting on his knees as a pillow for his head and the cup dangling from two fingers. Christopher adeptly rescued it. "I told my sister I would come to see her when I could, and now I've just disappeared off the face of the planet. You should throw me overboard now and get it over with. It would be better for everyone."

Christopher patted his shoulder, almost saying *there, there*. But then he asked the real question, one that perhaps wasn't entirely fair in this moment, given the state Ari was in. "Can we trust you?"

Ari's head was still in his arms. For a moment, Sam wondered if he had even heard, so lost was he in his drunken despair. But then he pushed up so they could see his face. "Yes, you can trust me. I will not betray you. How could I?" His head returned to his arms.

Christopher, for his part, met her gaze, and she could see him weighing all they'd heard, as she herself was doing. Since they'd gotten on the ship, Ari had seemed more human and relatable. And now, for the first time, he had her believing he was who he said he was.

At the dinner in the pavilion that first night, Sam had tried to talk to Ari, to get his take on leaving behind everything they had ever cared about in order to live in this alternate world. He hadn't wanted to talk and had simply shrugged, as if he was completely okay with taking everything in stride—*oh yes, we've just time traveled to Earth Two, don't mind us!*

The reality of time traveling was so much more than Sam had imagined, so much more ... *everything* ... than she'd been prepared for, even with all the videos she'd watched, descriptions she'd read, and conversations she'd had. It didn't honestly matter that she had been working towards this trip from the moment she'd accepted a job at the Bangor Institute. She'd known Sophie for some time now. Even before Chad picked Sam to travel to Earth Two, the other woman had been up-front about her experiences here. Andre and Sophie had coached Sam even more in the hours leading up to her departure in the helicopter, staying up late going over everything and anything she might encounter.

As if that could ever have been enough.

Ari was right. Sam did blame herself.

Could she have taken the controls and stopped the flight?

That first night, like Ari, she had confessed her regret, apologizing to

David for all she'd failed to do. She couldn't stop thinking she should have known sooner that Marie was one of the hijackers.

At first, Sam had been frozen in her seat by the arrival of the gunmen, not wanting to do anything to jeopardize the lives of her passengers. By the time she'd realized something wasn't right about Marie, the other woman had locked her out of the controls. Sam had been trained on Chad's helicopter. She could fix it and every one of the gadgets and machines they had brought with them. But if anyone had been expecting her to perform some kind of hand-to-hand karate move in the cockpit of a time-traveling helicopter while machine guns were pointed at her head, they were always going to be sorely disappointed.

As, to tell the truth, was she.

It looked to Sam as if Ari was drinking on the job because he was feeling the same regret about the time traveling, and what he had or had not done, as she was.

17

25 September 1297

Johnny

By mid-afternoon, what remained of the Flemish army in this region of Flanders—at least what of it that could be marshalled in a few hours—had gathered roughly a mile from Poeke Castle. The AZs saw no reason to wait to begin retaking what the French had stolen, and had been nothing if not vocal about their wishes. Pausing to catch their breath for even a full night and half a day appeared to them to be a waste of time and had them champing at the bit.

They were quiescent, however, for now. Johnny didn't know how long any of the AZs would be willing to listen to him personally, but they did seem to understand that it would do little good to recapture one of the castles the French had taken if they didn't have men to hold it afterwards. The AZs wanted to change the course of history; they wanted to ensure their beloved Zeeland remained free of foreign rule for many centuries. But even with their wonderful flying machine, there were only four of them. Whether they liked it or not, they needed Johnny, his family, and all the men who could be brought to bear against the French.

After extensive consultation yesterday evening, they had settled on Poeke Castle as the place to begin, with what the AZs called *a demonstration*. The castle was located near the village of Aalter, roughly ten miles west of Gravensteen. The distance was short enough that the cavalry gathered at Gravensteen or in the nearby City of Ghent could easily reach it in a couple of hours. Once a few scouts raced around the country on horseback to let everyone know they were needed, any who could travel on their own reconnaissance could arrive by the time the sun was setting. The Flemish servants who remained at Poeke, acting as spies for Guy, had reported that the castle was held by fewer than thirty—rough, rude, dirty, and otherwise much-hated—Frenchmen.

Jos was supremely confident. "Your villagers should come to see the spectacle, but we will not need them. They should know that before we begin."

"They should not know that." Count Guy had never suffered fools gladly. Jos wasn't a fool, but he was inexperienced in war. "They need to be prepared to fight, so if—"

"When."

Guy overrode Jos as if he hadn't spoken, "—it does come to pass that they are not needed, they will be grateful."

Jos's lip curled, and Johnny just knew he was going to say something impolitic, if not outright unwise.

Before he could, Marie stepped directly in front of him, effectively cutting off his retort. "They are your men, and we will give way to your wisdom and experience." She paused. "As I hope you will see, once we demonstrate our capabilities, we should have the final say over the employment of our flying machine."

Guy studied her, not assenting but not denying her either. Maybe he, like Johnny, had noted the *our*. Then he said, with a slight shrug, "We can discuss this after Poeke is ours once more."

Jos opened his mouth again, but Marie dragged him back towards the helicopter before he could speak.

Beside Johnny, Guy's mouth worked. "They do not take kindly to direction." By now, the AZs had moved away. By the look on his grandfather's face, he was suddenly as worried as Johnny about what they could be discussing. "I see how they look at me. They bow to me only because they think I can give them what they want. This last day has made me realize we must watch them at all times, and we can't trust them."

"Trust depends on what we are hoping they will do. They are full of rage at King Philippe. They want his head on a pike. We can give them that."

"I want it too."

Johnny grunted under his breath. "Can you trust them to obey every order you give them? No, you most definitely cannot. You can't think of them as mercenaries, like those we have employed in the past. These men cannot be bought, by you or anyone else. They have their own code, opaque as it may be. They could easily turn on us if we prevent them from proceeding as they see fit."

Count Guy's eyes had all of a sudden become very wary. "What have you brought me, my boy?"

"A flying machine and people who can fly it," Johnny said simply. "However, I fear their natural disdain for us is going to get worse before it gets better, if it ever does. A victory tonight will embolden them."

"If their further arrogance is the price of that victory, I might call it a fair trade."

Privately, Johnny wasn't so sure. Nevertheless, he saluted his grandfather and went after the AZs. Marie didn't like flying at night, but nighttime was the best time to attack if surprise was the aim. That's why they had brought the helicopter within striking distance of the castle before the sun set, to be sure of their terrain. Having put down in a field, they had set a wide margin of men to watch for stray French soldiers and spies. For the time being, the men within Poeke Castle thought they were well-protected by their high walls and towers.

It would never occur to them—and why would it?—that the Count of Flanders could simply ignore all of that and send his forces over the top.

18

Paris

25 September 1297

Ted

"This part always seems a bit unfair," Ted said. "You've done all the work, but I get to do the talking."

"I find hiding my light under a bushel perfectly acceptable." Elisa pecked him on the cheek. They were having this conversation in American English while waiting for their audience with King Philippe. In the French court, it was so rare as to be shocking for a woman to speak on issues of state. Thus, the need for Ted to take the lead. "You are Garfunkel to my Simon."

Simon and Garfunkel had always been one of Ted's favorite music groups, though they'd broken up before he'd been born. Some people said Ted even looked a bit like Garfunkel, so he appreciated the reference. "It is still wrong, even if you don't mind."

Elisa waggled her head. "Think of it as a way instead for you to lovingly protect your wife by taking all the heat."

Ted scoffed. "And the credit."

"I fear nobody will be getting much in the way of credit today. I'm actually more than a little concerned about what King Philippe's reaction to our news is going to be."

Three hours ago, when they'd arrived at King Philippe's palace on the Île de la Cité, they had just been two among a dozen people loitering in the hallway that passed for an anteroom outside King Philippe's receiving room. Now, they were the only ones left. All the rest had been let in, shared their business with the king, and left. And still, Ted and Elisa waited.

They'd asked to see the king every day since their conversation with David—and been roundly denied every time. They had come in person today only because King Philippe himself had floated the idea that it would serve his interests and his future relationship with David to finally greet them. That had given Matthew the opportunity to argue against the idea one more time. King Philippe had subsequently overridden him.

By now, Ted had no real expectation of actually seeing the king.

A certain measure of King Philippe's unreceptivity was David's fault for asking Matthew to hide their close relationship in the first place. Matthew had risen to the station of one of King Philippe's primary advisers after the events of two years ago. Even if David had completely saved King Philippe's bacon at that time and should have been viewed as a hero, to do so would undermine Philippe's sense of himself and France as preeminent.

Matthew had understood this from the start, and thus had subtly encouraged him to hold David—and thus England—at arms' length. Furthermore, he understood the king's mind enough by now to realize the best way to ensure he did what Matthew really wanted was to urge him towards the opposite idea so vehemently that King Philippe himself began to have second thoughts. Particularly after falling so deeply under the spell of Nogaret, Philippe sought always to be his own man.

After David's initial warning, Matthew had attempted to convey to Philippe the urgency of their need to consult with him. But since Elisa and Ted hadn't been willing to impart any of the details, King Philippe had been happy to refuse them. As always, Matthew had been working hard to maintain the façade that the three of them didn't get along, and that he was hosting them at the Paris Temple on sufferance. Thus, he hadn't been able to push the king any more either. Nor tell him the actual nature of the problem.

And really, the news that King David had traveled to Avalon, been hijacked on his return by a rogue group of modern Zeelanders, and then had his flying vehicle stolen by those same mercenaries who were hellbent on murdering Philippe himself, could not be shared with the King of France in any fashion but in person. And that wasn't even to mention the hijackers' other goals: to free Zeeland from foreign rule and avenge Flanders' defeat at the Battle of Furnes. Ted thought they had an even chance of convincing him of the danger he was facing. That chance went to zero if he wouldn't hear them out.

The key was to get into the room. Once there, Ted had his speech prepared.

For the AZs to take the position that the conquest of Flanders by King Philippe was the beginning of the end for Zeeland wasn't unreasonable. Truly, Ted could sympathize. David had changed the course of Wales's history. He hadn't assassinated King Edward himself, but he'd been on hand when it happened and had to take some of the credit (or blame) for the motivation of the man who'd poisoned a significant sector of the English court. David had given whole peoples in Earth Two a new vision for their lives. Even before his speech last week in Seattle, he had done the same for people in Avalon.

And thus, the AZs had taken matters into their own hands.

At long last, the door to the receiving room opened one more time, and Matthew himself appeared. "Please follow me." He turned on his heel, to all appearances barely maintaining a veneer of politeness. He also didn't look back to make sure they followed.

Other than Archbishop Romeyn, who until recently had been England's official ambassador to France, no member of David's court had been in King Philippe's presence since David had bent the knee to him two years ago. It was because of those events that David could not return to Paris again, regardless of what Philippe promised. Ted knew his nephew wanted to trust the French king, but even if he understood the extenuating circumstances that had made King Philippe behave as he had, he couldn't put the throne of England in jeopardy that way. His responsibility to the people he ruled was too great.

If David were ever to meet King Philippe in person again, it would have to be on neutral ground. Traditionally, negotiating parties met at the ford of a river running between their two territories. King Philippe owed David his life and those of his whole family. This fact was probably the only reason he hadn't declared war on England already for interfering in Normandy. He could still feel grateful for all David had done for him.

In turn, David had thought he could trust him enough to send his aunt and uncle to Paris. Ted thought there was an even chance he and Elisa were going to end the day in chains.

Upon reaching the far end of the hall where King Philippe waited on his golden throne, Ted halted, a half pace ahead of Elisa. "King Philippe." He bent his head while Elisa curtseyed. "Thank you for seeing us. It is an honor."

That was the kind of vague and yet respectful greeting King Philippe liked. Ted had become good at diplomacy long before he'd come to Earth Two. Chief Financial Officers didn't have to be quite as charismatic as their CEO counterparts, but it was an important skill to be able to reply in such a way that what you said meant nothing substantial while encouraging your listeners to see your words as respectful.

At Ted's platitude, King Philippe nodded stiffly (not a good sign), at which point Matthew stepped in to speak. Ted wasn't surprised since Matthew had warned him that the king often had his councilors speak for him. "King Philippe has graciously agreed to hear your petition today. What is it you have to say?"

The subtext of that was *spit it out and don't waste my time!* Matthew really was very good at expressing disdain. Ted was glad he didn't have to believe him.

The moment had come. Ted called upon all the confidence those many years of hobnobbing with powerful executives had taught him to show, even if he wasn't feeling entirely confident inside. "King David of England has sent us news that touches upon the safety of the King of France. A force may be on its way to Paris that intends the king harm."

As seemed to be his mandate, Matthew started to speak again, but this time King Philippe put up a hand to stop him. Leaning forward from his seat, he asked, "A force? What kind of force?"

Ted bent his head. "If you could bear with me, I would be happy to explain. You are aware, I'm sure, that King David originated in Avalon?"

"We are aware." It was the royal *we,* and King Philippe's expression implied he could have added, *and we are from France.* As if that somehow was equivalent.

Ted nodded. "Several agents of a malevolent organization managed to ride on David's coattails when he returned from Avalon, and then they escaped. We believe they are on their way to Europe, if they are not here already. King David feels himself responsible for being caught unawares and offers you whatever of his resources you will accept in order to deal with the threat."

David had been aware that this particular phrasing—in other words, admitting fault—would put him at a disadvantage with King

Philippe. He had decided he didn't care, and he couldn't pretend the situation was better than it was. He did feel responsible. He was also entirely sincere about offering to help, even as he knew Philippe would refuse it.

Which he did, with a wave of his hand. It was almost as if the whole scene had been scripted. It wasn't just Ted's words, which they'd lined out in advance, but King Philippe's reply too. David had to offer, and King Philippe had to refuse. In this moment, he was no more able to break out of the mold that had made him than any previous French king.

King Philippe had managed to put aside his pride twice in the past: once on the battlement of Chateau Niort when Gilbert de Clare had attempted to assassinate him and David both, after which the two kings had made their way across Aquitaine together. At that time, David had felt them to be almost like brothers. Those events were what had allowed King Philippe to reach out to David a second time, believing when he asked for David's help to save his wife and children that David would come through for him.

As he had.

But that was then. This King Philippe was not the same man he'd been two years ago. It wasn't just that he was older. He was harder than he had been then, or maybe that's just what he had to tell himself. He *couldn't* be in David's debt again. It would be too shameful.

Ted had to try anyway. "King Philippe—"

"We fear for your safety, my lord." Elisa stepped forward, not as they'd planned, but because they had nothing left to lose.

King Philippe blinked twice. "Madam." Then his expression softened, and he bowed his head to her, which was probably the most positive thing he could have done. In the English court, the idea that a woman couldn't speak before the king was laughable. But even King Philippe's queen, Joan, rarely put in an appearance in these public exchanges. Women's voices were best heard in private, if at all. "I am well protected. Have no fear for me. My sainted grandfather is watching over me." And then he unbent even further. "We do appreciate your concern. My wife will be glad to know that our bond with England remains strong."

"We are pleased to know it too." Ted bowed a little deeper this time. As he came up, he was ready to try again with the plea that King Philippe accept their aid, but Philippe had already risen to his feet and was turning towards a door located in the wall behind the throne.

They were dismissed. Ted knew it, but he still couldn't let it go. The French king was being stupid. Some part of him had to know it. So Ted broke protocol in order to try again—even as a spasm of pain crossed Matthew's face to see it. Protocol was *everything* in the French court.

"My lord—" He used the honorific, since King Philippe needed to listen. If that meant throwing himself at his feet, so be it. "These men are not your usual mercenaries. They are from Avalon. Imagine four men like George, willing to do anything and be anything to get their way." He didn't bother to mention that one of the *men* in question was really Marie, a woman. "They have weapons and abilities far beyond what any of your men possess or can array against them. They might even come at you from the air. If so, you will not be able to stop them. Let us help you."

At first, it looked as if Philippe wasn't bothering even to listen, since he was at the door before Ted had finished his plea. Matthew, who'd stayed behind, growled a bit under his breath, trying to get Ted to turn away. "It's too late. Let it go."

Ted resisted, continuing to stand in the middle of the hall. He was an Avalonian and an American to boot. All men were created equal in his world, and no protocol was going to stop him from doing what was right. He kept his gaze on the king.

At the last moment, King Philippe glanced back and their eyes met. For two seconds, Ted thought Philippe was going to soften, like he had earlier with Elisa. But then his expression returned to granite. "We do appreciate your warning, as I said, but France can take care of itself."

Then he was gone.

The three of them turned as one and left too. They knew better than to say another word within the confines of the palace. It wasn't until they were out the gates and in the street again that Elisa sighed. "For just a moment, I thought he might break the pattern."

"I know. I hoped for it too. If he had, right now we could have been standing around a plan of the castle, plotting how to counter an attack by helicopter." Ted shook his head. "But he is who he is."

It was these glimpses of an inner man that kept giving them the hope real change was possible. But then Philippe always reverted back to the person who in Avalon had destroyed the Templars and expelled France's Jewish population, all so he could take their money.

"I agree with Elisa." Matthew looked more worn than usual. "I'm sorry, but it was always going to go this way."

"We know that. So did David," Ted said. "We had to try. We could have been wrong this one time."

"What are we going to do now?" Matthew said.

"What we've been doing," Elisa said. "What we've always done. Philippe's newly sainted grandfather might be watching over him but pardon my thought that he'll need a bit more tangible protection too."

Ted nodded. "And that means we're going to help him anyway, whether he wants our help or not."

19

25 September 1297

Robbie

Robbie turned as he hit the gangway and held out his hand to Samantha to help her off the ship. "We'll rest at the castle here in Portsmouth tonight and leave tomorrow morning. If all goes well, we can be in Rouen a few days after that. I know it took two days to get here, but that's good progress so far. No need to worry."

They'd left Carew within hours of the helicopter's disappearance. They couldn't catch it, but constant failure wasn't going to prevent them from trying. Having ridden to Pembroke, they had then borrowed Cardinal Francesco's ship (with his blessing) at the Pembroke dock. They had mostly been blessed with winds that had pushed them in the right direction at the right time. Robbie had been born a nobleman rather than a seaman (a fact for which he could be endlessly grateful), so he didn't know any more about sailing than that. The ship had carried them from *point a to point b* as the Avalonians had been known to say, from Pembroke to Portsmouth, and that was good enough for him.

Up until now, Robbie hadn't approached Sam, beyond a few isolated instances, even within the close confines of the ship. He hadn't been avoiding her so much as struggling with how to talk to her. He'd never met a girl his age from Avalon before. The only reason Robbie had turned to her even now was because it would have been unchivalrous not to. Somehow, the others had disembarked ahead of them, and there wasn't anybody left to make sure she navigated the gap between the ship and the dock with ease in her dress that was still soaked from the knees down.

To be fair, Christopher had been first off the ship, supporting Isabelle. Ari had marched off with Huw immediately after. He had already apologized for his drunkenness and for the things he'd said. By now, they hadn't found it hard to forgive him. Even Robbie, who had never time traveled, could appreciate how traveling to a different world could put a man out of his depth.

Which left Robbie with Sam, who looked up at him, smiling. "I don't know that I would have said *worry* is the right word for what I'm feeling, but I appreciate the reassurance." She squeezed his hand. "And the help."

"My sense is you got more than you bargained for in flying here with David."

Sam let out a laugh of surprise as a splash of water from a rogue wave sloshed over the dock and wet the hem of her dress even more than it already was. "Is it that obvious? What about you? This can't have been your first choice for how to spend this week. How are you holding up?"

Robbie found himself blinking back his surprise. He couldn't remember the last time someone had asked him how *he* was doing. "I've truly had a good few days, compared to the previous ones." Then, when she looked confused, he said by way of explanation, "King David almost died from eating walnuts and went to Avalon. We are all doing great now that he's back."

Though she'd laughed a moment ago, and he'd seen her flashing smile numerous times before that, this was the first time she'd directed her smile at him. It was as if her soul was shining through her eyes. "And to think we in Avalon were excited because we had a chance to see him, if only for a few days."

That stopped him too. "It never occurred to me to think about it that way. I'll remember that the next time David *travels*, if there is a next time, which I assume there will be." He shook his head. "One world's loss is another's gain, and maybe, because of it, knowing everyone there is happy to see him, I can worry less about him not being here."

"I don't know if you should be that content. He has been chased across the planet a bit." By now they were off the dock, the wind at their backs, with a force that might indicate a change in the weather.

Robbie kept hold of her hand as they paced after the others. "And thrown out of an airplane, so I hear."

"That too. You worry about him, and we worry about him." Sam wrinkled her nose. "Most of the time he leaves unexpectedly, and it's hard to accept that we can't know what he has fallen into here."

"Or there," Robbie said.

"Now that I do know, I can't say it's going to make me worry any less!"

"Same." Robbie let down his guard enough to make an exaggerated fierce face, which made Samantha laugh again. "Nonetheless, we're keeping him."

Then Huw returned, huffing to a halt in front of them. At that point, Robbie realized he'd kept hold of Sam's hand and quickly dropped it.

Huw, meanwhile, shot Sam a grin, forcing Robbie to swallow down an inappropriate—and out of character—growl. Women always fawned over Huw. It could have been annoying if he wasn't so gracious about it. Sam, however, was merely looking at Huw expectantly.

"There's been a development," Huw said.

"Can't you tell us?" Robbie said.

Huw grinned again. "I could, but I'm not going to."

Resigned to letting Huw have his fun, the three of them hustled towards the castle where they would be spending the night. Portchester Castle, Portsmouth's primary fortress, was one of many similar edifices built over the centuries along the southern coastline to defend England. According to those who knew more than Robbie, the Romans had been the first to build a fort here, to protect their shipments in and out of Britain. In short, Portsmouth had been a chief port for a very long time.

Once inside the castle's receiving room, Robbie himself laughed at the sight of the two old friends, Henri and Thomas, both Templar knights, waiting to greet them. Henri was quite a lot older than Robbie and years ago had ridden across France with David in haste to prevent the usurpation of David's throne by Gilbert de Clare. Thomas was slightly younger than Robbie and had encountered Meg more than ten years ago at Hadrian's Wall, when he was a boy. Both men had become staunch allies and belonged to the inner circle of people who knew real truths about David and his family. If Robbie couldn't have William de Bohun and James Stewart at his side, these two were the next best thing.

Robbie hugged each of the men in turn, grinning as widely as Huw at the sight of them. Sam, by contrast, remained hovering by the door where Robbie had left her. She looked as uncertain as Robbie sometimes felt amongst strangers, and he made a point of bringing her closer and introducing her to his friends.

Once the formalities were over, Henri didn't make them wait for his news. "Early yesterday morning, the helicopter you're looking for flew over London, heading east above the River Thames."

"That was yesterday morning?" Ari ran a hand through his hair. "How does that make sense?"

Henri didn't understand why the timing was bothersome, so Robbie explained, "We are not questioning that it happened. We're puzzled because we expected the helicopter to have reached London sooner."

Henri's expression cleared. "That's partly why we are here. Master Godfrid spoke to King David on the evening he returned from Avalon, and then a second time after these ... what did you call them?"

"AZs," Christopher supplied.

"AZs stole the helicopter. He asked us to inform him if we heard it passing overhead. At that point, we hadn't, but once we knew it might come, we put out sentries and scouts. As it turned out, the whole of London heard it when it came!"

"Fortunately, Londoners consider themselves old hands when it comes to Avalonian vehicles and were mostly unimpressed." Thomas picked up the tale. "Afterwards, Master Godfrid tried to speak to the king again but he wasn't there, so we talked to Queen Lili." He then explained about the king's journey to the clearing where the helicopter had landed for a time, concluding, "The AZs lost many hours caring for their wounded comrade."

Sam looked pensive. "Maybe the rest of the time they were re-fueling."

Ari nodded. "Regardless, we have to assume they have reached Flanders or Paris by now."

"How is it you were in London at all?" Robbie put aside what they couldn't help, as they always had to. "Last we heard, you were in Aquitaine."

"Master Godfrid recalled us," Henri said. "At the time, he didn't say why, and we didn't question him. He needed us, so we came."

"Honestly, I was hoping we would arrive in England in time to come with you to the king's tournament at Carew," Thomas said. "I had to swallow my disappointment once we reached London, since you had already left. Now, I see it was just as well. If we had gone with you, we wouldn't have been on hand for Master Godfrid to send to Portsmouth with our news. Lili says you can use our help, and we should join your adventure."

Robbie held back his first impulse, which was to scoff. It wasn't that he didn't welcome their company. Both were proven companions, as their sixty-mile ride since yesterday from London to Portchester Castle revealed. He was just reluctant to accord Master Godfrid with *the sight*. That was for those with Celtic blood, and a tiny part of him was even a little offended that a Saxon would be so blessed.

But, as with all of God's gifts that He'd bestowed on David and his companions, Robbie chose to be grateful. Some of those gifts had also been bestowed on Robbie himself. And besides, Queen Lili did have *the sight*, and she wanted Thomas and Henri to join them.

So he nodded. "You want an adventure? You two get to go with Huw and Ari to Flanders."

20

25 September 1297
Johnny

"I t's *go* time." Zee was practically jumping up and down with glee.

Johnny wasn't feeling quite as enthusiastic about the coming endeavor as his cousin, but he was on board enough not to object to Zee's phrasing. Johnny's English wasn't exceptional, but he'd spent enough time with English speakers this last week to fill in some gaps and develop a desire to learn more. Zee had been an even better student.

And really, given the fact that England was his country's biggest trading partner, it made sense to learn the language.

Neither Zee nor Johnny was in line for the throne of Flanders since they had been born to Count Guy's daughters. Johnny himself had always been content to be his grandfather's ally, since he was a duke in his own right. That meant he theoretically outranked his grandfather when viewed from the perspective of the hierarchy of nobility in Europe. To think that was true in practice, however, would be a mistake. The mercenaries from Avalon had arrived in Flanders due to Johnny's and Zee's efforts, but they'd gone first to Gravensteen because Count Guy was the driving force behind the movement towards independence from France.

"Are you sure about participating, my lord?" That was from Jos, who appeared much more content now that they were on their way. All of the AZs had come on this mission, the two wounded refusing to be left behind. Marie, of course, couldn't be left behind, even if anyone still thought to view her as a woman. She was the pilot. She was flying them in. "Once we arrive at the castle, you are welcome to remain in the helicopter."

"Of course, I'm sure." Johnny gestured to Arne, who still had a tight bandage around his leg. "Marie, Arne, and Zee are more than enough to protect the helicopter."

When they'd discovered the stash of weapons, the AZs had warned Johnny—and subsequently Guy, his grandfather—that unless a contingent of David's men joined the fight and brought similar weapons, their ability to defeat any number of French forces would be limited by a lack of ammunition for the weapons.

For now, though, for this, he had been assured, they had enough.

While his grandfather's forces moved into place around Poeke Castle, the few of them in the helicopter were going to take it all on their own. Before the arrival of the AZs, the very idea would have been ludicrous. Now, it was a dream come true, not only for Johnny, but for his grandfather and all the men who waited down below. And, apparently, for these strangers from a strange land too.

Since leaving Carew, time and distance had become no object. They'd stolen the helicopter just two days ago. They'd made the plan they were currently carrying out *last night*. They could fly two hundred miles in a few hours. People were transformed into messenger pigeons.

And because of this capability, eight people were thought to be enough: Johnny and Zee; the four AZs; and two other companions, Willem and Erik. These last two were in their middle-thirties, seasoned soldiers, with eyes that, up until this morning when they'd been selected by Johnny's grandfather for this mission, implied they'd seen everything. By now, they had managed to rein in their incredulity at the AZs' mode of transport and weapons. They were here as two more hands and as further representatives of the interests of the Count of Flanders. And, maybe, to watch Johnny's and Zee's backs.

"Keep your focus on Paul and me," Jos said. "Stay behind us at all times. I don't want you caught in any crossfire. There will be no casualties on our side today."

"I will be careful. Do not worry about me." Johnny chose not to express any degree of the skepticism he still retained that any castle, no matter the weaponry brought to bear against it, could be taken with no casualties. Plans were all very well and good. Necessary, even. But they didn't last more than a few moments once the enemy engaged. Any good soldier knew that. Johnny might be young, but he had survived multiple battles against the French. He was not as young as he looked anymore.

"We're approaching the wall." Marie spoke through her *headset*. Jos (somewhat magnanimously) had once again given Johnny one of his own, so he could hear what they were saying to each other and speak in a normal tone. Johnny felt he had mastered the terminology, even if the words he had learned referred to ideas and things that three days ago would have been nonsensical.

The headset muffled the sound of the engine. He ignored it, as he had been ignoring everything he didn't understand or had trouble comprehending. That he was trepidatious about the theft of the helicopter and its ultimate impact on Flanders' relationship with England had no effect on his attitude towards this mission. Poeke Castle had been taken by the French. As an agent of his grandfather, he would do everything in his power, and use any weapon or personnel who came to hand, to take it back.

He would take it all back. Only then would all this be worth it.

The helicopter soared over the walls and hovered above the highest tower, prompting Paul to slide open the door. Arne was ready with his weapon and, within a heartbeat, had shot the lone soldier standing on top of the keep, gaping up at them. Such was the power of the weapon that the back of the man's head exploded like a ripe plum thrown against a stone wall. Down he went.

With one shot, the first stage of their attack was over.

"Go! Go! Go!" The spoken command wasn't all that different from what he had heard at the tournament in English, and Johnny took comfort in the idea that the distance between him and King David might not be too vast to cross. Their roots were the same. In the

end, David would understand why Johnny was doing what he was doing.

That confidence, misplaced as it might be, alleviated some of his terror at the prospect of sliding down a rope from the hovering helicopter to the top of the keep. Paul had tied knots every few feet to give them something to hang onto and arrest the suddenness of the drop. Like all of them, Johnny wore gloves, which would help with his grip and minimize rope burns.

Once Jos reached the tower, Johnny started after him. Marie would stay in the helicopter with Zee and Arne, whose job it was to shoot anyone he saw that wasn't one of them.

As Johnny's feet hit the wooden walkway, Arne shot a guard on the battlement below, who'd recovered enough from the sight of the helicopter flying above him to try to counter their attack with a crossbow. He got off his shot just before he died. The bolt hit the side of the craft with a bang and then fell harmlessly back to earth.

Johnny held the bottom of the rope, as he'd been told to do, first for Paul, who followed immediately after him, his wound to his upper arm seemingly forgotten, and next for Willem and Erik. Then, also as instructed, he stayed to the rear of the two AZs. The trap door flew open as they reached it. Jos shot the man who poked up his head—and then a second climbing up the ladder behind him.

The dead men fell to the floor below. Johnny followed Jos and Paul down the ladder, across the floor of the guardroom, to the stairwell that would take them down through the keep. He didn't avert his eyes as he stepped over the bodies. This was what he'd signed up for. He could say one thing for the way Jos meted out death: the men he killed died quickly.

Jos had not entrusted Johnny himself with one of the Avalonian weapons, but now that he was on his own two feet, he held his sword bare in his hand. That he was on this mission at all was as much a sop to his sensibilities as because his grandfather had insisted on it. It was the Count of Flanders who was taking this castle, not these Avalonian mercenaries, and Guy wanted to make sure they were clear on the command structure from the start. The black lion of Flanders would be raised above the tower, not the Zeeland banner or whatever flag these AZs held dear.

The AZs were fine with that. Even Zee, who was the Count of Zeeland, was fine with that. Zee was Guy's grandson, the same as Johnny, and the AZs had no quarrel with Flanders. It was their common enemy, the King of France, who concerned them. For Johnny's part, he was the Duke of Brabant, Lothier, and Limburg, all territories either already taken or under threat by France. The only reason Zee wasn't coming down the stairs behind Johnny was because their grandfather had also decreed he wasn't going to lose both grandsons to this mission, if it went awry. And besides, Zee was still only thirteen.

Bang! Bang! Bang! Every man who poked his head out of a room or was encountered coming up the stairwell was killed before he could draw breath. The rate at which the AZs were meting out death was unprecedented.

Although they were still within the tower, as they descended through the stories, *clearing* each one, to use Jos's words, Johnny could also hear Arne continuing to pick off French soldiers from the air. Over it all came the continuing beat of the helicopter.

With the two AZs in the lead, their party surged out of the keep to find themselves at the top of the old motte, no longer surrounded by its own ditch and wall but squatting in the center of the bailey. The ground below them was littered with bodies of dead French soldiers. At least a dozen lay within Johnny's current field of vision.

At long last, the helicopter settled onto the sparse grass and dirt between the buildings. Arne continued to sit nonchalantly on the floor of the helicopter with his legs outside and his feet hanging. Zee crouched beside him, his sword in his hand, though there was nobody on whom to use it. Marie stayed in the pilot's seat.

Jos motioned with his fingers towards the great hall. "Shoot anyone with a weapon. There may be friendlies among them. The count won't thank us for killing his own people."

"We got it," Paul said, and he and Erik headed off in that direction—Erik with a sword like Johnny.

Jos ordered Willem to stand guard at the top of the steps, ready to shout a warning if anyone poked his head out from the surrounding buildings. Then Jos and Johnny approached the waiting helicopter.

"How many in the keep?" Arne said without preamble.

"Twelve, including the one you neutralized on the battlement. I count fourteen on the ground. How many on the wall-walk?"

"Another six. They weren't prepared to be taken from the air."

"How could they be?" Jos said simply. Then he turned to Johnny. "We were told to expect thirty soldiers garrisoned here. We're at thirty-two now. How far off might our intelligence be?"

Johnny was still getting over the fact that the three AZs had *neutralized* thirty-two men in hardly more than a quarter of an hour. "I don't know. We trust the spy who gave us that number." He looked past Jos to Arne. "How many came from within the gatehouse?"

"Two."

Johnny nodded. "They would have been guarding the main gate as well as the Flemish prisoners in the basement."

"We'll free them presently. Time to open the gates." Jos made a little bow, possibly his first, in Johnny's direction. "My lord, I present to you Poeke Castle."

21

26 September 1297

Ted

"Open the door in the name of the king!"

No person, whether medieval, modern, or somewhere in between, could hear those words and not have a momentary heart attack at what it might foretell.

Not really by coincidence, since Ted was something of a morning person (unlike Elisa), he had been standing on the battlement of the Paris Temple, watching the sun illumine the city with the dawn. He had heard the company riding towards the temple before he'd seen it, but he hadn't known that the riders were making for the Paris Temple itself until they arrived at the gatehouse. It was roughly a mile as the crow flies from the heart of Paris on the Île de la Cité. Those riders could have been headed anywhere. Really, right up until they arrived at the door, they could have been a delegation from one of the other Templar commanderies in France or elsewhere. Maybe even from Master Godfrid in London. That would have been something to be happy about. As it was, the riders were dressed in the king's livery.

In Avalon, the Paris Temple had been demolished long since, along with the Templar Order itself. All that remained was a metro stop on the M3 (Gold) line. In Earth Two, the Paris Temple, still in all its magnificence, was located on the right bank at the northern edge of the city. The commandery's southern gate led directly into the city, while a northern gate gave access to the countryside and effectively protected that side of Paris. Sixty-odd years from now, the walls of the city would be extended to enclose the entire commandery (though by then, of course, it no longer belonged to the Templars). For now, the commandery was like a square appendage sticking out from the main body of Paris.

Ted had time to warn the men who guarded the gatehouse that the king's men were coming. While one of the monks ran to wake Matthew, another greeted the newcomers, and Ted stayed at his post. His position as ambassador (or husband to the ambassador) was fraught enough that he didn't want to miss hearing firsthand what this delegation was about.

Although the seat of the Templar Grand Master, Jacques de Molay, was in Cyprus, it was the Paris Temple that was the center of the Templar world in Europe. For the King of France to take it upon himself to send a company of riders to pound at the door when it was barely light enough to see was a serious breach of etiquette. That was especially true since Matthew was one of the king's own advisers. King Philippe might be displeased with him in some fashion, but this was taking that displeasure quite a long way too far.

Ted couldn't help flash back to a movie he'd seen in Avalon that reenacted King Philippe's destruction of the Templars. That had been in 1307, ten years from now by Earth Two's reckoning. If King Philippe was moving up the timeline, their best bet was to use the tunnels beneath the commandery that had facilitated the flight with Paris's Jewish community two years ago. That would be better than having to watch Matthew burn at the stake.

Matthew knew that history now. Nonetheless, the soldiers were admitted quickly and with grace. Besides which, in and of themselves, they were not numerous enough to take over the commandery. They milled about in the bailey for a minute or two while Matthew got dressed, which also gave Ted time to make his way down from the battlements. Whatever arose from this intrusion, it had the promise of being a bit more pressing than what was supposed to be his occupation this morning, namely looking over some financial documents for Matthew.

The leader of the squad of soldiers stood with his hands on his hips in the center of the bailey, waiting. When Matthew's adjutant approached to tell him he could be seen, he lifted his chin in what had to be described as a haughty manner and marched after him.

Ted stayed in the shadows, hustling down a corridor and two sets of stairs to reach the back door to Matthew's receiving room ten seconds before the soldier was ushered inside. Matthew saw Ted come in and waved him into a corner with a flick of his fingers. They were comfortable enough with each other that Ted had no trouble doing as he was bid, even if it meant hiding behind a pillar.

"How may I help you?" The Temple's receiving room was not unlike King Philippe's own, though smaller and far less ornate. Matthew spoke in the politest terms too, without mentioning the way he'd been rousted far too early in the morning.

The soldier had been arrogant with Matthew's people, but when faced with the Master of the Paris Temple himself, he stuck to the forms, beginning by bowing respectfully. The Templars remained a force to be reckoned with, at least for now. "I am not here for you or any of your people, Master Norris. I seek the ambassador from England."

"The ambassador is a guest in my house. Who summons him?"

"King Philippe, of course." The man paused. "I come to you with the request that you allow him to return with me to the palace. I would prefer you do not make me demand it. I respect you and your holy order too much for that."

Matthew studied the man for a bit longer than was polite. The newcomer was of below average height, a little dumpy, and had pulled back his fine blond curls into a tail at the nape of his neck. Ted already didn't like him.

Finally, Matthew said, "Do you know what is behind these summons?"

"It is not my business to know why the king requires something, only to obey his orders." What was left unsaid were the words, *that is also your duty*. This was the king asking, after all.

Matthew endeavored to stall. "May I see the exact wording on the summons? I assume it was written down." In addition to being David's representative in France, not to mention his uncle, Ted was the Earl of Gloucester and the Lord High Treasurer of England. It wasn't just some commoner Philippe was summoning.

The messenger coughed lightly. "No, Master, it was not."

"Who then passed the order on to you? Was it from the king's own mouth? I am asking purely for my own clarification, so when the King of England asks me why his ambassador was brought to the palace by armed soldiers, I can tell him."

The other man didn't like the question, but he squared his normally rounded shoulders nonetheless and carried on. "The order came from the king's chancellor."

Ted managed not to groan out loud. The adventures of two years ago had brought down Guillaume de Nogaret, King Philippe's most influential adviser at the time. He was still in prison as far as Ted knew. Although the exposure of Nogaret as a schemer had elevated Matthew and Archbishop Romeyn, it had left several other untrustworthy individuals in place. One of those was Pierre Flote, the Chancellor of France and the Keeper of the Seals.

That it was he, in fact, who'd sent the soldiers explained the heavy-handed approach and the obvious desire to put Ted (and Matthew) at a disadvantage. Flote would not be able to prove that Matthew was more loyal to David than to King Philippe, but Ted wouldn't be surprised to learn he felt it in his bones. It had been Matthew (and the Templars) who had gained the most once Nogaret fell.

Flote had been placed on probation and kept on a short leash. Apparently, that leash had been lengthened or dropped entirely.

When Matthew didn't immediately give way, the messenger cleared his throat and spoke again. "I would not want to return to the king with the news that you refused to give him up. Is that what you wish?"

"Of course not. I have no reason to refuse the king. I am just concerned about how it will look to King David."

"You mean, the *Duke of Gascony and Aquitaine*?" the messenger said, this time with a genuine sneer he couldn't—or didn't bother—to suppress.

"As you well know, Ambassador Shepherd is not here on behalf of the Duke of Gascony and Aquitaine," Matthew said gently. "He is here as a representative of the King of England."

And the High King of Britain, Matthew could have said, but Ted didn't hold it against him for not throwing that in too. If the messenger had known what was good for him, he would have taken a step back to hear Matthew's tone become that dry. Ted knew his friend well enough by now to realize it meant his patience was at an end.

There seemed to be no help for it, however. Before Matthew said something he might regret, or worse, blew his cover, Ted stepped out from behind the pillar. He was counting on Matthew to get him out of whatever danger this represented, which he wouldn't be able to do if he was exposed as an agent for David or England. "I am pleased to consult with King Philippe on any topic that concerns him. As I told him yesterday, we are at his service."

Matthew held the soldier's gaze, rather than telegraphing his concern by glancing at Ted. "I will accompany the ambassador as well."

"That won't be necess—"

"Are you questioning me, Enguerrand?"

It was only then that Ted realized he was looking at Enguerrand de Marigny, currently not much more established at court than any other retainer in the king's household. In a few years, he would become one of King Philippe's most trusted men. In fact, in Avalon's past, he fully supported the annexation of Flanders and re-placed Pierre Flote as Chamberlain after Flote's death at the *Battle of the Golden Spurs*—a battle fought in 1302 between Flanders and France. A battle France actually lost.

Not that the victory had helped Flanders in the end. The de-feat served only to entrench King Philippe's conviction that he had to control Flanders and the whole of what in the future became the Netherlands. He renewed the war, and Count Guy died in prison in 1305.

All of that was still to come, *or not*, in Earth Two.

Ted put up a hand to imply surrender, and two seconds later found himself surrounded by soldiers. With Enguerrand in the lead, they marched out of the receiving room, down some stairs, out the door of the keep, and then across the bailey to the gatehouse, above which less than a half-hour earlier Ted had been standing admiring the sunrise. Matthew followed close behind, and his own men were attuned enough to the situation to already have two horses saddled: one for Ted and one for Matthew. It was a mile to the palace, after all. Enguerrand could hardly expect Ted to walk.

Or maybe that was exactly what he had expected. Enguerrand's eyes narrowed as Ted mounted, showing a measure of discontent that implied the Frenchman had been looking forward to urging him down the street on foot as he and his men rode towards the palace. Ted shot Matthew a grateful look that he'd been spared that humiliation.

He also had to send up a prayer of thanksgiving that Elisa had slept through the whole thing. She might be upset to find him gone, and a little worried once she learned why, but she wouldn't be marched to the palace herself. He really was lovingly protecting his wife, just like he'd suggested.

Then, he had a momentary panic at the risks she might be willing to take to get him back.

As they rode towards the Île de la Cité, Ted tried to keep in mind that being summoned to the palace at dawn wasn't quite tantamount to a declaration of war. Two years ago, King Philippe had imprisoned David and his family, since his own family was being held hostage by Nogaret and his ilk. It could be that something similar was happening now. For the time being, Ted was willing—yet again—to give Philippe the benefit of the doubt.

Like all of them, the King of France was a product of his own upbringing. There was always the hope he could rise above it.

Maybe he was simply going to rake Ted over the coals. Maybe he had some grave news to impart. What was definitely true was that King Philippe was feeling more confident in this moment than he had since David's departure from Paris two years ago. David had saved his life. King Philippe had been grateful.

Too bad that gratitude had taken him, and all of them, only so far.

22

26 September 1297

Ted

Ted and Matthew arrived in the king's receiving room, unchanged from the day before, except for the addition of Pierre Flote, who was standing at the king's right hand. Yesterday, the person in that position had been Matthew.

Two years ago, David had been frog-marched out the door of the palace and into captivity at the behest of King Philippe. At that time, Philippe was being blackmailed and forced to act against his will. Today, he didn't look like he was acting against his will at all. Today, he was standing on the dais, rather than sitting on his throne, and his expression was as intense as Ted had ever seen it.

"Lord king." Ted opted for a new honorific, choosing to ignore the fact that he had five soldiers around him. "I have come, as requested."

"Ambassador." King Philippe's tone was as stiff as his shoulders.

Flote stepped to the fore. He appeared even thinner than he had two years ago, with grayer hair. Ted could see why the intervening period might have been difficult for him. "This morning we received some startling news that our beloved king is concerned you did not share with us yesterday."

Ted tipped his head and looked expectant. He had decided pretty quickly that in an unknown diplomatic situation, it was best to say as little as possible.

Flote, however, objected to his silence. "You have no reply?" He came off the dais so he was on Ted's level, though still a good six feet away.

"I did not realize you had asked me a question that required an answer. I do not know what news you have heard, so I did not think it would be wise to comment on it." Again, he was filling his sentences with stuff that sounded good while saying nothing.

"Poeke Castle has fallen to the Count of Flanders." The words exploded from King Philippe, causing both Flote and Ted to whip their heads in his direction. "They came with a flying machine!"

King Philippe was the same age as David, born earlier in the same year, with the long nose and high forehead of his ancestors. History knew him as Philippe le Bel—Philippe the Fair, in reference to his handsome looks rather than because he was a just ruler. Speaking as a loving wife, Elisa had said she didn't think he was particularly attractive.

Ted had been in many high-level meetings before he'd come to Earth Two. He'd worked for Chad Treadman once upon a time. So he did a quick canter around the possible replies he could or should make and decided his best option was to speak the entire truth as he saw it, come what may. "Thus, our petition to you, that you heard yesterday. Though, if you recall, we had requested an audience the moment we learned such an action had become a possibility. We were repeatedly turned away."

Flote made no effort to swallow his anger, which was really in mimicry of the king's. "Are you blaming *us* for this treachery?"

Ted looked at him hard. "We asked for an audience with the king days ago. Master Norris brought our request to the palace and spoke it directly in the king's ear. Was it on your advice he denied us?"

Flote's mouth worked, giving Ted the answer he needed without Flote having to actually say it. Even Matthew hadn't related that observation. Though, in truth, Ted's guess hadn't been that far-fetched.

Looking past Flote to where King Philippe had resumed his seat on his throne, he added, "This may be the first of many castles they take, my lord. I don't know that we can be of assistance to you in Flanders—" *nor want to*, he could have said, "—but we would be wise to look to the defenses here." Then he spoke again to Flote. "When did Poeke fall?"

"Last night." Flote still stood on Ted's level, with his back to the king. His face had a tenseness to it, like he thought Ted was trying to deceive him in some way, but he wasn't sure how.

To be honest, Ted couldn't have told him. Deception had never been his strong suit. "How is it possible you know this already? Poeke Castle is two hundred miles from here."

"They sent a pigeon," King Philippe said. "We have spies all through Flanders, with instructions to warn us if Count Guy attempts to regain the upper hand."

Messenger pigeons had been used for communication across long distances since ancient times. The message being sent had to be written on a tiny piece of paper or the pigeon couldn't carry it. A message along the lines of *Poeke Castle under attack by Guy,* however, could easily be relayed.

"Could it be that Count Guy was not involved?" Ted said. "Unless you are certain of that too?"

"The word came only that a flying machine took the castle," Flote said, as stiffly as ever.

"Were those the exact words sent?"

Flote threw up his hands. "Why do you need to know exactly?"

"I can't help you if I don't have all the information."

Flote looked back to King Philippe, who made a motion with his hand, resigned now, rather than angry. "Show him."

With evident reluctance, Flote pulled out the little scrap of paper. Ted's written French had been passable when he'd come to Earth Two, not having had call to use it except in dealings with foreign transactions, but it had quickly come up to speed. He read, *Poeke Castle fallen. Many dead. Reports of steel bird carrying men.*

Ted let out a breath. "I am pleased you are no longer questioning the truth of what I've been saying."

"I knew it was true when you told me of it." King Philippe was back to being disdainful. His nose couldn't have been higher in the air.

"Is that because you had spies at the tournament in Wales, also with pigeons to send?"

Again, Flote gave away the answer, this time with a curl of his lip, before King Philippe confirmed it with a shrug. "We should not be at such a disadvantage that we have to wait for this news. You should have told us the moment you learned Poeke was a target."

Ted blinked. "But I didn't know it was until you told me."

"Flote assures me you have a communication device at the Paris Temple that allows you to speak to distant lands, including where King David currently resides."

Ted didn't risk a glance at Matthew to see how he was taking this revelation. For all intents and purposes, Philippe was telling them he'd placed a spy in the commandery.

King Philippe then brought the full weight of the royal gaze down on Matthew. "My respect for you and your order is such that my men did not take it this morning. That you did not tell me the ambassador brought such a device with him has caused me to question your loyalty."

Matthew kept his back straight. "My apologies, my king. I thought you already knew about it. The English have had these devices for years."

"But not in Paris! Not right under my nose!" King Philippe was back to roaring. "I expect you to deliver the device to me by

Nones today. Meanwhile," his eyes went again to Ted, "the English ambassador will remain our guest here at the palace."

In the Middle Ages, *Nones*, as a delineation of time, meant three o'clock in the afternoon. Ted had long since given up questioning the fact that *Nones* was in later centuries corrupted to mean *noon*, and thus midday. That must have been confusing when it happened, but it was not his problem in this moment.

Despite the danger, not just to Ted but possibly to the Templars as a whole, Matthew didn't immediately acquiesce. "My lord, are you sure you wish to antagonize the English king? We don't have a commensurate device. You won't be able to talk to any of your own people with it."

King Philippe was back to glaring at Ted. "Will I be able to talk directly to David, wherever he may be?"

"Yes." There was no point in lying about that. "If you know how to use it."

"You will teach me."

That wasn't a question, but also not something Ted wanted to counter with *will I?* This was going to play out as it would. Instead, he opted to divert King Philippe. "What does our communication device have to do with the taking of Poeke Castle?"

"Everything!"

"My apologies, but I still don't understand. Why antagonize the English king when you are faced with a renewed war in Flanders?"

King Philippe answered in a way that at first appeared to be a digression. "David is entirely unwilling to commit troops to the continent. In fifteen years, not one English soldier has landed on our shores. I admit he has proved himself to be more expert in diplomacy than I would have preferred, but he cannot touch me here. He won't. *I want that device!*" These last words were a command not to be refused.

Matthew bowed. "As always, I am pleased to do your bidding." He turned on his heel and strode from the hall.

A moment later, Enguerrand was on one side of Ted and a nameless soldier on the other. Each grabbed an arm, as had happened when David had bent the knee before King Philippe two years ago. Then they marched Ted away. Their path took them into the palace proper, up some stairs, down a corridor or two, until finally they arrived at the southwest corner. This location was almost exactly opposite the rooms in which David and his family had been held. Ted had no expectation he would find hidden corridors in the walls this time around.

The king had sauntered after them, which seemed unusual behavior to Ted. By the time Ted was standing in the center of his new room, straightening his tunic and robe, King Philippe lounged in the doorway, his arms folded across his chest. With a flick of his fingers, he dismissed everyone else, leaving the two of them alone. Even so, beyond the doorway, Ted could see Flote and Enguerrand with their heads together, talking seriously.

In the faint hope Philippe might change his mind, Ted kept his tone gentle. "Are you sure this is the course of action you want to take?"

"I am quite sure." Philippe tsked. "For what reason should I stay my hand?"

"I would think there are several."

King Philippe's eyes narrowed. "My wife and children for a country, is that it?"

"I am unsure—"

"Gascony, Aquitaine, Normandy." King Philippe ticked the names off his fingers. "Where else do I need to be worried about? Burgundy? Brittany?"

Ted could have told him the latter was definitely in doubt, since it was the domain of the Earl of Richmond and his son, John Jr., who'd also been involved in the events of two years ago. He knew in this case to keep his mouth shut.

King Philippe shook his head. "Flote has persuaded me that my gratitude is misplaced, and David means to rob me of half my kingdom—or perhaps all of it—before he's done."

"Flote has a silver tongue. He cares for his own power and knows it will grow as his influence with you grows. David, you will have noticed, has both the brains and the power to be a tyrant and chooses not to be."

"I dislike the implication that I am not my own man." As usual, King Philippe had heard only the slight to his character and not the positive message. "I assure you, I know exactly what I'm doing."

He turned abruptly and left the room, leaving Ted alone in his comfortable prison.

Immediately, Ted set about exploring the room, not giving up on the idea that King Philippe could have reworked his secret tunnels, and there was a doorway somewhere to find. The room contained a bed, a wardrobe, and little else. He had a moment of hope when he realized a portion of the molding and wallpaper had been cleverly installed to disguise a door, with the keyhole behind a metal flower, one of many, which he initially assumed to be simply decoration. Because medieval locks were rarely robust, disguising the lock in this way was another form of security. Heart beating, he squatted down so he could look through the keyhole.

Beyond was another bedroom with similar bare furnishings, though oddly curved walls, indicating it was within the corner tower.

In addition, about three feet away, also crouching down to look through the keyhole, was a young woman. At the sight of him, she said, "Hello. I'm Philippa. Who are you?"

Yet again, just when Ted thought he had King Philippe figured out, he surprised him.

23

26 September 1297

David

"Why on earth did Uncle Ted just go along with it?" David had always disliked scenes in books and movies where the condemned man doesn't fight his captors all the way to the guillotine, or even kneels on his own volition with his back to his executioner, waiting for his head to be lopped off. He hoped, if it ever came to that for him, he'd make those who'd passed judgment on him work for his death.

Then again, Uncle Ted's current situation wasn't a death sentence any more than it had been for David when Philippe had taken him prisoner. With that thought, David waved a hand Elisa couldn't see and said, "Never mind. It's hardly his fault, and I know why he did it. He bought us time."

"Nones is coming," Aunt Elisa said. "What am I going to say to Philippe?"

David imagined his aunt throwing her cloak around her shoulders in that exasperated manner she had, getting ready to confront one of the most powerful men in the world as if born to it. It wasn't only David and Callum who'd discovered who they were meant to be in coming to Earth Two.

"How do we refuse the King of France outright?" Matthew was in the room too and equally a part of whatever would come next. His position as an adviser to the King of France was on the line too, as was, perhaps, the survival of the whole Templar order.

Ever since the Johns had stolen the helicopter, David had been continually tempted to board the next boat to France. He had been persuaded (for now) of the foolishness of that plan. While he wanted to go, and every fiber in his being told him he needed to go, he was on his way to London instead. It wasn't just the fact that it would take days to get to Paris that stopped him. He could have gone with Robbie and the others. It's possible he might even have been able to make a difference.

But he also might have ended up becoming a pawn in Philippe's game like Uncle Ted. That David would end up in prison was everyone else's understandable concern too. In the end, Lili had been the one to tell him in no uncertain terms that he had to trust his people to do the job he'd given them, else why give them the job in the first place?

He had conceded the point.

His one other concern, which he hadn't shared with anyone, not even Lili, was that none of the people currently involved in this adventure could time travel. Was that a flaw in the plan? Would going himself have ended up saving someone's life because he still had this one, spectacular, *get-out-of-jail-free* card?

"If the theft of the helicopter was a worst-case scenario for twenty-firster weaponry," Aunt Elisa said, "for King Philippe to demand our radio is a commensurate disaster for our communications."

"Honestly, half the reason I allowed myself to be persuaded to stay behind was because of our ability to talk with you, as I'm doing right now. Once we do as Philippe wants, even that advantage will be lost to us. Unless—" David paused to think, "—unless it isn't."

"Unless it isn't—what?" Aunt Elisa said.

"Unless it isn't lost to us. What if we do exactly as Philippe asks with a smile on our faces?"

Matthew scoffed. "We give him the radio and show him how to use it?"

"Yes."

Their skepticism couldn't have come through more clearly if the three of them had been in the same room.

"How can you even suggest that?" Aunt Elisa said. "Without it, we can't talk to you. It will be like he's holding you hostage all over again."

"We would have Uncle Ted back."

"Unless he doesn't give Ted back," Aunt Elisa said. "Unless he requires Ted to stay at the palace so he can work the radio."

Oddly, every counter argument further warmed David to the idea. "Would that be so bad? We're in this for the long haul, aren't we? That helicopter is coming and, whether Philippe admits it or not, he needs us."

Matthew tsked loud enough for David to hear. "Are you really suggesting we walk into the palace and just hand the radio over?"

"Yeah, as a genuine gift." This idea had started out as a whim. Now David was sure. "We can lock it to a single frequency, one of our choosing. He won't be able to listen in on our communication otherwise. He would be able to talk only with me."

Neither Matthew nor Aunt Elisa replied immediately, which was a good indication of how strongly they disagreed. David let the silence lengthen, which anyone who has ever made a phone call knows can be really hard to do when all that is coming from the other end is breathing and a bit of buzz. Even fifteen seconds without conversation is a long time.

It was Aunt Elisa who ultimately replied, speaking slowly as she considered the ramifications. "Gifts of state require ceremony."

"Such was my thought," David said.

"We could spread the word throughout the city that we will be transporting the radio from the Paris Temple to the palace. People will come out to see this great treasure from Avalon. It would be like a little holiday."

"What is the point of that?" Matthew asked.

As always, Aunt Elisa had made David's idea better. "Everyone will know what we are doing, and it will burnish David's reputation in a way that makes Philippe beholden to him once again. There is literally no gift Philippe could give David that can match it, and it will also be so public that if Philippe does something untoward—like keep Ted captive in the palace—then he will look small. Philippe hates looking small."

David found himself smiling. "That will be what Philippe is thinking, anyway. For our purposes, once the radio is up and running, I'll be waiting to talk to him."

"King Philippe could easily see the radio as tribute." Matthew's disapproval reverberated down the line.

"We don't care how he sees it." Aunt Elisa really was coming around. "The radio would be like the hotline to the Kremlin in the White House."

Matthew had no idea what she meant, which unfortunately might be usual for him. Thus, he ignored it. "What's to prevent King Philippe from taking your aunt hostage too? He has created a situation where no member of your court can ever set foot in his presence again. You were absent for two years, and the first thing he does is set a ransom for one of your family members."

"Believe me, I noticed that too," David said. "That Archbishop Romeyn is a churchman may be the only reason he was never used this way. Philippe has been in enough hot water with the Pope as it is that he didn't dare imprison him. You have to do this for me, Matthew. Please."

Matthew was silent for another long moment. When he finally spoke, David could hear his sigh down all those many miles. "King Philippe is certain you won't cross the English Channel. His tone was full of mockery at the very idea."

"Why would I invade?" David said. "Armies are ready to go on the borders of Gascony, Aquitaine, and Normandy, each filled with people with longstanding hatreds that a thimbleful of tinder could spark into a conflagration. Each and every one is longing to lay waste to his country."

"He acts like that isn't true," Elisa said.

"He can act how he likes."

"Which he does," Matthew said. "I, of course, will do as *you* ask."

"Thank you," David said.

Aunt Elisa gave a little laugh. "You can get the better of him all day long, David. In fact, as I see it, with this move you have already defeated him without having to lift a finger yourself."

"Now I really don't understand what you're talking about," Matthew said. "We are giving up the radio. How does that mean we won?"

"Because this isn't about what Philippe thinks it is," David said. "You are going to put *my voice* at the center of his existence. Any time he wants, I can be right there to talk with him."

"To say what?" Matthew still wasn't getting it.

"That kings rule only at the consent of the governed." Aunt Elisa had a smile in her voice. "He'll talk of democracy, Matthew. Of freedom of speech and religion. Of the equality of men and women. All in subtle tones, of course, in the guise of being a listening ear. It isn't deceit, since it's the only advice he could give anyway. David went all the way to Avalon to speak to the people there of hope and peace, just as he has brought both to the CSB. These are wars that aren't won on the field of battle, but in people's hearts and minds. And really, they are the only wars worth fighting in the end."

"Tell that to King Philippe!" Matthew said. "And the people of France!"

"Now you're getting it." David laughed. "That's exactly what I intend to do."

24

26 September 1297

Ted

For as long as there had been warring groups, hostage-taking had been a tried-and-true method of controlling the opposition. The medieval period had its fair share of warfare, and Philippa was hardly the first child held hostage to her father's good behavior. In Avalon, she wasn't released even after the surrender/peace treaty deal Pope Boniface negotiated that gave Flanders to France, nor after her father's death in captivity in 1305.

At that time, her brother, Robert, their father's heir, who had also been imprisoned, was freed. But not Philippa. King Philippe's continued hope had been that he could use her to control her brother. In Avalon's history, she died in her prison, never released nor even married off to one of France's allies, as might actually have made some sense. The Flemish believed she was poisoned, but the historical record was unclear on the exact means of her demise.

It was a bit of a shock, then, for Ted to come face-to-face—or rather eyeball-to-eyeball—with the girl. At twenty-two, she was lovely, her chestnut hair piled artfully on top of her head and her dress of the latest fashion, even though nobody would ever see her. It was a little daunting to know her fate, like she was a dead woman walking. He didn't like it. She looked hardly old enough to drive. She shouldn't be dying in a few years on the whim of the King of France.

He didn't know what he could do about it, however. Yet.

"Hello." It seemed like a good beginning. "My name is Ted Shepherd, King David's ambassador from England." He set aside the fact that Elisa was really in charge.

"I saw you come in. I was hoping you were here to tell Philippe that England was coming into the war on the side of Flanders." Philippa scooted backwards to sit on the edge of her bed. "Are you? Is that why the king imprisoned you too?"

"No. I'm sorry. Not yet anyway." Ted cleared his throat. "Before I get to that, how is it you saw me come in? I wouldn't have thought your window faced towards the main gate."

"It doesn't, but I'm allowed at the top of the tower whenever I want." She pointed with her finger towards the ceiling. He tipped his head, craning to see what she was indicating, but the keyhole wasn't that big. "There's a ladder against the far wall that goes to the roof. I know it is unladylike to hitch up my skirts, but it is the only way I can get up there. I spend most of my time outside. If I follow the wall of my turret all the way around in a circle, it's thirty-four steps."

"And nobody minds?" Ted was still confused. "They allow you out without supervision?"

"It's a tower with a trap door. There's nowhere for me to go but down."

Or up, Ted had the sudden thought, but didn't say. Now that he knew what he was looking at, he understood why the walls of her room were curved. This fact also explained the strange arrangement of doors in the corridor he'd noticed when they'd brought him in here. The door to her room was set at an angle in the wall. The guard outside in the corridor could thus watch Ted's door and Philippa's without moving from his post, since they were all of a few feet apart.

It also wasn't unusual for rooms in the medieval period to have connecting doors. Corridors were wasted space, as long as you didn't mind people walking through your room to get to the next one. Corridors were designed more for servants, so they didn't disturb the elite members of the household with their daily activities. Servants should be neither seen nor heard.

In happier times, a guest could have stayed in Philippa's chamber while Ted's was used for business or as a sitting area. He'd been put here not because there was anything special about the room but because it was conveniently located next to where King Philippe already had a prisoner. And if there was no way out for Philippa, there was no way out for Ted either. His first thought was that King Philippe had put him here because he wanted him to free Philippa. Maybe he did. Maybe he thought Ted was that good. Doing so was going to be a little difficult, though, if he couldn't even free himself.

"Do you have another door in your room that leads to the next room on the other side?" he asked her.

"No." She shook her head sadly.

"Do you know where the key to this door is?"

"No. They've never opened it while I've been in here."

That fact wasn't of real concern to Ted. He could break through the door with the heel of his boot if he had to. The walls between the rooms were wooden, not stone or steel. "Has anyone spoken to you about what happened yesterday?"

She shook her head again. "Hardly anyone speaks to me at all."

"The king summoned me here because your father and brother retook Poeke Castle last night. One of King Philippe's spies sent a pigeon with the news."

She drew in a breath. "They are restarting the war."

"So it seems. I'm sorry."

"Why?" Her chin came up. "I'm not."

Ted blinked. "Even if it means—"

"—my death?" She interrupted him.

"I probably wouldn't have stated my fears so starkly, but yes."

"If King Philippe kills me, he can't use me as leverage anymore, can he? Then my father and brother will be free." She made a motion with her head. "As will I."

There didn't seem much Ted could say to that. She wasn't wrong, when it came to it. After that, once they'd chatted about trivial things like the weather and the food, Philippa left him to walk about on the top of her tower. At that point, though his knees were not enjoying the hard floor, Ted studied the lock itself. That medieval locks could be bypassed with relative ease was why the guard remained stationed outside his door. This was a warded lock, as was typical for the era, and eminently pickable with the right tools.

Which he happened to have.

They'd taken his sword, something he wore as a matter of course (even if he, quite frankly, had little real use for it), but they hadn't patted him down. In particular, they hadn't confiscated his key ring, which had a few real keys on it as well as three basic skeleton keys. He'd been carrying them around for years now after a conversation with Callum about learning lockpicking in college and how he'd like to be prepared for every contingency. When the second key he tried did the trick, he opened the door between his room and Philippa's three inches, just to be sure he could, and then closed it again without relocking it.

Just as he stood up, relieved to be off the floor, the door to the corridor opened, and three of King Philippe's men entered. They were followed by Pierre Flote, whose smile did not give Ted confidence that he was going to like what happened next.

He was right. They were here on Flote's behalf, not King Philippe's.

And they didn't seem particularly interested in talking.

25

26 September 1297

Elisa

"I still don't think this is a good idea," Matthew said as he and Elisa headed down the stairs side-by-side. "David wouldn't like it."

"That may be, but he isn't here, and I didn't hear him forbid me." Elisa made a motion with her head. "I realize this might seem foolish to you, but I can't *not* go."

Matthew bit his lip. "You know what he would say. I notice you haven't called him again to warn him of your plan." He really was getting the terminology down.

"David isn't going to be able to talk to us every five minutes anymore, is he? We won't be able to clear everything with him. *I'm doing this.* Begin as I mean to go on, I say."

Matthew still didn't look happy. "You didn't see how King Philippe looked at me. He suspects our relationship isn't what I have led him to believe. If you are discovered, it could be disastrous."

"It's already disastrous, and why would anyone look twice at me?" Elisa said. "Anyway, even if they did, Ted and I are staying at

"

the Paris Temple because Philippe himself ordered it. You and I are in-laws. Of course, you must be friendly. You are trying to convince us you are on our side—"

"—all the while trying to reassure King Philippe I'm on his." Matthew groaned. "This is madness. I hadn't realized how much so until today."

"Today is when the rubber hits the road."

Matthew couldn't be familiar with that reference either. Still, he nodded. "After today, things will at least be clearer."

"I want my husband back. I would prefer not to be at war with France. But really, what happens next doesn't depend on us."

"I hope King David can find the right words. He couldn't when he was here."

"In public, he couldn't," Elisa said. "In private, he said and did exactly what King Philippe needed."

"David might not have the same privacy today. Flote is a jealous man."

"It also looks as if he is feeding King Philippe's ambitions and fears again, and going about it more cleverly than Nogaret did."

"Promise me you'll be careful."

"Of course."

Matthew didn't necessarily look reassured.

Having reached the bailey of the Paris Temple, Matthew escorted her to her place next to the litter on which rested the shortwave radio. The intent was to carry it like it was the Holy Grail or the Ark of the Covenant, with numerous guards all around it holding the handles. One of those guards was going to be Elisa, dressed in an enveloping Templar robe and helmet, both of which she planned to shed once she was inside the palace.

Matthew inspected her once more. "I'm worried about what happens when you take off that helmet. For now, you look like one of my men. Just because I can admit it doesn't mean I think this is a good idea."

"I can't sit idly by while the King of France does who knows what with my husband. If I'm discovered, you must claim you knew nothing about what I was doing, as we agreed." She paused as she and the five men holding the handles of the litter picked it up in preparation for the upcoming procession. "I appreciate you bending the rules for me."

Matthew scoffed under his breath. "What rules? You Avalonians not only act like the rules don't apply to you. Half the time, it's almost like you don't believe there are any rules."

"We do have a saying in my country: *rules are made to be broken.*"

He laughed. "That explains a great deal."

Matthew then mounted his horse and, as the great gate to the commandery opened, he took his place at the front of the procession. Elisa was wearing the helmet and hood to hide her face, but they had the side effect of making it nearly impossible for her to see or hear anything. Thus, as she paced forward beside the litter, her first thought was that no citizens of Paris had shown up and their plan was a bust.

But then she took her first step into the street, and a great cheer went up. The streets of Paris were narrow, like little canyons. When lined with people, the sound was concentrated. There was even music playing somewhere off to her right.

Elisa kept her head down, afraid to meet anyone's eyes lest they realize one of the litter bearers was a woman. Matthew had deliberately chosen men who were on the shorter side to carry the litter with her, so she wouldn't look out of place. And it wasn't as if the radio was heavy. Nonetheless, it was a mile to the palace, which was a long way to carry a litter when she was unaccustomed to carrying any weight at all. Elisa sweated under the cloak. After five minutes, she was swearing to herself that if she never wore a war helmet again, it would be too soon.

Finally, close to an hour later, they reached the palace. The gate opened ponderously to admit them. All the while, people cheered and waved little banners and handkerchiefs. It was gratifying, honestly, that they would be so enthused about an Avalonian object. And maybe thrilled that their king was going to have it for himself. It served to augment the already high opinion the French had of themselves and their king.

Once inside the palace, Elisa was almost rocked off her feet by the ringing of bells, first coming from Sainte-Chapelle and then followed by every other church in the city. With thirty-five parishes serving over sixty thousand households, it was the very definition of cacophony.

As soon as she caught her breath, however, she realized the bells weren't ringing to celebrate their arrival but because they had arrived at the palace exactly at Nones, as promised. The men guarding the great hall pulled open the doors, Matthew dismounted, and everyone started forward.

She was in.

26

26 September 1297

Matthew

"You came." This was the extent of Enguerrand's greeting. It was disturbing to see him here and realize he must have been promoted. Now that Matthew knew his future history, he would be more on guard with him.

Matthew could also have been offended by Enguerrand's implied doubt that he would obey the king. Instead, he found himself amused at his pettiness. It could be that some of the Avalonian recklessness was rubbing off on him. "Of course I came. I seek only to serve." He was pleased to be able to counter with the implication that Enguerrand was seeking something other than service to the king.

Enguerrand might have tsked under his breath in the same moment he turned on his heel and marched up the aisle to where King Philippe was waiting for them on his throne. The hall was packed with every single court official, lackey, and hanger-on in the palace. All except for Flote, who was uncharacteristically absent. There was also no sign of Ted.

King Philippe wanted—equally with David, as it turned out—everyone to know he was receiving the Avalonian radio. That he had a completely different interpretation of the events leading up to this moment was unimportant. For now, David was happy for Philippe to think he'd won this round.

Even the servants had been summoned to stand against the side walls. That boded well for Elisa's upcoming transformation into one of them.

"We were hoping we would see the ambassador today," Matthew said to Enguerrand's back.

Enguerrand acted like he hadn't heard him. By that point, they had reached the throne anyway.

King Philippe did not rise to his feet, but he had an excitement in his face Matthew hadn't often seen. The King of France worked very hard to portray a certain *laissez faire* attitude towards everything, so as to never give away when he was interested in what anyone else was saying or doing.

The bearers set the litter before the steps up to the throne and, with a wave of his hand, Matthew dismissed them. They backed away, not so much melting into the crowd as being overwhelmed by the onlookers pressing forward to see the radio. In truth, the machine didn't look like much, which was why Matthew had arranged for this elaborate presentation. The radio itself was quite compact, even in its protective case, roughly one foot on a side and six inches high, absent its solar powered array. Without it, the radio would last ten to fourteen hours of continual use. That gave them a few days to figure out if David's plan would work.

They'd brought it in an ornate chest on top of an ornate litter, not unlike those on which the ancient rulers of Rome might have once been carried.

Matthew bowed before the king, as did everyone else. "My lord. I have brought the Avalonian radio." Then he opened the case and turned on the radio with a flick of his finger, as he'd been taught.

Little lights sparked all over the device, and the crowd gasped, pressing even closer. In order for Philippe to approach, Matthew stepped a bit to the side too. As he did so, he glanced to his right to see Elisa shedding her Templar helmet and robe behind a pillar. Another Templar who'd come with them, a good man named Emile, blocked the view of her form from other watching eyes and then took the gear from her. All of a sudden, Elisa was dressed in an apron and coif and looked much like any other of the palace's servants. A moment later, she disappeared through a side door, not even waiting to see the outcome of the proceedings.

If Ted had been present in the receiving room, her plan had still been to remove her gear. Had he been released into Matthew's custody, she would have left the palace on the heels of the Templars. Now that they knew he remained captive, her goal was to find him and determine the nature of his situation. Once that was clear, she and Matthew could make another plan.

Or so she had said. He thought he had the measure of her now and was inclined to think she would improvise in some unexpected and likely risky way.

Matthew forced his attention back to the issue at hand. "King David hopes you accept his gift in the spirit in which it was given."

The king still hadn't spoken and now tipped his head. In that moment, Matthew saw cunning amusement enter his eyes, indicating he understood that by making the radio a gift, David had made a virtue of a necessity. Now, with his own wave, King Philippe indicated Matthew himself should pick up the case off the litter and come with him. Even though the receiving room was full to the brim of people anxious to interact with the radio, Philippe turned on his heel and left by the private door at the back.

Radio in hand, Matthew followed on his heels.

27

26 September 1297

Elisa

Although King Philippe had reworked his secret passageways in the wake of the events of two years ago, he hadn't redone his receiving room. The little door Elisa went through still led to a bare corridor that allowed the servants to move about the palace without disturbing the king. Thus, while everyone else was oohing and aahing over the radio, Elisa slipped away.

Their preparations had been hasty, but careful. Underneath her Templar garb, Elisa had put on a cream-colored apron over a plain gray kirtle that barely covered her ankles. Servants in this era didn't wear uniforms, but they also didn't wear sweeping gowns. The shortness of the dress, necessary when a woman's job was scrubbing floors, also meant it conveniently hadn't been visible under the Templar robe.

Following the map in her head, memorized from what Matthew had drawn for her, Elisa worked her way through the labyrinth of corridors and stairs, moving deeper into the palace with every step. At one point, she heard voices up ahead, but when she turned the corner, nobody was there. She had almost been looking forward to encountering someone, as a trial run to know she could pass as a servant.

By the time she reached the top floor of the palace, she had started walking brazenly down the center of the corridors. This particular area was fully decorated, indicating nobility were housed here. More voices up ahead had her finally treading a bit more warily, conscious of her footfalls, even on the thick carpet. Before coming to Earth Two, she hadn't known carpet was already a thing, if one had the money. Really, Philippe's palace on the Île de la Cité was ahead of its time, much more resembling a seventeenth century country manor house than a castle. This resemblance had been made all the more pronounced with every iteration.

At long last, she poked her head around a corner to find she'd reached the end tower. Two guards were just coming out of a door, a man hung between them, barely able to walk. Behind them strolled Pierre Flote. Elisa gaped through a moment of disbelief that the injured man could possibly be Ted and that Philippe had actually been so foolish as to harm him.

But it was Ted, and while his face was unmarred, the way the guards continued to drag him along indicated he'd had a very rough afternoon. Tears pricked at the corners of Elisa's eyes, but she wiped them away and refused to allow any more to fall, telling herself this wasn't the time. Instead, she slipped into a nearby unoccupied room. Once the men were past her, she poked out her head again and silently followed them.

As they went down the stairs, she hung back so she wouldn't be noticed, and had just come out of the stairwell when her husband was turned into a room at the far end of another long corridor. A second before he disappeared inside, Ted turned his head and saw her. His eyes widened.

Then he was gone, and the guard closed the door behind him.

28

26 September 1297

Matthew

Ted's manner as he stood before the king told Matthew more about his character than anything he'd done during their acquaintance up until this moment. Matthew had watched him come in and couldn't mistake, either from the pleased look on Flote's face or from the two guards carrying him, that he was in intense pain. The instant he'd crossed the threshold and saw the king hovering over the radio with his back to the door, he had straightened. By the time King Philippe looked around, Ted was fully upright and standing on his own recognizance.

"I trust your accommodations were more than adequate," King Philippe said, turning back to the radio after a single glance. "I assume you will be reporting to David that you were treated with the utmost courtesy."

If anyone else had been speaking, he could have been being facetious. Ted blinked once, the only indication he had just realized, as had Matthew, that King Philippe had no idea what Ted had experienced while in captivity.

Ted smiled. "Of course."

He did not add the appropriate honorific, which couldn't be an oversight. Ted didn't make those kinds of mistakes, not after that smile.

Flote, meanwhile, stepped to one side, his self-satisfied demeanor turning to puzzlement. With Ted denying any injury, there was no room for Flote's own triumph over him.

King Philippe then gestured for Ted to sit in a chair placed in front of the radio. A second chair was drawn up for the king. "If you would explain everything you're doing as we proceed."

Ted walked to the chair and sat. He was hiding his pain well, but because Matthew had seen the beginning of his act, he noted the measure of gratefulness and the slow way he eased himself into the chair.

It was just as well Ted had sat down, the better to weather the storm that blew into the room a heartbeat later in the form of his wife. Having removed her servant's coif and apron, she stood in the doorway, quivering with fury. And while her attire at first made her appear dowdy and middle-aged, the fire in her eyes was all anybody could see.

"How dare you!" Her French was perfect, and only after she spoke did the king recognize her, having swung around again as the door banged back against the wall.

"Madame, I—"

Elisa overrode him. "You say you want peace with England, but your treatment of the ambassador is shameful, even for you!"

King Philippe looked genuinely bewildered. "Madame, I—"

"Look at him!" Her voice thundered as she pointed at Ted.

Ted put out a hand in a desperate attempt to deflect her ire. "Elisa, it's okay."

"It isn't okay! Were you or were you not beaten half to death at the hands of the king's men?"

"Well, not *half to death*."

"Don't quibble with me Theodore Shepherd! They *beat* you." Striding up to her husband, she pulled open his robes and yanked up his shirt to reveal a mass of bruises that made even Matthew, who'd seen plenty of injured men in his time, blanche. "Anyone should have been able to see how gingerly you were sitting there. You have at least one broken rib, maybe a bruised kidney or two." She swung back to the king. "We are leaving, and we are taking our radio with us!"

As she bent to the radio, Flote, who had been initially as stunned as the rest by Elisa's entrance, waved to the two guards at the door, who moved into a ready stance to block her departure. "Do not touch that. It is ours."

She glared at him. "It was a gift from King David."

"If you take it, you will be imprisoned too."

"Go ahead. Try it. I'll scream bloody murder, you vile fiendish cessbucket!"

Flote blinked at her insult, naturally taken aback, which gave Matthew room to step forward. "What is happening, Flote? What did you do?"

"I will tell you what is happening!" Elisa wasn't letting anything get in the way of her control of the room. Such was her rage that nobody was questioning how she had come to be in the palace in the first place. With a wide gesture, she swept away Flote's protests. "It was he who ordered this abuse of my husband! Don't bother to deny it. I see the truth in your eyes!"

Flote's attention was on the king. "I was only doing as I believe you wished."

At last, King Philippe rose slowly to his feet, like a cat stretching before eyeing up the mouse on which it intended to pounce. "What was your plan, Flote?"

His voice was calmer than it should have been. The king always wanted to be three steps ahead of everyone else. Matthew knew few men as clever and none as calculating. He definitely did not like being caught unaware.

Flote gestured to Ted. "He knows more than he has said. We can't believe for a moment he didn't know about the taking of Poeke. What's next? Are we to lose Male too?"

Flote didn't seem to realize how badly he had blundered. Had he thought the king would be impressed with his treatment of Ted? Had he not realized how badly his men had hurt him? Or had he been so pleased with his power over England's ambassador, blaming him in lieu of David for all his woes these last two years, he hadn't thought that far ahead?

"Do you seek to style yourself after Nogaret?" King Philippe asked, in a tone hardly more intent than if he were inquiring about the readiness of his next meal. "Was it your plan to step into his shoes? You think me a fool, is that it?"

"N-n-no, sire." Flote tried one more time. "We barely touched him—"

Philippe snapped his fingers at the two guards, who a moment before had been working for Flote. "Take him to the Louvre. I should have known better than to trust you again. You're right. I was a fool."

"My lord—" Flote's eyes flicked from the guards to Ted to the king and back again. "I thought—"

"How many times do I have to make clear that you are not to think on your own?" King Philippe's voice, in contrast to Elisa's, was thundering in its softness. "I will deal with you later."

He turned his back on Flote, who now had the two guards on either side of him. With another motion of his hand, the king sent Matthew with them. "Go. See that they do my bidding. Once again, I find myself in a position of distrust."

"At once, my lord." Matthew bent his head, using the moment to contain his own expression. He had feared for Elisa, coming to the palace. He hadn't known he had to fear for Ted. It had honestly never occurred to him that Flote would beat Ted on his own initiative. Matthew could regret Ted's wounds, but Flote himself had played directly into David's hands.

Once at the door, Matthew looked back to see the king seated before Ted and Elisa, his hands clasped before his lips. King

Philippe's head was actually bowed in what appeared to be real contrition. "My friends, I am so sorry …"

29

26 September 1297

David

"He's on!" Bronwen waved a hand from the back of the covered wagon housing the shortwave radio. They had been taking turns waiting for Uncle Ted to open a channel.

Since the call was coming a bit sooner than expected, David had to be summoned from where he'd been riding his horse, his son Alexander in front of him.

They were making their way back to England at something of a leisurely pace. This particular shortwave was now David's dedicated connection to Philippe. He had a second with him by which to speak to everyone else, which included Carew at Carew Castle; Llywelyn, David's father, wherever he might be at any given moment; and Math and Anna. Given how portable these radios were, they all could bring them with them everywhere they went, a little like being attached to a cell phone.

Although David had left Avalon at the age of fourteen, before the use of smart phones was widespread among his age set, he'd nonetheless carried his flip phone with him everywhere. It was a tether that had taken more than a minute for him to adjust to severing when he'd come to Earth Two. Mark Jones still had the phone in the technology storage in London.

David passed Alexander off to Lili and climbed into the back of the wagon, followed a moment later by Ieuan, Callum, and Michael. The rest of his friends and family had mostly scattered to the four corners of the CSB. Each had people and estates of their own to see to in a similar kind of seasonal round for which David was responsible as King of England.

Settling himself with a released breath, David picked up the microphone. "Uncle Ted. How are you?"

"Good to hear your voice." Uncle Ted spoke in English. "I have been better; Flote arranged for a beating. Additionally, I have met our prisoner in the tower."

This came out all in a rush. King Philippe didn't understand English, but he would recognize Philippa's name if Uncle Ted had said it. Even with that short preamble, the French king's patience was at an end. "What are you saying? Speak plainly!"

Ted immediately, and with admirable smoothness, switched to French. "King Philippe is here and would like to speak to you."

"Thank you, Uncle," David said in the same language. "Be well."

David really wanted to know more about this beating. The fact that it was the first thing out of Ted's mouth indicated David needed to set the correct tone for this first conversation. "Hello, Philippe. How are your wife and children?"

"They are well." Philippe's voice sounded tight. "And yours?"

David tried to reply, but Philippe was still holding down on the button that kept the channel open on his side. David simply had to wait until Ted intervened, at which point he caught the tail end of his sentence, "—release the button, my lord."

Once able to be heard, David said, "They are well too; the whole of my family is well." He paused. "Except for my uncle, it seems."

"He is my guest. I would never have ordered one of my people to harm him." It sounded now like Philippe was speaking through gritted teeth. "It was entirely Flote. Still, he is under my command, and thus my responsibility. I have apologized to the ambassador. I must do the same to you." He paused now too. "I will, of course, return your radio."

Philippe's management of his court was not coming off as he would like, that was clear. The last thing the King of France wanted was to be perceived as ineffectual or easily manipulated.

David reminded himself not to make that mistake with him either. "Thank you for your apology, but given this initial gross misunderstanding, I see all the more reason for us to have a direct way of communicating with one another. Please keep it."

"Such was my thought from the start. I too believe that is for the best." Philippe acquiesced, a bit of the stiffness leaving his voice.

"There have been too many misunderstandings between our countries over the years."

"On that topic, what can I do for you?"

Philippe didn't pause for breath this time. "I would like to know exactly what happened in Carew."

David had never had a problem with the truth, so he explained again about his unexpected visit to Avalon and subsequent return.

Philippe, however, appeared to have been waiting for David to stop speaking with renewed impatience. "Yes, yes. Your uncle told me all that. What I want to know is *why* these mercenaries are here?"

David hesitated. "I am not sure I understand the question."

"Why would anyone from Avalon care what I do here?"

Here it was again. David had never lied about what Avalon was. He just hadn't told the whole story. He thought back to all the times he'd wanted to talk about the real situation, and now that the opportunity was again before him, he met the eyes of each of his companions listening in the back of the wagon with him. They all knew, as he did, that the time was coming when the whole of Earth Two would have to be told the real truth—the same truth everyone in Avalon now knew as well. Still, it was important to drip-feed the information, rather than dump it out all at once.

Beside him, Ieuan said in an undertone in Welsh, "Speaking of Avalon to the King of France isn't to be done lightly."

"It has to be done. It's why we're here." Callum gestured towards David as if to say, *Go on. We're with you.*

David took the plunge. "Avalon is a world much like this one, to the point that there is an equivalent version of Flanders in it. Because of my traveling back and forth, these mercenaries know you have attacked this world's Flanders. They don't like it." As soon as David finished speaking, he let out a huge breath. He was even feeling a bit light-headed. This conversation had been such a long time coming.

In his mind's eye, David imagined Philippe settling back in his seat. He expected next to have to tell Philippe he was from the future too, but that wasn't the question he asked. "They know this because you told them?"

"Yes, though to be clear, I did not tell them personally. I had no idea they existed until they hijacked the helicopter."

"How did they learn of it then?"

David almost laughed. *How was he going to explain this one?* "In Avalon, everyone has a radio like you are using now. They allow total strangers to communicate with one another across the whole world."

"Everyone has one?"

It was time to get back to the main point. "Suffice to say, they heard about it. Once we were back at Carew Castle, I spoke to my aunt and uncle and asked them to warn you about the mercenaries and that they were coming. We believe they seek to assassinate you."

"Before they took Poeke Castle, I was more likely to be dismissive of their activities."

Then, in the background, David heard some muffled French, cut off by a sharp word from Philippe. "I will tell him what I choose to tell him. It is not your concern, Enguerrand." He had kept his finger on the button, allowing David to overhear. This time, Ted didn't correct him.

The other speaker appeared to protest again, prompting Philippe to exclaim. "Leave me!" Followed by, "Not you, Ambassador."

There was more scuffling about, and then the sound of Aunt Elisa's laugh, followed by what was unmistakably Philippe's own.

From the other side of the wagon, Bronwen said, since it would be impossible for Philippe to overhear, even if he did understand English. "Maybe it's best he doesn't know we're from the future, David. He would want control of it, to the extent that he might decide to start assassinating people in advance of a future we've told him about. You'd spend the rest of your life putting out fires he started."

Before David could properly process that thought, Philippe was back. He and David's aunt and uncle were once again alone in the room with the radio. It felt remarkably intimate, like they were sitting around the kitchen table rather than hundreds of miles apart.

Philippe said, "Tell me about this flying machine."

"It can travel long distances quickly, like a bird. The mercenaries also have weapons that can kill many men very quickly."

"What do you suggest I do?"

"Leave Paris."

"Never! I will not run." But then Philippe continued, "I have already sent my family to Vincennes. Knowing what I know now, they will be moved farther out of the city today."

"Good. For starters, my advisers suggest you post very few men on the battlements, and all of them under cover. The Avalonians can't shoot what they can't see. The moment you hear the sound of the helicopter ..." David released the button, letting his last thought hang in the air and waiting for a response from Philippe.

"Will it sound something like the airplane when it flew over Paris two years ago?"

"Somewhat. Ted and Elisa can explain."

"If you were here could you take me to Avalon?"

That was unexpected. In light of what Bronwen had just suggested, it was unwanted too. "I could. I thought we might have gone years ago at Chateau Niort, but we did not."

"Are you suggesting Avalon rejected my request for admittance?" Philippe's tone had gone from polite to outraged in a heartbeat.

He was tapping into a legend of Avalon, which had circulated throughout Earth Two over the years. It included the idea that only those who were worthy of Avalon would be admitted.

"I don't think it works that way," David said. "I think my life wasn't in as much danger as it was last week, so you and I fell into the river. I must tell you also that traveling to Avalon is never exactly fun."

"Because you die every time you do."

"Yes," David said carefully. He wasn't sure how Philippe had learned about that aspect of the situation, but he wasn't wrong.

"I would meet these mercenaries in their own castle."

"They can't go to Avalon without me, and I am very far away from you. By the time I could get there, it will all be over anyway."

"Would you come if I asked?"

"Yes." David spoke the truth, come what may. "When have I not?"

It seemed like Philippe might have wet his lips. "Don't come. Stay safe yourself. You sent me your aunt and uncle. That will have to be enough."

30

26 September 1297

Sam

With the arrival of Thomas and Henri, everyone had felt a renewed urgency in their mission. With Huw's group sailing to Flanders and Sam's to France, they hadn't waited until the dawn to leave Portsmouth, choosing instead to sail just after midnight at the next turn of the tide. Unfortunately, almost immediately the tide turned on them.

"What are we doing?" Sam shouted at Robbie, whom she'd discovered was far nicer than she'd expected. He was busy tying a rope around her waist so he didn't answer until he'd finished.

"Saving our lives."

Sam wasn't sure how a rope was going to save them. They needed life jackets. Or to time travel. But without David or one of his family members, that wasn't going to happen.

"Help me with Isabelle." In the murky light that was all they appeared to be getting today, Christopher's face looked gray, which was only slightly better than the greenish tinge that had taken over Isabelle. Sam was glad Ari wasn't with them any longer, though, since his ship had left at nearly the same time as theirs, bound for Bruges, he'd be caught up in the same storm. On the last journey, which hadn't even been that rough, Ari's darker skin had looked almost purple, like the vomiting had bruised him from head to foot.

"I can't move," Isabelle said. "Leave me here."

"We are not going to do that." Christopher's eyes were full of fear. "The ship is leaking. If it breaks apart, you'll die down here.

"I would rather die than spend another minute on this God-forsaken boat."

"I would really rather you didn't die at all, but if it's going to happen, let's do it on the deck." He lifted his wife to her feet.

With Robbie on the other side, they mostly carried her up the ladder.

"We're in the eye of the storm." The captain was there as they reached the top, taking Isabelle's hand to help her up the last few rungs.

Sam arrived on deck with a sense of relief. The last time she'd been up here, she had become instantly soaked from the rain and waves. "It's calmer than before, and the ship is running with the wind."

"It isn't calm. Don't you dare call it calm." Isabelle settled herself gingerly against the side of the ship. The rope around her waist was connected to Christopher's, same as Sam's to Robbie. If they were going to die, they would die together. Sam couldn't fault the principle. She just didn't think it would do them much good if the ship really did break apart.

"Sam said calm*er*." Christopher stayed next to Isabelle, holding onto the rail above her head.

For her part, Isabelle returned to the fetal position at his feet. She had been so ill, Sam feared it was the same norovirus that had left Birdy behind. If this was the virus, rather than seasickness, it could lay waste to half the population of Earth Two. And it would be their fault for spreading it.

Then again, Robbie was also native to Earth Two, and he was fine. He'd brought the binoculars up on deck with them and now put them to his eyes, for possibly the hundredth time today. This time, he said, with a catch in his voice, "I see land."

Isabelle's head came up. "Really?"

Sam peered as hard as she could into the distance. Maybe she was so desperate she was seeing things, but ... "Could that be the mouth of the Seine?"

As she spoke, the ship dove into a giant trough. All they could see was water on every side. It came up again, as it had each time up until now.

Then one of the crew shouted from the top of the mast. "Land, ho!"

Against all expectation, Sam was suddenly feeling quite cheerful. "I didn't know sailors actually said that."

She had come close to dying more times in the last five days than in her entire life, but instead of being paralyzed by it, she found herself laughing. It could even be, though she hadn't known it until now, that her whole life had conspired to bring her to this spot, right here, right now. She wouldn't be the first person to think it, nor be comforted by the thought. The idea dissipated the fear that had roiled her belly every few minutes since she'd come to Earth Two.

Once again, the captain of the ship rolled his way towards them. "We are through the worst of it now. We'll be in Rouen before you know it."

Christopher held out his hand to Robbie, asking for the binoculars. "How did we get here so fast? If I didn't know better, I would almost say we time traveled."

"The storm came from a direction we could work with," the captain said simply.

Within the next hour, although the weather continued to torment their ship, tossing it around like a rubber duck in a toddler's bathtub, it brought them to the shores of Normandy. Then, almost before they knew it, they were sailing up the Seine to Rouen. Bedraggled and exhausted, they each managed a bit of sleep for the first time since they'd left Portsmouth.

By morning, a little more than forty-eight hours after they'd left Portsmouth, the four of them came down the gangplank towards Amaury de Montfort, Master of the Rouen Templar commandery. In his early fifties, he still had the dark hair and athletic physique of a much younger man. In fact, he bore a striking resemblance to Sam's father, who had worked his farm every day of his life. It was barely dawn, but Amaury had come down to the dock the moment they sent word they'd arrived.

Christopher had described to Sam in some detail his and Isabelle's first encounter with Amaury. They had been in fear for their lives, and he had given them shelter in the commandery, though not before some intense questioning as to their identities. Even before they'd met, Amaury had been an ally, both to David and to the Jewish community of France. Like so many who encountered the twenty-firsters, Amaury had turned his back on old fears and hatreds and embraced the future David was charting.

Christopher and Isabelle had thus been in Normandy when it had thrown off the yoke of France. Really, it wasn't any wonder the two Flemish Johns had come to David for help to counter what they viewed as their common enemy. They may even have thought the fact that he hadn't helped Flanders was in some way an oversight. They wouldn't know it was a deliberate attempt not to repeat the mistakes of Avalon's past.

At least, they hadn't known it when they'd come to Carew. They might know it now, depending upon how much the AZs had told them.

"Welcome, though the fact that you are here means you are in need." Amaury surveyed the motley group before him. At least Isabelle was finally standing upright, her eyes brighter than they had been in days.

"We are in trouble, in more ways than we should discuss out here." Robbie's Scottish accent had become more pronounced as the journey had progressed. "Truly, we are lucky to be alive."

The lines on Amaury's face deepened as he took in their faces. For some reason, Sam got a look of concern equal to the one he directed at Isabelle. "I am having rooms prepared for you at the commandery as we speak. You can freshen up, and we'll discuss your needs over breakfast."

Which was how Sam found herself an hour later sitting around a table, eating the best meal she'd had since she'd arrived in Earth Two. The meat was roasted to perfection; the bread light and fluffy; and the butter sweet and salty at the same time. Of course, they were in France now. She should have expected it. No offense to David's table, but a Templar like Amaury, whose father had been for a time the *de facto* King of England, would want to eat well.

Amaury let them fill their plates before giving them the bad news. "We've had word Artois is moving his army south."

Robert d'Artois was the general of the French forces, as he had been two years ago during the war in Aquitaine.

Isabelle settled more into her chair beside Sam, a pastry on her plate at which she'd actually been nibbling. As the only two women on the expedition, they had made a concerted effort to get to know each other as best they could between Isabelle's bouts of sickness. It helped that Christopher was a twenty-firster, so who and what Sam was hadn't been a complete unknown to Isabelle. Now, she buttered a piece of bread for Sam without asking if Sam wanted it (which she did) and said to Amaury, "Do you fear Artois is turning his attention to Normandy?"

"That would be logical from the direction reports say he is moving."

"Logical if King Philippe wants a war with the whole CSB," Robbie said. "Does he?"

"King Philippe wants what he once had," Amaury said. "Artois' victories this summer have renewed Philippe's confidence. I'm telling you this now in case it has a bearing on your mission."

Robbie looked at Christopher. "Callum should have kept Artois in prison."

"Or killed him," Amaury said, "though to say so isn't very Christian of me."

"We all know Callum was never going to do that. That's why he's Callum." Christopher nodded at Amaury. "As you guessed, your news is relevant to our problem. David sent my parents to Paris in response to the annexing of Flanders and the surrounding counties. We are here for the same reason."

And with a frankness Sam hadn't expected about twenty-firster-only details, he laid out what they knew. Because their ability to communicate throughout most of the medieval world was still limited, Amaury had heard none of this. He didn't have a shortwave radio anymore, since Ted and Elisa had taken theirs to Paris, and David hadn't wanted to risk sending one of the new ones with Robbie or Huw, in case it was intercepted.

Amaury turned one hand palm upright. "I would have thought if King Philippe was going to come at us, he would have done so earlier, before we were so well established ... before we were part of the Confederated States of Britain!"

They hadn't changed the name, even though the countries now part of the CSB included Ireland, Normandy, Aquitaine, and Gascony. Maybe they should just call themselves the *United States* and be done with it. Then they could include any number of countries in their confederation.

"King Philippe is very good at waiting and planning. He's like a cat in that." Isabelle definitely was feeling better if she was able to talk politics. She hadn't quite grown up in the French court, but she knew it well. "He'll watch until the time is right to strike, which he did at the Battle of Furnes."

"While he won that battle," Christopher said, "I have to ask why he thinks he can win in Normandy. Does King Philippe truly think the CSB wouldn't rise up to defend you?"

"My guess is he doesn't really understand what the CSB *is*. I barely do, and my country is a part of it." Amaury looked at Christopher. "When you see your parents, you must warn them what might be coming."

Christopher spread his hands wide. "You know I will, but you also know as well as I that my parents can take care of themselves. That said, it has been four days since we left Carew Castle, and we don't know what's happening there any more than they know what is happening with us."

Isabelle leaned forward. "Paris is seventy miles by road from here. Do you have the means to get us there?"

"You are limited only by how fast you can ride. The Templars have stations to change horses every ten miles." Amaury paused. "That said, you've had a long journey. You need to rest."

"We didn't die on that boat, and we made it here from England in record time." Isabelle met Sam's eyes, and then her husband's and Robbie's. She wasn't saying anything the other three could disagree with. "I can't help but think that's for a reason."

Amaury took in the determined faces of the young people before him. "But what reason? I admit the last time you were here, you accomplished a great deal with few resources other than an excess of grit and luck. But what are the four of you really going to be able to do against the vast powers ranged against you?"

"David sent us to Paris so we could be there when the AZs reach it, which they will. And there are only four of them too." Christopher put a hand on Amaury's shoulder. "We are going to be there at the end, just like we planned. And we're going to take that helicopter back."

"When a person has grit and luck," Sam said, "what more does she need?"

Suddenly, all four of them were laughing.

31

27 September 1297

Huw

The ship surged up the River Zwin, a natural channel that, in the thirteenth century, led from the sea to Bruges itself. Nobody could possibly have been more relieved than Huw to finally be arriving, except perhaps for Ari, who once again had spent the entire journey seasick. The city had been established initially to defend the coastline but had gone into decline when the river had started to silt up. It had then been reborn a hundred and fifty years ago when a storm had reopened the channel. Since then, it had become a major port, if not *the* major port, in Flanders.

The storm they'd just survived was a good explanation as to why the channel remained open. The weather had turned into something pretty terrible within an hour of leaving Portsmouth. Unlike their friends who were sailing southeast to France, Huw's ship had sailed directly east first, before tacking northeast to the Flemish coast. He could only hope the other ship had survived too.

That fear for their friends' lives was evident in his companions' eyes, and likely in his own. He might have called death an old friend if there was anything friendly about it. None of them could time travel but, as it turned out, their lives hadn't been in so much danger they'd lost them—even if Ari had openly stated at times that he would prefer to die.

Huw had to put the fate of the other ship from his thoughts. They were on their own, and had to act like it. Though Huw would never accuse Dafydd of being cavalier with anyone's life, he'd sent one group to Flanders and one to Paris to cover all his bases, as Christopher might say. Yes, Dafydd wanted representation in the court of Flanders, but he also didn't know where the AZs intended to go. Spreading out the best they could across Europe made sense. But to do so also meant that if one party failed to achieve their objective, the other might still survive.

Their ship had been able to sail all the way to the city walls, making them one of several boats pulled up to the dock. But even though it was late afternoon, it was not a time of great activity. Instead, other than a few men associated with loading a nearby vessel with cargo, the area in front of them was deserted in a way that Huw didn't think could be fully explained by the rain that was still falling. More soaking than storming, it couldn't have been unusual weather for the residents of this region.

As the captain put out the gangplank, a man dressed in a thick cloak and wearing a wide-brimmed hat against the weather came out of a little hut on the dock and approached. The captain's expression cleared to see him, and he said to Huw and the others, "Wait here."

He walked down the gangplank and met the dockmaster about ten yards away from the ship. They talked for a count of ten, if that, the captain handed the dockmaster a purse, and then they separated. The dockmaster snapped his fingers, and a boy of perhaps ten ran over. Again, they conferred for a couple heartbeats before the boy ran off, this time towards the main gate that allowed entrance to the city. Then the dockmaster returned to his hut, and the captain walked back to the ship.

"You bribed him?" Thomas, as always, was good for a little naïveté.

The captain didn't take offense. "I paid for our moorage, as is customary, with enough for the city fee and him for his troubles. He'll leave us alone. That's what you wanted, isn't it?"

"Yes," Huw said firmly. "Do we have free passage into the city?"

"Again, that's what the young lad was sent to ensure. He'll tell the guards you have passed inspection. Lift a hand to them in greeting as you go by. If need be, you can remind them Marc knows about you."

"Thank you."

The captain pursed his lips. "What do you want from me now? Do I stay or go? I've been here before, which is how I know Marc. I can tell you right now something isn't right in this city."

"We know of no immediate threat to you. Keep your head down. All we ask is that you stay as long as you can," Huw said. "If we come back, it might be in a hurry."

The captain glanced at Henri for confirmation, as he had done throughout the voyage. To him, the will of a Templar trumped that of a king's man. In addition, Henri was at least fifteen years older than Huw. Once the trend had become apparent, Huw and Henri hadn't fought it. When Henri nodded too, the captain said, "I will try."

And then Thomas and Henri began to strip off their Templar garb, which they'd worn on the boat as a matter of course. Templar law had once been that no Templar knight could ever be seen in public without identifying himself in some way as a Templar. For Henri and Thomas, that law had been put aside numerous times once Dafydd had told Jacques de Molay how in Avalon it had been used against them by King Philippe when he'd destroyed the Templar order in 1307.

The Templars as a whole had been inclined to be Dafydd's allies already, and the knowledge that he was trying to save them put them in his corner to a degree no other king had ever experienced. Godfrid de Windsor, brother to Nicholas de Carew, even acted as regent for Dafydd when he was not in England.

"Why aren't we heading straight to the Templar Commandery?" Ari waved a hand to encompass the both of them. "Why are you taking off your gear?"

It just went to show how much more comfortable Ari had become in the Templars' company that he could ask so bluntly. It could also be that Henri and Thomas hadn't been immediately comfortable with Ari, either. Everyone had warmed up considerably over the course of their journey. Shared peril had the tendency to do that.

Henri and Thomas looked at each other, and then raised their eyebrows at Huw. Yet again, it was up to him to explain. "They do have a commandery to the northwest of Bruges, quite a large one. It is unlikely it's on the way to wherever we can find Count Guy, but we could ask them for help. At the same time, this is a moment when Thomas and Henri are more agents for King Dafydd—and Master Godfrid—than for the Templar Order as a whole. Peter, the master of the Bruges Temple, is a chief adviser to the Count of Flanders."

Ari scratched the back of his neck while he thought about that. "So, Godfrid advises David and is loyal to him; Matthew advises King Philippe but is loyal to David; and Peter advises Guy and is loyal to him. That about right?"

"Their highest loyalty is to God and the Order, but when it comes to politics, it is not always clear to everyone which is the proper path to take." Thomas cleared his throat, as if *this* truth was one he hadn't thought about before. "Henri and I think it would be best to steer clear for now. Regardless of whether or not Count Guy is involved with the AZs, Peter will be at *his* side, not ours."

Thomas and Henri had been brought into the Avalonian circle of trust long ago. They knew that King Philippe had wreaked the same destruction on the Templars in Flanders as he had on those in France. It would be all the more reason for Peter to oppose King Philippe now and support Guy—and for the Flemish to wonder why Dafydd and all of his men weren't doing the same.

"I don't like it any more than you do, Ari," Huw said. "It goes against my instincts too. It isn't only Dafydd who puts a premium on being honest."

Ari raised his eyebrows. "You misunderstand. I have no problem with lying. Often it's easier than telling the truth. I just want to be very clear about why I'm doing it."

"Hopefully, you won't have to," Thomas said. "Lie, I mean."

"We are counting on you to get us through this, Ari," Huw said. "You're the one who speaks Flemish. For now, we aren't sure who to trust—or who might trust us."

Ari looked disgruntled for a moment. "That's the only reason I'm here, isn't it?"

Huw looked at him more closely. "Is this going to be a problem?"

"No." Ari let out something of a laugh. "I know the difference between being *used* and being *of use*. And even then." He gave a shake of his head. "Until a few days ago, none of you knew me. I can't blame you for thinking you don't really know me even now. Why should you take me at face value and on such short but fraught acquaintance?" Now he bobbed his head in Henri's direction. "He's here for a reason. As are you. And you." He indicated Thomas and Huw. "We each have a particular skill set, and you certainly didn't bring me along for my expertise with a sword."

Huw opened his mouth to protest (though in this instance Ari was right), but Ari waved it away before he could speak. "Any team to which I have ever belonged had to be carefully constructed so each member could contribute. I know the AZs. I speak Flemish. And, despite David's concerns about my safety on the Continent, that I'm Jewish could be helpful here in Bruges." He let out a low laugh. "When has that ever been the case?"

Huw found himself grinning at the other man. "Welcome to Earth Two."

For a moment Ari's brow furrowed, as if he couldn't believe Huw had actually said that to him. But then he replied, "Happy to be here," and he genuinely seemed to mean it.

32

27 September 1297

Robbie

After eating and bathing, the four of them mounted the horses Amaury had provided for them and began their journey down the road to Paris. Since then, they'd changed horses twice at Templar way stations, eaten, and rested once again. By late afternoon, they had come thirty miles. Robbie was riding beside Sam, who somehow looked far more alert and happy than Robbie had any right to expect.

"Only forty more miles to go!" she said. "We've made better progress than I hoped."

They had started out at a gallop, but as the miles had worn on, they'd settled into more of a canter, which the horses could keep up for hours. A trot was too slow and would have been teeth-rattling for seventy miles. It also would have prevented much in the way of conversation.

"You're not sore?"

"Of course I'm sore. What I wouldn't give for an earthquake to suddenly bring Paris thirty miles closer to Rouen."

Robbie felt his eyes cross at the unfamiliar phrasing. "I'm not sure what you mean by that. *An earthquake?*"

Sam tipped her head. "That's when the ground shakes from movement deep within the earth."

"I do know what it means, though I've never felt one. I just don't understand what you mean about one bringing Paris closer to Rouen. Is such an event possible in Avalon?"

"No." Sam waved a hand before returning it to the reins. "And really, if Rouen were closer to Paris, then it would be that much easier for the King of France to invade. I was just making a dumb joke. I'm sorry."

"Don't be sorry. It isn't your fault I didn't understand." He paused before adding, "For nation shall rise against nation, and kingdom against kingdom: and there shall be famines, and pestilences, and earthquakes, in diverse places."

"I could do without famine and pestilence. Is that a quote from the Bible?"

Robbie looked at her a bit sideways. "The Book of Matthew."

Her expression cleared. "Of course. Sorry."

He waved that apology away too. It wasn't the first quote from scripture that an Avalonian didn't know. When he'd first come from Avalon, Christopher had been ignorant too. It made Robbie wonder what kind of education they had there. They lived with wonders, but not one had ever read Matthew. Or Aristotle. Instead, he said, "You don't need to apologize to me. I've noticed you do it quite a lot."

"I'm sorry—" she started to say, but then stopped when Robbie gave her a mockingly hard look. She laughed. "I'll try to stop."

Ahead of them, Christopher slowed. "We are coming up on our first real test." He spoke now to Sam. "A lot of the time, guards are for show, but getting past them can be a little like trying to get through TSA: you never know how the rules could have changed overnight and what might trip you up."

Robbie had no idea what TSA was and thus identified it, like so many of the things that came out of Christopher's mouth, as yet another esoteric Avalonian reference. He understood the gist of what Christopher was talking about, regardless, and had been waiting for this moment, enjoying the intimate conversation with Sam because he knew he'd soon have to think about far more momentous things.

They had reached the River Epte, which marked the boundary between Normandy and France. As he'd been told to expect, it was guarded on both sides. It was at the ford here that an ancient French king had signed that first treaty giving Normandy to the Normans so they'd leave the rest of France alone. The Kings of France had taken it back only in the last hundred years. And then, in this world, lost it again.

Chateau de Saint-Clair was controlled by the French and was located on their side of the river. Once across the bridge, Robbie and his companions would have to pass right under the castle towers if they were to stay on the road to Paris. Farther east, higher land could be seen beyond the river.

The Normans, out of fear of attack, had recently thrown up their own castle on their side of the river, within line of sight of the French castle. Even more, they had constructed a gate right on the road and set men to guard it, with the idea of stopping every person who passed in either direction. This move hadn't exactly been a boon to trade, since it could put the fear of God into anyone who had something to hide. At the same time, the soldiers weren't taxing the travelers, merely stopping each one and questioning them.

As to be expected, the French had countered with an outpost of their own, in what Sam called *a mini-arms race*. As usual, Robbie didn't quite follow the thought until she explained what she meant.

Robbie took the lead on the Normandy side, relying both on his Scottish accent and the letter from Master Amaury to get them through. The guardsman couldn't read, but he recognized the seal, and with hardly more than a quick thanks, let them pass. They were leaving Normandy, after all, so would soon be the problem of his counterpart on the other side of the river.

"You're up, Isabelle," Christopher said. "We need a home run."

Robbie had played many impromptu games of baseball with Christopher over the years, so he knew the source of the phrase. *You're up* was a shortened way of saying, *You're up to bat*. Since he'd started paying attention, Robbie had come to see that Avalonian speech was littered with baseball metaphors.

Isabelle shot her husband a dry look. "I know how to hit it *out of the park*. Don't worry, darling. This isn't my first rodeo."

"Different event altogether, Izzy." Christopher grinned at his wife.

Beside Robbie, Sam shook her head and laughed. "You two."

Her cheerfulness served to bolster everyone as they approached the barricades constructed by the French. Robbie had played this role when entering Rouen two years ago. He could again, but they all thought Isabelle was a better choice this time. To that end, she stuck her nose in the air, in her best impression of a lady of the French court, and pranced her horse right up to one of the two guards on duty. "I am Isabelle Norris, daughter of the Master of the Paris Temple. Let us pass."

Although she was dressed in traveling clothes, hers were far finer than a common person would wear. In the old days, she would have been given free passage without any question.

But times had changed, and there was indecision in the guardsman's face. "How do I know you are who you say you are? What were you doing in Rouen? What business could you have had there? Who do you have with you?"

Isabelle turned her head to look back, first at Christopher, who could not reveal his true identity under any circumstances, and then at Robbie. She opened her mouth to speak, but the guard cut her off. "I want to hear it from them."

Sam urged her horse closer, metaphorically stepping *up to the plate,* so to speak. "I am my lady's maidservant. The other two are her sworn bondsmen." Her voice suddenly became lighter and sweeter. And, if Robbie wasn't mistaken, she batted her eyelashes at the guard. She also spoke in excellent French. "We have been traveling for days and have ever so far to go." And then she added in something of a conspiratorial tone, while Isabelle pretended she couldn't hear, "My lady is anxious to reach the commandery at Vigny before dark. If we are late for dinner, she'll be cross! I'm so sorry to trouble you, but might you please let us pass?"

For once, the apology was appropriate. The guard looked at Christopher, who bent his head respectfully, and then at Robbie, who put his hand to his heart and did the same. Then they all held their collective breath.

After another agonizingly long moment, the guard stepped out of the road and waved them through. They passed by at a walk, trying not to look like they were in a hurry, and then picked up the pace. In point of fact, they could have run down the guard if he hadn't let them through. Of course, that would have called attention to themselves more than anything else could have done, short of identifying Christopher as the Hero of Westminster and cousin to the King of England.

When they were some yards along, Robbie glanced back to see the two guards standing in the middle of the road, face-to-face and speaking in a heated manner. Then the second guard, with whom they hadn't interacted, shoved at the other and ran off, towards the guardhouse. A moment later, he was mounted and galloping towards the French castle.

"Go. Ride now." Robbie spurred his own horse.

The others didn't question, just obeyed, bent over their horses' necks as they galloped. The village of Saint-Clair-sur-Epte, which hugged the riverbank and clustered around the church to the east of the castle, flashed past. Then the road turned sharply southeast, and they climbed towards the hills beyond the village.

"Is anyone following?" Christopher said from up ahead.

Robbie glanced over his shoulder once more. "Not that I can see. I regret now not taking the time to go around. As it is, we ought to get off this particular road sooner rather than later, just in case."

"Is this my fault?" Sam asked, once they crested the rise and could catch their breaths, since the road remained empty behind them. "Did I do something wrong?"

"You were great," Robbie said. "You behaved perfectly."

"You did way better than I would have," Christopher added. "I come off as American no matter what I say."

Robbie gazed back down the road. "Rather than casting blame, we need to consider what this incident tells us."

Isabelle nodded her understanding first. "They're on high alert, preparing for war is my guess. I'm wondering if the French guards had been warned that someone like us, though not seemingly us specifically, might be coming through."

"How?" Sam said. "Nobody could have beaten us here."

"No person," Robbie said, "but a bird could have. And King Philippe has the best pigeon corps in the world."

33

27 September 1297

Huw

Huw kept pace beside Ari, as had become something of his self-appointed job. He'd stayed close on the boat too, though, in that case, it was more because Ari had spent the entire time with his head over a bucket—when he wasn't begging Huw to throw him overboard because he was too weak to do it himself.

"I agree with the captain that there's a heaviness to the air that can't be explained by the rain," Henri said from his place a few paces behind them, Thomas at his side. "We need to find cover and regroup, the sooner the better."

That was Huw's preference too. But while the area of the city just past the docks was the logical place to start looking, every door was closed to them, and nobody answered when they knocked. Somewhat disbelieving, Huw led his friends up one street and down another, on a quest for an inn that would allow them entry, simply to get off the street. They were turned away in every instance. It was as if the city was abandoned or, at the very least, everyone in Bruges was hiding in their cellars.

Except, Huw knew people were still present by the twitching of the curtains in the windows on the upper floors, or a sense of movement in the back of rooms when they peered through front windows.

Giving up on finding a solution himself, the time had come to see what they were really dealing with in Ari. "Can you take us to Jacob? You're the only one of us who has ever been in Bruges before, and the only one who speaks Flemish."

"Though I'm starting to wonder if it's the right Flemish, the city isn't so different from when I was last here." He eyed them all for a moment before adding, "Two weeks and seven hundred and twenty-eight years ago."

"How could it be so much the same?" Thomas said. "London and Paris are very different, so we have heard."

"They've preserved it as a World Heritage Site, like Caernarfon or Conwy." Ari gave a shake of his head at the looks of non-comprehension. "They've kept it looking medieval on purpose, though based on how the city was a hundred or more years from now. Still, the streets haven't changed that much. While Bruges in Avalon never had much in the way of a Jewish community, I still think I can find it."

Rather than dwelling on the oddity of even having this conversation, Huw could be happy Ari was from that different world. Right now, they needed him to be. And if the signs on the streets and the plethora of storefronts showing Jewish symbols were anything to go by, he was taking them in the right direction.

Finally, Ari stopped in front of a red door, not unlike a dozen others they'd encountered in the last half-hour. Next door was an inn with the painting of a ram on the sign, with (Huw was guessing) the word *ram* written in Hebrew underneath.

"When Aaron gave me this address, I was pretty sure it was in an effort to get me to stop arguing." Ari held his knuckles in front of the door, waiting to knock. "Now I'm not so sure. If all other doors are closed to us, this seems to me a good place to start."

"To us, too." Huw had known about Jacob's group before they'd left Carew, though, without ever having been to Bruges, he couldn't know exactly where to find it. Ari was right that Aaron had given him the specifics to appease his pride and get him moving in the direction Dafydd wanted. On the whole, it was pretty good thinking on the old doctor's part. "Given the lack of a warm welcome everywhere else, I have fewer doubts now that it was the right decision to come to Bruges than when we made it. We don't know what's happening in this city. We need information, and if we're going to get it anywhere, it's here."

At first, nobody answered Ari's knock, but after Ari persisted, the door to the adjacent inn opened, and a man poked out his head. Perhaps all he intended was to check the street, but Huw was quick to leap the few feet between them in order to put a foot in the door before the man could close it again.

Ari spoke rapidly in a foreign language Huw presumed to be Flemish, though it could have been Hebrew or something similar too. The longer Ari talked, the more the man's expression eased. But it was the mention of Dafydd, the only word Huw recognized, though Ari had said it the English way, *David,* that had him pulling the door wide. It was as if all Ari would have had to do was say David's name from the start, like it was a secret password. "Come, get off the street. It isn't safe for strangers in the city today."

Huw was the last one through the door, to ensure his companions were admitted too. They huddled in a small foyer with a long, narrow hallway heading into the recesses of the house and a set of stairs going up. To the right at the bottom of the stairs was a second door, beyond which Huw could hear voices. Since they were safe from prying eyes, he didn't press through it on his own, waiting for the innkeeper to open it.

Instead, the man stood resolutely in their way and switched to English. "You say King David sent you, and you have just come from Wales, but by your accent you are not from there. Where are you from?"

Thomas took it upon himself to answer first, since he was the only one of them with a real Earth Two English accent. "I am from England. My name is Thomas Hartley." And then he introduced Henri, Ari, and Huw. He didn't immediately identify himself and Henri as Templars, nor mention that Henri was French, born and raised. Henri's accent would give him away in an instant, and he had the wisdom in this moment to keep his mouth shut.

"Still," the innkeeper kept his eyes on Ari, "you are different. Not one of them. Not one of us."

"That's because he is from Avalon," Thomas said, never afraid to speak the truth as he saw it.

"I had heard that our people are in Avalon, but I'd scarcely dared believe it!" The man's expression turned to one of hope.

"Yes," Ari said, following Thomas's example, even if, as he'd told them earlier, lying came more easily. "Millions of them."

And it was that truth that finally had the innkeeper opening the second door.

The inn's common room was full of people chattering to each other. Huw could tell from the clothing styles and hair that every man present, except for Thomas, Henri, and Huw himself, was Jewish.

"It looks like we've come to the right place," he said in English under his breath.

"You most definitely have."

These words were in English too, and not from a voice Huw immediately recognized. He spun around to see a man of about thirty, with a huge grin on his face, standing behind them.

The man spoke again. "I have prayed this day would come! It seems a gift from God that it is today of all days!"

"Jacob!" Huw put out a hand, which Jacob ignored in order to wrap him up in a hug instead.

That prompted a man at one of the tables to ask, "Who are these people, Jacob?"

Jacob shot him an intense look. "They are among the righteous." Then, his arm still around Huw, Jacob turned him towards the expectant faces of those in the room. "May I introduce my friends, Huw, Henri, and Thomas. They all serve David. They all were with us in Paris."

As one, the other men in the room surged to their feet in order to greet them—Ari included, whom they accepted without question—less, Huw thought, because he was Jewish too than because he was with Huw, Henri, and Thomas.

Ari had gotten them in the door, however, and for that Huw could be grateful. Now, Ari leaned in and said to Huw, under his breath, "that an inn of Jewish men in Bruges could welcome two Templars, a Welshman, and a spy from Israel merely at the mention of David's name indicates how I, and everyone else in Avalon, have grossly underestimated the esteem in which he is held here. I'm embarrassed for myself and everyone else for their past treatment of him."

If Huw hadn't seen the same events with his own eyes (and heard Ari's confession with his own ears), he might not have believed it either.

Finally, Jacob asked, "How did you know to come tonight?"

Huw frowned. "We didn't. I mean, what is happening tonight?"

"We have received word from the Count of Flanders that he is taking back Male Castle from the French. We're going to take all of Bruges back at the same time."

"How?" That was from Thomas again, bless his heart.

Jacob lowered his voice, out of instinct at the gravity of the mission. "We are charged with killing the French soldiers as they sleep in their barracks. It will be our special pleasure, given their treatment of us."

Thomas looked stricken, but once again, Ari was right in Huw's ear, whispering in English: "What Jacob describes is almost exactly what the people of Bruges perpetrated on the French before the Battle of Furnes in 1302 (in Avalon). In May of that year, they rose up and killed every Frenchman in Bruges, including the entire garrison. As far as I know, no Jewish folk were involved that time."

"How do you know all this?"

"This story was bread and butter to the members of the Zeelandic Revolution. They held it up as inspiration for what they themselves planned."

Huw chewed on his lower lip. "It makes me wonder if the AZs were the ones to propose the action in the first place. And what other stories they've told themselves."

It was Ari's turn to look concerned. "I don't know. I guess we'll find out."

Just then, three gentle taps, one long and two short, came at the door, prompting the men in the room to move towards it.

"That's the signal," Jacob said. "It's time to go."

"For us, too." Huw put a hand on Jacob's shoulder. "We need to get to Male Castle."

"It's two miles outside the city." Jacob stood irresolute. He wanted to leave, but he wasn't willing to abandon them either, not with the great debt he owed Dafydd. "I was hoping you'd come with us."

"We can't." Huw was regretful.

"It's that important?"

"Yes," Huw said. "Life and death, I might even say."

"I might be able to arrange for horses to get you there quicker." He paused to think and then fumbled in his purse for a wooden coin. "Just outside the east gate is a man named Chaim. He runs a stall that sells haircloth. If you show him this coin and tell him I sent you, he will get you what you need." He paused while he shook everyone's hands. "Thank you for coming. It is good to know King David stands with us once again. Good luck to you."

"And to you," Huw said, without correcting him as to the exact situation. None of the others chose to dissuade Jacob of his assumptions either. It would serve no purpose tonight. A moment later, they were back out in the street, watching Jacob's small army trot away in the gathering dusk.

Henri spoke for the first time since they'd entered the inn. "While you were talking to Jacob, I chatted with the innkeeper's son at length. Two nights ago, the Count of Flanders took Poeke Castle with his flying machine. We should assume that is how they will be attacking Male too."

"How far away is Poeke from Male?" Thomas said.

Huw had never heard of it, but Ari, once again, was there with the information they needed. "As the crow flies? Less than fifteen miles. They could have had riders racing back and forth between here and there all day."

"As well as pigeons," Henri said. "Fifteen miles is a good day's walk for a fit army, but it sounds like the count's forces were not pressed at Poeke, and most of the recruits would have been collected from the countryside along the way. Or, now that I think about it, from Bruges itself."

"No wonder it was such a party in there," Ari said.

"Was this what we signed up for when we agreed to come to Flanders?" Thomas gave a shake of his head as he set off side-by-side with Henri heading east, the opposite direction from Jacob and his men. "If he were here, what would David do?"

"What he had to," Henri said flatly.

"Somehow, we seem to have joined Bruges' rebellion against the French," Huw made his voice milder than Henri's had been, "whether we intended to or not."

34

27 September 1297

Thomas

"Here we go again," Thomas said, "heading straight into the lion's den!"

"Is that you complaining? You're the one who is always suggesting we take unnecessary risks," Henri said.

Thomas was still grinning. "Just trying to keep up with you, old man."

Even Thomas had been a soldier long enough to realize the danger inherent in roaming the streets of a city about to experience a regime change. Even worse, as Thomas had said to Henri, they were riding towards battle instead of away from it.

"There it is." Ari cut through their jesting, pointing ahead to Male Castle, which was suddenly visible in the distance. "Still standing for now."

A few torches on the battlements were beating back the rain that continued to fall. The sight of it had them slowing their horses, more wary now that they were so close. They were wet from head to foot, as they had been for days, but at least the water coating them was no longer salty. With the setting of the sun, it had grown very dark, and Thomas spared a thought for Jacob and his band of men, moving secretly to do their part to oust the French. Thomas didn't like the unchivalrous nature of what they'd planned, even if he could understand it. He was glad he and his companions had a different task.

On the whole, Thomas was not unhappy about lending his own aid. It wasn't as if anyone *liked* the idea of King Philippe stealing an entire country. David wanted them at the court of Count Guy, and if Thomas had any say in the matter, that was what he was going to get. He was honestly pleased they might manage it on the very evening they'd arrived.

Huw put up a hand for everyone to stop. Up ahead Thomas could hear dozens of voices. There were so many, in fact, that he couldn't really make out individual conversations. Through the hubbub, however, he could hear men talking in Flemish, French, and even English.

Henri pulled up beside him. "Are you thinking what I'm thinking?"

"I'm thinking the four of us have just become the Count of Flanders' newest recruits. That is what you were about to say, isn't it?"

"Of course."

From behind them, Ari said, "Me too. *Great minds think alike.*"

That was a phrase Thomas had heard from Avalonians before. It had taken him a while to understand that whenever one of them said it, it was like he was laughing at himself and everyone else too. Did Ari think he had a great mind or didn't he? When most men boasted, they meant it. But while, to a man (or woman), the Avalonians were even more confident, they never bragged.

Being French, Henri probably thought Ari was being serious. "We will say we have just come from England. Even with Ari's Flemish, I think it unwise to pretend to be other than we are."

That was Thomas's preference too, of course, and they took a few moments to straighten their clothing and adjust their gear in order to present themselves as well as possible.

"It will be a fine line we're walking," Huw reminded everyone. "We are ambassadors from Dafydd. We are not really here to free Flanders from France!"

"In addition, we aren't going to be able to ride right up to Count Guy, if he is even here," Henri said. "There will be many layers of men between him and us. Be patient."

"It would be nice not to be killed before we get that far," Ari said.

Again, it seemed he was being facetious.

Thus, for now, they were just knights. This was an army, after all, and all armies needed soldiers. Thomas, as always, could act as Henri's squire. Ari was obviously their Flemish contact. And Huw was their sworn companion, which was an accurate description regardless of where they found themselves.

As they approached the encampment, it became clear by the number of men milling about that a significant action was in the works, as if they hadn't known it already. Most of the soldiers before them were properly armed, many with a giant weapon with a long shaft and a steel spike, the better to hack apart any Frenchmen they saw.

Henri echoed Thomas's thoughts. "This is no casual army."

"They put it together quickly, too," Thomas said. "They took Poeke Castle two nights ago. And they're already here."

"The AZs are in a hurry," Ari said. "Say what you will about them, but they have a sense of purpose and an urgency for that purpose. If they didn't move quickly, Robert d'Artois could have had time to return and further fortify their stolen possessions. Better to retain the element of surprise. It's a very mod—" he broke off. "It's a very Avalonian perspective."

"Moving too fast increases the risk of failure," Huw said. "It can stretch out supply lines too far."

"They are in the heart of Flanders," Henri said. "Count Guy is well supplied with men and goods. He should have no trouble keeping every castle he takes."

"Besides, they have the helicopter and Avalonian weapons," Ari said. "Unless something goes drastically wrong, they aren't going to fail."

The companions trotted their horses along the edge of the encampment, though that was perhaps too robust a word to describe the gathering. There were neither tents nor fires, nor a host of torches, for fear of alerting the men in the castle as to what was coming at them. Some soldiers were eating, but their food was being consumed cold. While at long last the rain had ceased, the clouds remained, and it was dark within the shadow of this stand of trees.

Thomas could feel the anxiety, as well as the anticipation, in the men around him as they waited for the action to start. He and his three companions finally found the cavalry, gathered on the other side of the road in a similar clearing. There weren't very many of them for a military action, maybe a dozen. Some had dismounted and were talking quietly. As Thomas and the others rode up, one of their number stepped to the fore with his hand up.

"Wie gaat daar?" Thomas knew enough Flemish—and human behavior—to understand that meant *who goes there?*

He urged his horse closer, leaning down to speak to the soldier who wasn't mounted. "We are friends." He spoke in English, because that was what they'd agreed. That they were foreign would also excuse whatever manners or statements they made that weren't quite right, like Ari's Flemish.

One of the cavalryman's companions had a lantern, which he'd been holding down low at his side. Now he raised it higher to illuminate Thomas's face. "You are English?" He said *English* more like *Englische.* It wasn't as if Thomas didn't know what he meant.

"Yes. Come to stand by you." Thomas gestured to his friends. "If you will have us."

The second man let out a snort and relayed Thomas's words to a third man, better dressed and armored, indicating he might be the commander. This was confirmed when he subsequently let out a *hup* sound, which the soldiers around him interpreted to mean it was time to mount their horses. As they began moving onto the road that led to the castle, the second man, the one who'd understood Thomas's English, gestured that the four of them should fall into line.

Thomas had been worried about ending up a corpse in a ditch so the Flemish could appropriate his horse. Instead, they were being included in the Flemish cavalry as if foreigners asking to join their army was a daily thing. Maybe it was.

"They didn't even ask for our names," he said in an undertone.

"We timed our arrival perfectly," Henri said.

From Thomas's other side, Ari said, "Again."

Thomas could sense him shaking his head. In truth, Thomas tried never to grow used to the coincidences that gathered around David's companions, even as he was grateful for them.

Just in front of him, a young man similar in age to Thomas asked his neighbor, in Scot-accented English, of all things, "How many have come, do you think?"

"Don't be fooled by the small number of cavalry," replied the older man beside him. "We have hundreds of men on foot with us."

Given their inclusion, Thomas thought it might be safe to risk a question. "How has your night gone so far?"

"We just arrived too," the older man said.

"Why so few cavalry?"

"More might come, but they say we won't need them." He scoffed, knowing as Thomas did that more men was always better. But then he explained further: "We have few cavalry due to the large number of defections amongst the nobility. We lost so many at Furnes, the rest were cowed. They think the King of France is their future and could not be convinced otherwise."

"That was before two nights ago," the younger man said. "A few have returned since then."

"Do you know the plan?" Thomas said.

Maybe that was a dangerous question to ask because of concern about betrayal, but the older man seemed to think nothing of it. "We are charged with riding right up to the castle. We're the distraction. Or, if you prefer, the bait. As we speak, others are taking back the city."

The younger man nodded vigorously. "Some of our companions were sent to the mayor's house. Them Frenchies won't know what hit them."

"Are they Scottish too?" Thomas said.

"We brought an army in ourselves. It wasn't looking too good for a while, and many wanted to go home. We find ourselves glad we stayed." The older man bobbed his head towards Thomas. "Especially now we know England is coming in on our side. I'd take the Flems any day over the French."

Flems was a nickname worthy of Bronwen. Thomas didn't enlighten him either that the English weren't exactly coming in on the Flemish side.

"How about you?" One of the Scots' companions with a set of particularly bushy eyebrows leaned past the first man. "What brought you here?"

"We've been tracking Artois' army." Thomas didn't know how much sense that really made.

It satisfied the strangers, to the point that the older Scot nodded. "He's gone to Normandy, leaving the field clear for us." There was an element of glee in his voice.

Then their commander stood in his stirrups and spoke in Flemish, which Ari was right there to translate. "He's urging us forward. We are to approach the gates."

"Robert is as brave as they come," the older Scotsman said. "He never asks his men to do what he won't."

It was only then that Thomas realized who this was: their commander was none other than Count Guy's own son. Thomas was quite sure that when David sent them as his ambassadors to the court of Count Guy of Flanders, he had no expectation they would be within touching distance of Guy's heir on their first night.

If the goal was to be there when the AZs overplayed their hand, Thomas and his companions were well on their way to being in the right place at the right time.

35

27 September 1297

Ari

From the moment he'd arrived in Earth Two, Ari had experienced one surprising and unexpected situation after another. Honestly, for all of the uncertainty, the moment he'd felt most in control had been while walking through the streets of Bruges, even though the only time he'd been in a town that deserted was in Avalon when he'd traveled through France at the end of January one year. In the little communities south of Paris—some even built within the walls of former Templar commanderies—only one shop in ten was open and no restaurants. He'd ultimately had to pick through the offerings at a gas station to find something to eat.

He wasn't walking anymore, but riding, so he was back to barely hanging on for dear life. Really, it was Ari's own fault for not reminding everyone he was not an expert horseman. When he'd learned they had to ride all of two miles from the city walls to Male Castle, he'd thought at first *how bad could it be?* He'd ridden farther than that the first day out of Carew Castle to Pembroke.

As it turned out, it was a good thing it was dark and raining much of the time. Five days ago, he'd been fresh out of the helicopter from Avalon and ready for action. Today, he was operating on too many days of little to no food or sleep. Both deficits would have to be remedied eventually.

At one point after the conversation with Jacob, Ari had thought about suggesting they save the wooden coin and just walk. They would have had to do so anyway if Chaim hadn't given them horses. But knights didn't walk. None of the others would have been happy about it.

Well, Ari wasn't a knight. Pretending to be one didn't count. For all of the horribleness of the boat, at least there he'd been able to shed the mail armor. He was wearing it again, though without the tunic sporting Carew's sigil or the helmet. At some point during his ordeal, a seaman had given him a hat with a wide brim, which kept the rain off his face and shielded it from prying eyes. In Avalon, he'd prided himself on his ability to hide in plain sight. Here, it was extremely uncomfortable to know they weren't hiding at all.

In truth, that he was able to sit on a horse was something of a miracle. If they hadn't landed when they had, if he'd had to stay on that ship even one more hour, the man who'd infiltrated the Zeelandic Revolution would have been entirely gone, replaced by a wet rag. And now, here he was, half a head back from the front line next to the heir to the County of Flanders, trying not to think about the last time he'd been in combat. Although he was on horseback this time and not in a personnel carrier, the feeling in his gut was entirely the same: fear, anticipation, uncertainty, and determination above all else:

"Get ready to return fire!" *The call came from their leader, Franc, who was standing with three points of contact at the front of the makeshift armored personnel carrier.*

Then the truck leading their convoy blasted through the heli-port's eight-foot-high chain-link fence. It had worked to perfection, in that it had kept at bay the army of reporters in the street who were anxious to get a glimpse of David. But it was no match for the truck's massive bull bar.

The two personnel carriers had started life, possibly decades earlier, as farm vehicles hauling onions (by the smell), one of the State of Washington's chief crops. Even after being repurposed, the odor remained. The ZR had affixed metal plates to the sides, each separated by a gap wide enough to allow those inside to fire their weapons. Ari clutched his AR-15 with one hand and the rail of the seat with the other as the carrier jostled over the downed fence.

Then they were inside the grounds. The men in the lead truck were tasked with pinning down airport—and Chad Treadman's—security, while those in Ari's truck hijacked the helicopter. The ZRs had the advantage in this fight, in that the FBI pilot was a compatriot.

Even one of the richest men in the world could be terribly naïve. Chad hadn't disguised the extent to which he was throwing his wealth and power behind anything David needed. He had spent hundreds of millions of dollars developing the most advanced helicopter in the world. Although he was recouping his investment by selling it to governments and organizations, its real purpose had always been to take David, if he were to grace this universe with his presence again, back to Earth Two. Everybody knew it. Thus, Marie the Mole.

Which meant the ZR's plan had worked. Granted, they'd had a lot of good luck, beginning with the fact that they'd based a large part of their organization in Seattle in the first place because that's where Chad's factory was located. It was also a large city within striking distance of both Portland, Oregon, where David had grown up, and Pendleton, another of David's known locations. Marie had excelled both in the FBI and as a pilot. She was smart, driven, and focused. It was almost as if she had willed Chad to choose her.

Now, she kept the helicopter on the ground as Ari and his companions piled out of their vehicle, weapons at the ready. Ari fired at the refueling truck, which went up in a huge spout of flame. Really, he'd done it so as to appear at the center of the fight while also avoiding killing any of Chad's people.

"Go! Go! Go!" That was Franc again.

Ari ran towards the helicopter, reaching it just as Jos, Franc's second-in-command, slid open the door. Franc leapt inside, but Ari kept back in order to be the last one in. It was his job to lay down a field of covering fire. He knew how to do it so nobody would get hurt. What he really wanted was for Chad's people to keep their heads down. What he really wanted was to not have to kill anyone ...

It had crossed his mind a moment ago that he was additionally lucky none of the AZs had been attached to Robert's retinue. They would have recognized him immediately. To them, he was a traitor and/or spy for David. If only to be their translator, Ari had meant to stick close to his companions/friends. To be honest, it had been a long time since he had spent substantial time with anyone he could genuinely call a *friend*. But somehow, in the jostling about that horses by nature did when scrunched together, he found himself nearly at Robert's side.

"Are you ready for this?" Robert was speaking to his second-in-command, the one who spoke English, but Ari found himself nodding too.

Robert glanced at him out of the corner of his eye, they were almost to the drawbridge. It was pulled up, the moat lapping below their feet, so there was no way to reach the castle. Several French guardsmen had gathered at the top of the gatehouse to look down on them. It would have been impossible for them not to have noticed the sixteen men on horseback coming towards them, torches blazing brightly against the night sky. The brightness of the guards' own torches was ruining their night vision too. As the Scot had said, the cavalry were the distraction, keeping French attention on them so the Flemish foot soldiers and crossbowmen could creep closer to the castle. Count Guy wasn't entirely relying on the helicopter to get this done.

"Who goes there!" A tall guardsman leaned over the battlement wall.

Ari couldn't help grinning to hear the words again, though coming from the French this time. People really did say that in the Middle Ages!

"I am Robert, the Count of Nevers and the son of Count Guy of Flanders. I request an audience with your commander."

This caused some consternation among the guardsmen, who conferred before the original one spoke again. "It is late. You should return to Bruges for your billet for tonight. You may see our commander in the morning."

The men around Ari shifted, murmuring their disgruntlement at the reply. Even Ari, a novice when it came to medieval politics, knew this to be a major snub. It was a little funny that the cavalrymen were automatically behaving as if any of what was happening on their end was real. The goal was to get the commander to come out onto the battlement so he could be shot by one of the AZs in the helicopter. The Flemish cavalry didn't actually want to enter the castle until that happened.

Robert pretended to be unconcerned about being so discounted. Instead he lifted a hand, implying acknowledgment and also to prevent the guard's departure. "If that is really your commander's wish, of course we will leave. But I would like to hear it from his own lips. Since we have no billet, as you say, in Bruges, we can just camp right here tonight."

Nobody on the battlement liked that idea either. They didn't want to disturb their commander; they *liked* snubbing the son of the Count of Flanders; but they didn't want sixteen Flemish cavalry camping at the end of their drawbridge either. After further discussion, the guardsmen sent one of their number away.

Everyone waited, taking easy breaths, at least for those around Ari. These were seasoned soldiers for the most part. They weren't fearful. Yet.

Then the French commander appeared on the battlement, wearing a high hat with a feather. Even through the dark night, Ari thought he could see his sneer. "What is it you want?"

At that moment, the moon came out from behind the clouds for the first time, shining down on the scene with an eerie white light.

Robert raised a hand above his head. The commander might have thought Robert's motion was a means of acknowledging his presence, but really it was a signal to a horseman to Ari's left. He raced away through the fields beyond the castle, leaping two successive stone walls. Then he disappeared into a dip in the landscape. He'd gone perhaps two hundred yards at a breakneck pace.

The French commander had to have seen him too. He leaned through a crenel, his eyes glaring. His mouth formed to speak, but then the sound of the helicopter came unmistakably through the night air.

Even if the commander had no idea what the noise signified, he couldn't mistake the menace it represented. The sound also momentarily distracted him from the cavalry before him, who took the opportunity to retreat. They didn't want to be anywhere near the castle when the AZs began firing their weapons.

A moment later, the helicopter rose above the fields like the giant flying grasshopper it was.

When David had summoned Ari to warn him of the dangers he might face, he likely couldn't have imagined their current situation. Still, he had looked at Ari with those cool blue eyes of his and seen right through him. Only now, sitting here next to Count Guys' heir, about to participate in the attack on Male Castle, did Ari finally have an inkling of what David had really been asking.

Can I trust you?

Even more, *can I trust you with being a representative of Avalon, no matter what you face and how dire your circumstances?*

Can I trust you not just to save yourself?

36

27 September 1297

Johnny

Unlike at Poeke, where Johnny had stayed in Jos's wake, he had his own mission this time: to stop, if not kill, all the French messenger pigeons kept in the castle. A counterpart was doing the same in the city. The two hundred miles from Paris to Bruges would take a rider on horseback days to cross. A healthy pigeon could do it before morning.

The moon had been a sudden, though not unwelcome, respite from an otherwise very dark night. Since they were no longer needing to hide their forces, the fact that the countryside around Male Castle was nearly as brightly lit as the castle itself meant their own men could position themselves without fear of tripping over each other. Two miles distant was the City of Bruges, where even now their people should be swinging into action. If they were to take back this region of Flanders for good, this needed to be a coordinated attack.

Conveniently, the French defenders on the battlement were illuminated even further by their torches. Johnny didn't know which of the six men who gaped up at them from the top of the gatehouse was the commander. He chose not to care. By now, he had hardened his heart to the death toll. The near elimination of their enemy's forces served to spare his own.

Jos gave Arne the signal to begin firing.

As before, the sight of the bullets ripping through the men reminded Johnny of a scythe cutting through wheat at harvest time. Then Marie circled the helicopter over the whole castle, Arne chewing through another dozen defenders before they had the sense to retreat inside their protective walls. The castle's defenses included an exterior moat, an outer curtain wall, an outer bailey, and then an inner curtain wall and inner gatehouse that protected the keep, hall, and private quarters of the noble family. The fortress was eminently defensible—unless one had the capability, as Johnny all of a sudden did, to come at the castle from above.

They'd known Poeke Castle was a practice run from the start. It was meant to be a display of might, in order to prove what was possible with the marvelous machine and silence the naysayers in Count Guy's court. To take the castle with such ease was a nice bonus (as Marie had said). Johnny's vocabulary had increased significantly since he started *hanging out* with the Avalonians, not just the AZs but starting at King David's tournament in Wales.

By contrast to Poeke, Male Castle *meant* something to Johnny's entire family. It had been the seat of the Counts of Flanders for generations. Guy had lamented its loss from the moment the French invaded, and he wanted it back above all others. At one time, the castle had been built in wood, fortified as a motte and bailey castle against Danish attacks three hundred years or more ago. Some time after that, it had been rebuilt in stone and had since been remodeled several times with all the latest modern features, including an English toilet. Johnny understood now, having been to Carew Castle, that its design came from Avalon.

Johnny's quick *crash course* (again, words from Avalon) on effective resistance to superior numbers had changed his perspective on warfare entirely. Pitched battles should be a thing of the past. Once he learned that Avalon had its fair share of warfare, he had listened intently to what the AZs had to teach him. He understood far more now how David had managed to take and hang onto his power in Britain—and why he was loath to cross the English Channel to risk it on the Continent. Even though the AZs had been angry with David for not allying with Flanders, they admitted that, in Avalon, no English king had ever achieved lasting success in Europe. It wasn't ambition these kings lacked. It was an issue of too few men and resources to wage war far from home.

Taking Male Castle would have been far more difficult if Robert d'Artois hadn't marched the bulk of his army away, under the false impression that all Flemish resistance had collapsed. Johnny supposed Artois hadn't necessarily been wrong at the time. All open resistance *had* collapsed. Over a month had passed since the fall of the Flemish army at Furnes, and King Philippe thought he had Flanders well in hand. Johnny, Zee, and Count Guy were his vassals, and that was all there was to it. He was holding the region with forty men in the castle and another two hundred quartered in the city. As long as he kept Philippa hostage, he didn't see a need for any further gar-risoning.

Jos had asked, with the lack of tact and an abundance of frankness they'd grown to expect from him, if one life was worth the loss of a country. He'd meant Philippa's life and Flanders respective-ly. Even if the AZs hadn't arrived, the peace couldn't have lasted for-ever. The answer to Jos's question always had to be *no, it isn't*. His grandfather had been quiescent since Philippa's abduction, but very soon King Philippe would learn of the renewal of the war—and then her life very well might be forfeit.

But that didn't mean they weren't going to try to save it, as best they could. The hope was to take Male with the helicopter and then beat the news of its loss to Paris.

By now, all the other men who'd come on the helicopter had dropped down a rope to the battlements below. Jos led half from the top of the keep, and Paul charged with the rest along the wall-walk above the barracks. Each man intended to work his way down to the bailey. Opening the gate and letting down the drawbridge was Zee's job. Johnny's destination was a spot along the southern wall-walk. All the guards who'd been posted along it were dead, thanks to Arne's accuracy with his weapon.

"Can't we just take these pigeons out from the air?" Arne was looking through his scope as they circled the castle. *Take out*, of course, was a euphemism for *kill*. Johnny still wasn't clear on when Avalonians thought it was appropriate to be blunt, and when it wasn't.

"The roost isn't on the top of the tower. It's along that balcony there, facing the bailey." Johnny drew Arne's attention to the place he meant. Until they had control of the castle, they weren't prepared to land in the interior. Even as Johnny had the thought, a crossbow bolt clanged against the bottom of the helicopter, fired from a bowman Arne hadn't yet eliminated.

"You're sure you can handle this?" Arne said after casually firing in the bowman's direction.

"If I can't do this, I don't deserve to call myself a knight." Maybe that was an exaggeration and a bit bravado to boot, but with the others murdering their way through the castle, Jos couldn't spare any of the Avalonian weapons, even if Johnny knew how to use one. Johnny also thought Jos didn't quite appreciate how important it was to stop these pigeons, not only to Johnny's family but to the AZs' mission. The less the French king knew about their doings before they arrived in Paris, the better.

Descending the rope still felt hair-raising. Johnny managed it without dying—or getting pierced by a crossbow bolt. Several of the French soldiers had set up in the second floor of the barracks, which was as good a place as any to mount their defense. They had to know the castle itself was lost, and they would be better off surrendering. Jos might be more bloodthirsty than any of them were comfortable with, but he had accepted Count Guy's, and thus his son Robert's, authority. It was Robert who was in charge here, leading the cavalry outside the walls. He was simply waiting for Zee to open the gate.

Johnny hit the stones of the wall-walk a bit harder than he intended, twisting his ankle slightly. The footing was also slippery from the recent rains, so he had to modify his loping run even further to account for it. When he reached the door into the nearest square guard tower, he found it unlocked. He went down the interior stairs with his sword out, glad he was circling to the right, which would force anyone coming up the stairs to fight more awkwardly. Again, no castellan ever expected his castle to be attacked from the air.

Unlike Castle Poeke, Johnny knew Male like the back of his hand. He couldn't count the number of times he'd played at sneaking about the castle, pretending he was an invader. Well, now he was one.

He came out into a corridor one floor down in time to see the head of a man poking out of the doorway of the dovecote to the left. Johnny ran forward, his heart in his throat, silence giving way to speed. The other man tried to slam the door in his face, but Johnny reached the threshold a heartbeat before the door sealed shut and got his boot between the door and the frame. Then, he put all his weight against the door and pushed it open.

The man fell back. He was of an age with Johnny's grandfather, which meant hitting the floor as he'd just done must have hurt. He had no weapon either, so merely held his hands before his face as he cowered next to a table on which sat two cages, one holding an anxious bird, fluttering and twittering.

"Where's the message!" Johnny shouted the words in French, his sword pointed at the man's throat.

"There!" the man pointed to the bird in the cage. "Over there!"

Johnny needed two hands to open the cage door, which meant he had to set his sword on the table. He kept it within easy reach in case the man decided to be heroic. Johnny himself was starting to breathe a little easier. It had been a close call, since the man had already put the note into the pigeon's carrier on its leg. Johnny fumbled a bit with the tiny piece of paper and then opened it to read, "Male lost; Guy." And then, on the back side, was a little drawing, done in ink, of the helicopter. Beside it was the word *Avalon*.

The drawing was a very good likeness. Johnny looked down at the man. "Who drew this?"

"I-I-I did. After—" He seemed to lose the ability to speak and simply gestured beyond the walls, where the sound of the helicopter was clearly audible, even through the stone walls of the castle.

"This is all you intended to say?"

The man frowned, not understanding the question at first. Johnny's French was perfect, so he knew it wasn't him.

He tried again. "You wrote the note, drew the picture, and then came here, is that right?"

"Yes."

Johnny would have allowed himself another breath if the man hadn't then added, "The sketch was my idea after I sent the first note."

Johnny's sword was in his hand again. "You sent what?"

Eyes as big as saucers, the man flapped a hand towards the table, indicating the second cage. Johnny's heart sank into his boots as he finally understood that it wasn't empty because the man hadn't had time to capture a second bird. The cage was empty because the second bird had already flown.

37

27 September 1297

Johnny

With a shout, the men who'd been waiting for the draw-bridge to drop surged across it and into the castle. Before they could set out across the center of the bailey too, those already within the castle guided them towards the sides, up onto the battlements, or into the great hall, all intended to keep them away from the Frenchmen still defending the barracks with their powerful crossbows.

Johnny's Uncle Robert dismounted within the shelter of the outer gatehouse next to a man Johnny almost thought he recognized. He refused to worry about it for now, accepting that many of these men should be known to him, but he wasn't very good with faces. Nor names. He did much better with numbers.

Leaving other men to take care of his horse, Robert made his way around the perimeter of the outer bailey to where Johnny was waiting with Jos in the tunnel within the inner gatehouse. Marie was the fifth among their number, having landed the helicopter in the inner bailey. While she remained partnered with Arne, Johnny had finally asked the right question and learned she and Jos were cousins. Although some of his grandfather's court had looked askance at her presence, she had been a part of the council every step of the way so far.

Robert halted in front of Johnny. "You are well?"

"We suffered no injury, if that's what you're asking," Johnny said. "I was not in time to stop a pigeon from being released."

Robert's chin hardened. "I feared I saw one fly away as the helicopter approached the battlement. Who sent it? The commander was killed moments later."

"The pigeon master. He sent the first as soon as the helicopter appeared. I was in time only to stop the second."

"They were smart." Robert gave a disgusted *tsk*. "Do not blame yourself. We were unlucky." Now he turned his attention to Jos. "Except for the pigeon, it went as you said it would. Well done."

While Robert might be in overall command, Jos's mind underpinned the entire mission. It had been his plan to kill the French soldiers within Bruges while they were in their barracks, and it was he who'd developed the strategy for taking the castle from the air. As far as Johnny could tell, ice instead of blood coursed through his veins.

"Thank you." Jos glanced at Marie once, received a nod, and then laid out what was happening now. "We guided your men away from the center of the bailey because French soldiers have barricaded themselves on the top floor of the barracks. Our only losses have come when someone comes within an angle they can hit with their crossbows. They appear to be fully supplied with bolts."

"How is it you haven't killed them with your guns?" Robert didn't even stumble over the new word. "I have seen the power of your weapons. We all have now. They can shoot right through wood."

"We are loath to waste bullets on men we cannot see," Jos said succinctly. "We may need them." He meant the bullets, not the men.

Johnny stepped into the conversation. "We commissioned several soldiers to break down the door that leads to their lair. Three of them were lost to bolts in the process. I would rather not lose any more men without a better surety of success."

"We have plenty of men," Robert said. "They know their duty. So far we have asked very little of them."

"We were hoping to come up with a new idea," Johnny said, "one that gets us what we want without simply throwing bodies at the problem."

"I suggested we could burn them out." Zee's eyes had momentarily widened at the extent of Robert's callousness. He worshiped him, as well he should. "But Johnny fears we might lose grandfather's castle in our attempt to gain it."

Robert put a hand on Zee's shoulder. "He's right. My apologies for appearing to care more for the castle than for our men. To take the castle, however, *is* why we are here."

"Whatever we decide, it needs to happen quickly. Already they tell me we might not reach Paris before that pigeon." Jos shook his head. "I had no idea they could fly so fast."

"King Philippe's broods are the best in the world—" Robert spoke at the same instant a bolt was loosed from the top window and hit a negligent soldier with such force it knocked him onto his back.

Robert started towards him, but Johnny grabbed his arm and pulled him back. "You can't help him. You'll only die too."

The bolt stuck straight up out of the man's chest as he lay on the stones of the bailey. He was gasping for air, but nobody dared leave his shelter to succor him.

"This is untenable." Robert finally understood the urgency.

"Speaking of untenable." Marie motioned with her head. "Look who's come to join the party."

It was the man who'd ridden into the castle beside Robert, now without his hat, revealing a face that could have been chiseled out of rock, with dark eyes and curly black hair cut close to his head. He was tall too, over six feet. He looked more noble than most noblemen of Johnny's acquaintance.

He also finally recognized him as the last Avalonian who'd flown in the helicopter. Though a spy for David and last seen at Carew Castle, he was, somehow, extraordinarily, *here*.

"Marie," Ari said. "Glad to see the helicopter remains in one piece."

"Just a few dents from crossbow bolts." Marie's tone was casual, but her look was intent. "Are you alone?"

"I am not."

"David?" Johnny's heart was in his throat again.

"Not this time." Ari's tone implied dismissal, as if whoever had accompanied him was unimportant. "I am here to offer my services. I can take out those men in the barracks for you. As you know, I have been trained as a sharp shooter. Arne is fine with his weapon, but he is only as accurate as he needs to be."

There was that phrase again, *take out*. And while Johnny hadn't ever before heard of a *sharp shooter*, somehow he knew what it meant.

"I admit, we have gone through more bullets than I would have hoped," Jos's voice was uninflected too, as if he wasn't speaking to a traitor, "but it would mean giving you a weapon."

"True, but you could keep your own gun trained on me while I did the work."

Robert made a chopping motion with one hand. "I see now we have not been properly introduced. You said you were from England. I took you at your word."

"His name is Ari," Johnny said, "and for our purposes, he is from England, sent by King David."

Ari bent his head to Robert. "A pleasure, my lord." Then he put out a hand to Jos, asking for his weapon. "Do you want my help or not?"

"We do," Robert said, answering for the AZs, all of whom looked a bit mutinous, "The sooner the better."

Ari had walked into their war with an enviable confidence. His manner implied he had been sure they wouldn't arrest or kill him. He offered them *his* help. And they were taking it. Although a traitor to the AZs, Ari was loyal to David. That was admirable, Johnny had to admit. He was not happy with being torn again about his duty and his choices. Before Ari's arrival, things had been a tiny bit simpler.

For now, Jos waved a hand for Paul to come forward from where he'd been waiting twenty paces away, out of earshot but not out of sight. Ari then went off with him and Marie, presumably to find an appropriate vantage point to *take out* the French soldiers on the upper floor of the barracks. At Robert's motion, Zee went with them too. Robert was of the generation of Johnny's father. He had been in many battles and led men for his entire adult life. He knew a volatile situation when he saw one.

Robert surveyed the bailey. "My father will be pleased at the work you've done today. You will be well-rewarded."

"We appreciate that," Jos said. "We also didn't do it for money. You know what we want."

Robert's jaw worked. "You must understand what I am trusting you with. I can put aside our sleight against King David for now. Once this castle is entirely ours again, I give you leave to fly to Paris."

Jos allowed himself what, in his case, passed for a smile. "That means you approve—"

Robert cut him off. "Your first job is to save my sister, if she can be saved. Only then is King Philippe's head yours for the taking."

38

Huw allowed Henri to take the lead as the three of them approached Robert, Johnny, and Jos, all of whom were still standing under the inner gatehouse, watching the bailey with grim expressions. It hadn't been Huw's first choice to have Ari make himself known, but they'd concluded it would be better to come forward openly than be caught like thieves in the night.

"About time you guys showed up!" A shout came from above them, Ari speaking in English. "Do me a favor and figure out a way to draw those guys in the barracks out, will you?"

Huw hugged the wall, craning his neck to see above him to wherever Ari was posted. "Are you kidding me?"

"What? Don't you trust me?" Ari's tone was all drawl. "I'll be quicker than him; I promise."

Then, before Huw could decide whether or not he did, in fact, trust Ari, Thomas set off across the bailey towards the dying man. In the heartbeat it took for the crossbowman to bring his weapon to bear, Ari fired a shot. And then a second. The bowman still managed to release the bolt from his crossbow but, at his death, it arched harmlessly through the air and fell onto the far side of the battlement. From where he stood, Huw couldn't see where it landed.

Robert took a half step forward, still not within line of sight of the barracks' windows, but closer so his voice would carry. "You saw what happened to your friend just now. If you surrender this instant, we will let you live. Continue to fight, and you will all die."

The Frenchmen inside didn't respond through a count of ten. Robert appeared happy to wait, since there was no immediate threat to any of them.

From above, Ari started counting backwards in French from ten: *Dix, neuf, huit, sept ...*"

"All right! All right!" One of the French soldiers had wrapped a piece of cloth around the end of a bolt and stuck it out the window. "How do we know you won't kill us anyway? You killed everyone else!" The Frenchman wanted to wrap himself in pride, but he also didn't want to die.

"They were in our way." Robert's tone was dry. "You have my word, as representative of my father, Count Guy of Flanders, that you will live if you surrender now."

This time the reply was immediate. "We are coming out. Don't shoot us!"

"You will not come to harm. Throw down your weapons and come out one by one. My men will escort you from the castle."

And so it was. It was another instructive lesson on the difference the Avalonian weapons could make to the outcome of any encounter. Huw was also beginning to understand more fully why Dafydd was so concerned about having these weapons available at all. They didn't just level the playing field, as Christopher might say; they *leveled* it.

At that point, Ari came down from his post on the battlement. He was followed by Marie, Paul, and John Secundus. The gun Ari had used was back in Paul's possession.

"So." Robert's hands were on his hips. "Who are you, really? And why have you come?"

Henri put a hand to his chest, introducing himself and Thomas. "We have most recently been attached to the London Temple."

"Templars!" Robert straightened. "We have no quarrel with your order."

"Such was not our concern," Henri said coolly. "We are interested, however, in what you do next, as the Templar Order does find itself having a keen interest in anything that involves the King of England and the King of France."

"Did David send you?" John Primus looked at Huw with a steady expression, admitting nothing.

"Of course he sent us. Christopher sends his greetings, by the way." Huw paused at the suddenly delicate moment. Other than the fact that Marie was not currently sitting in the pilot's seat, there was nothing to stop the AZs from heading to Paris right now. He could see in Robert's face that he was deliberating whether to consider Huw an enemy combatant too, an approach Huw himself had been striving to avoid. "I am here as a representative of the throne of England, as ambassador to the Court of Flanders."

An ambassador was a formal position. For a foreign leader to imprison an ambassador was a grave offense.

Robert shifted in his stance. He knew it too. "Why have you come?"

"To speak of the helicopter." Huw saw no reason to beat around the bush.

"It is ours." Jos sneered. "Possession is nine-tenths of the law."

Robert put out a hand to him, telling him to subside, which he did, if reluctantly. "But not all of it. Let Ambassador Huw speak."

"We aren't here to argue semantics. We are here because David couldn't come himself." For once, given the company he was keeping, Huw said David's name the English way.

"He is offering his support?" There might even have been a hopeful tone in Robert's voice.

Huw tipped his head. "Let's just say he is not refusing it. More than anything, he is trying to avoid more war."

"War has come." Jos couldn't bear to remain silent. "He can't avoid it. We will not be subsumed into France just because David is afraid to act. *We* have acted."

Robert turned on him more fully this time, and such was his authority—and his glare—that he didn't have to say anything to make Jos take a step back. Jos even managed an apology, his eyes on his feet: "Pardon, my lord. I spoke out of turn."

Robert returned to Huw. "So he is still not throwing in with us?"

"Not yet." Huw was careful to qualify what was really a hard *no*. "But he is not on King Philippe's side either. Quite the opposite. He is sympathetic to your cause. More than sympathetic, in fact."

For a moment, John Secundus's face held incredulity. "He is? He was careful not to imply that to us when we were in Carew."

"And is he still? Even after what we've done?" John Primus had maybe done a great deal of growing up in the last five days. "Why would he be?"

"Because he is also the son of the King of Wales," Huw said simply. "Most don't remember anymore that King Edward of England did his utmost to conquer Wales and make it part of England. David has not forgotten. Nor has Llywelyn, his father. They know what it means to fight for years against an enemy with superior wealth and numbers. When one is in that position, one must do what one can with the tools one has been given."

"That's why we went to him in the first place!" John Secundus said eagerly. "He—"

"Zee." Robert spoke quietly, but with authority. "You too, Johnny. Let him talk."

Huw was pleased to learn the two Johns had better nicknames than John Primus and John Secundus, with all respect to Bronwen. "David does want his helicopter back. I won't pretend otherwise. For now, he is willing to loan it to you, provided you include us—" he gestured to Henri, Thomas, and Ari, "—in your subsequent endeavors."

The hope in Zee's face was almost painful. He was ready to agree immediately. It did indicate also that he hadn't entirely transferred his allegiance to the AZs.

Jos, who had been listening along with everyone else, didn't say anything this time. Nor did the others, except for Marie, who leaned in to whisper in Jos's ear, words nobody else could hear. Robert's lips were pursed, and if Huw was reading his expression correctly, he still hadn't understood the full scope of the problem as Huw (and Dafydd) saw it.

Johnny, on the other hand, was looking at Huw through narrowed eyes. "That's it? He forgives our actions provided he can say we just *borrowed* his helicopter instead of *stole* it."

"He can choose to be hostile if you would prefer."

"No, no." Robert made a motion with one hand, telling Johnny to take a step back.

Henri did the same for Huw, which was probably just as well, since Huw had entirely run out of patience. Johnny *had* stolen the helicopter, and now they were quibbling about being forgiven?

"For now," Henri said, "provided the vehicle is not used against him or any of his people, and nobody is under the illusion that he is backing your endeavors here, then *yes*, David will forgive your actions. As Huw said, we don't want a war with Flanders. That's the last thing we want. But we are going with them to Paris."

That was finally enough to get Jos to lean forward, in this case to speak to Robert rather than Huw or Henri. "You promised me Philippe's head."

He could hardly have spoken in a fashion more likely to raise Robert's hackles. Not only was his tone demanding, but he hadn't included the obligatory *my lord*. Having spent so many years in King Dafydd's court, Huw knew the extent to which Avalonians found it difficult to accord any member of the nobility the basic amount of respect that was customary. It was obvious also that Jos had no idea what was wrong with what he'd just said.

Or, at least, he didn't realize it until Robert slowly turned his head one more time to look at him.

Seeing Robert's expression, Marie tugged on Jos's arm, accompanied by a bit more whispering, and finally managed to get him to ease away, leaving only her and Paul representing the AZs. To Robert, she said, "My apologies, my lord."

Robert turned back to Henri without acknowledging she'd spoken. "Why do you want to go to Paris?"

Henri kept things simple. "The helicopter is ours. Now that we have found it, we are loath to let it out of our sight. In addition, between you and me, we feel the need to be a moderating influence on its use." Diplomat that he was, he paused now for effect. "Perhaps we can be of service also in the rescue of your sister."

Robert's mouth worked. "We have been made aware of King David's own imprisonment and subsequent escape from Philippe's palace."

"And all that followed afterwards," Zee put in.

"The court of Flanders has no desire to antagonize the King of England," Robert continued. "We had no foreknowledge of my nephews' acquisition of the helicopter. Once we had it, however, we saw the sense in using it."

"Not that you could have stopped us." This was said in an undertone by Paul, in English, who was standing to Huw's right, implying it was for Huw's ears, not Robert's.

Even if he overheard, or understood the English, Robert ignored him. "We have been concerned about King David's reaction. That he has chosen not to war with us, is, quite frankly, surprising." He paused. "Someday, I would very much like to meet him. In the interim, I must warn you: while we appreciate the *loan* of this vehicle of the air, while we have it, we will determine how and when we use it. We will not tolerate any interference. You may go with my nephew and these men to Paris. But the helicopter is ours until we are finished with it."

"Understood." Huw answered this time, dipping his head to Robert before looking towards Marie, whom he'd concluded might actually be the leader of the AZs. "How long before we go?"

"The moment it's light enough to see," Marie said. "We have the fuel to make it that far."

Huw looked at Robert. "That will give us time to arrange for the return of our horses to the man from whom we borrowed them. With your permission, my lord, I would also ask to send a message to the captain of our ship to tell him we are leaving Bruges by a different method."

Robert made a sound along the lines of *huh*. "You Avalonians are a strange breed."

Huw wanted to laugh. Should he take Robert's misunderstanding of his origins as an insult or a compliment? Really, the man had spoken the plain truth. Avalonians *were* a strange breed.

And, somehow, almost while he wasn't looking, Huw had become one of them.

39

28 September 1297

Johnny

"Are you sure we shouldn't just kill them?" *Zee's words came low in Johnny's ear.* "There are easier ways to subdue the guards."

Spare me the casual bloodthirstiness of a thirteen-year-old squire. Johnny hadn't actually said those words to Zee out loud, just nodded his head. "I'm sure there are. But best not to harm any of David's men if we can help it. We don't want a war with England!"

"You can't really think King David will forgive us for stealing his air vehicle, do you? Not to mention his prisoners! They abducted him, after all. He must want to see them punished. Instead, we are freeing them."

And giving them free rein. Though that hadn't been what Johnny had been thinking at the time. In truth, he had hoped to mitigate the damage he was doing. He saw now how foolish that had been.

Rat-tat! Rat-tat!

Johnny woke with a start, certain he was awake because Arne was shooting again. That would have been especially disconcerting because they were flying many hundreds of feet in the air above the fields of France. But it had only been his dream skipping around from that initial morning when they'd freed the AZs to the taking of Male Castle.

There were nine of them in the helicopter: the four AZs, Johnny, Ari, Huw, Thomas, and Henri. Zee had been left behind this time, much to his dismay but at Robert's insistence. At the moment, Johnny was sitting shoulder to shoulder with Huw, who turned his head to meet his gaze.

Huw's look could have been full of disdain, but instead he showed concern. "Are you all right? You look like you've seen a ghost."

"Maybe I have," Johnny said before he could stop himself, understanding now why he had been dreaming of that first day. In his sleep, he was unable to hide from the truth of his betrayal. He *had* sullied his honor. Everyone knew it. King Philippe had convinced the Pope to canonize his grandfather, but Johnny's father had been a real saint, as judged by his behavior, the perfect knight. Johnny's betrayal of David's trust in him would ensure that no such accolades would ever be accorded Johnny himself.

Johnny could live with that. He had made the choices he had because there had seemed no other option at the time, and he would probably make those same decisions again, were he put in the same position. In many ways, it was far worse that David *had* forgiven him.

Johnny didn't deserve forgiveness, since in order to be absolved of a sin, one had to actually regret doing it.

Things hadn't improved since then, either.

Despite the agreement with Robert, once they were airborne, Jos and Arne had pointed their weapons at Huw, Ari, Henri, and Thomas while Paul stripped them of their weapons and bound their hands behind their backs. The *seatbelts* were acting as restraints, since none of David's men could reach the releases. Johnny had been forced to look on, aghast. He'd had no way to stop what was happening; he'd also understood the wisdom of saying nothing.

Huw didn't ask what ghost Johnny had seen. Somehow, it felt like he knew. Huw's history was no less righteous than many others of King David's retainers. His family had rescued David when he'd been a prince of Wales. His loyalty was unquestioning and unquestionable. It was no surprise it was he whom David had trusted to come to Flanders to find them.

Instead of chastising Johnny with the differences between them, he motioned with his head towards the window.

Johnny sucked in a breath to see a genuine army below them. "How many must there be—"

"I think we are looking at the forces of Artois." Huw was entirely matter-of-fact about what might enrage his king, given that Normandy was part of the CSB.

Ari, meanwhile, shook out his legs, which were the only part of him he could really move. "Jos wants King Philippe's head, Huw. Are you really going to just let him take it?"

Johnny glanced towards Jos, who was sitting in the co-pilot's seat and shouldn't be able to hear anything happening in the passenger area. The other mercenaries were seated in nearby chairs, each busy with some aspect of being an Avalonian. Much of this had to do with readying weapons. They were all wearing headsets and the conversation among them had been fairly nonstop since they'd taken off in the gray light of dawn.

"Are you?" Huw said right back to him.

The two men couldn't look at each other, given their restraints, but there were undertones here that Johnny didn't understand. It was as if, all of a sudden, they were no longer friends.

"You do understand why I'm torn?"

"I do."

It was as if they were speaking in a code to which Johnny wasn't party.

Now, Ari nodded. "We serve the same king."

"I'm glad to hear it."

With Huw's reply, both of them seemed to suddenly relax against the back of their seats in a way that implied they hadn't been nearly as content up until then.

Johnny, however, was more confused than ever. Had Huw been worried Ari wasn't loyal? *Were* they going to stop Jos from killing Philippe? Or not?

Even more, their conversation brought into sharp relief Johnny's role in the coming events. Was *he* going to let Jos murder the King of France? And was Ari and Huw's conversation actually directed at *him*?

It felt like Marie was flying them into a maelstrom. Nobody could predict how things were going to turn out.

Even, or maybe especially, Johnny himself.

40

28 September 1297

Thomas

Jos hadn't given Johnny a headset any more than he'd given one to Thomas or his friends. Thomas knew for a fact there were five, since the fifth was hanging from a hook above Arne's head. From what Thomas had sensed over the last hour, the four AZs had been having a fairly intense discussion, which was why they hadn't noticed or responded to the earlier conversation between Huw, Ari, and Johnny. Unfortunately, they'd been speaking Zeeland-ic, so even if Thomas could read lips, he wouldn't have known what they were talking about. He had a feeling he was going to regret not knowing.

Johnny, meanwhile, appeared to be in the midst of some kind of internal conflict. As far as Thomas was concerned, it was about time. If the AZs ever thought about anyone other than themselves, they would have noticed by now.

Ari met Thomas's gaze for a heartbeat, just a bit of confirmation between the two of them. He had probably seen what was happening with Johnny too. Thomas himself had always struggled to hide what he was thinking. Like everyone else, he'd had concerns about Ari's loyalties. By this point, even if they didn't agree on every particular, Ari believed in the mission as much as he did.

"What if Philippa isn't being held at the palace?" Ari said, projecting his voice so everyone in the passenger area could hear him. "What if King Philippe has taken himself off to the Louvre or any one of a number of fortresses he owns? You need intelligence to make a plan like this work."

Arne and Paul were the two AZs sitting in the back with them, guns at the ready. They either were outright ignoring him, or were so preoccupied with the conversation going on in their headsets they weren't listening.

"That's what I told them before we started flying," Johnny said, in what could have been an aside, but was also loud enough for everyone to hear. "You telling them the same thing isn't going to help. They appear to hate you."

"I'm a traitor in their eyes. Doesn't mean I'm not right."

There was definitely a special animosity the AZs appeared to reserve just for Ari. Paul had tied Ari's hands at the wrists far more tightly than Thomas's own. From the looks, the rope was biting so fiercely it might be breaking Ari's skin. Really, he and his friends had achieved far more than he had thought possible when they'd set out from Carew. They'd found the helicopter! And talked their way onto it. Such as it was. Thomas supposed they shouldn't have expected the AZs to take them to Paris willingly.

Since the AZs had bound them, Thomas had been entertaining himself by imagining various untimely ends for them. Whatever sympathy he might have felt for their cause was long gone. While, like Ari, they were stranded in a strange land, and must have families back in Avalon, they gave no sign they were in any way conflicted. Overall, they were as cold and unfeeling as any soldiers Thomas had ever met. Maybe they really were so focused on murder they couldn't think about anything else.

Thomas's own bonds were uncomfortable, but he had been uncomfortable before. Even so, Johnny looked more uncomfortable still, and he wasn't tied. Maybe Johnny himself wasn't entirely sure what side he was on anymore.

Ari was still trying to get a response from one of the AZs. Now, he motioned with his chin towards Arne. "How *do* you intend to kill the King of France, exactly?"

Arne had always been the most intense of the bunch, which had become only more true as the condition of his leg improved. He'd been badly injured a week ago, and now he was nearly back to full health. "The same as we've been doing."

For a heartbeat, a look of triumph flashed across Ari's face. "So your plan is to fly over the palace and take it like you took Male?"

"Something like that."

If Ari was looking for specifics, Arne wasn't forthcoming, and anyway became distracted again by the conversation going on in his headset. All of a sudden, Jos and Marie appeared to be shouting at each other.

Henri took the opportunity to speak to Ari. "Didn't you hear what Johnny said? Why are you engaging him?"

"I don't want to die because of their lack of a plan."

"Would you prefer to be killed for getting in their way?" Huw said through gritted teeth.

"They won't kill you." Johnny appeared entirely sure on this point. "They can't."

"You think they respect your uncle that much?" Ari said.

"They care about the future. An alliance with King David is necessary for our future. They know that."

"But do they?" Thomas meant to speak whimsically to himself, but he caught Johnny's ear anyway.

"They know I would tell my grandfather the truth about what they did, and then he would take action against them. He wanted Male back, it's true, but like King David, he is ambivalent about participating in the murder of another ruler. That is why he sent none of his own men but me. As I am a duke in my own right, I can make my own choices."

"Then what's to stop them from killing you?" Ari was nothing if not blunt.

"My family *is* Zeeland's future. Only we have any chance to withstand France. They want King Philippe very badly, but they are smart enough to know it will do them no good if they kill me in the process of killing him. Our people won't follow them. Without my family, they are just four more mercenaries. I am the leash between my grandfather and these hounds, as well as being here for Philippa, of course."

Thomas put forth another thought that might have been better spoken softly. "You want them to fail too, don't you?"

This time, Johnny made no immediate reply, instead gazing straight ahead without even a twitch in anyone else's direction.

Hardly three breaths later, the helicopter sank below the clouds in a sudden move that might have jerked Thomas out of his seat if he hadn't been belted in so tightly. Marie had been navigating by dipping in and out of the cloud cover every twenty miles or so to make sure they were still heading in the general direction of Paris.

As soon as the helicopter steadied, Arne rose from his seat. He stretched elaborately, took a look around the compartment, and then descended like a falcon diving for its prey on Thomas, ramming his fist into Thomas's stomach with a blow that nearly split him in two.

Johnny pushed upwards in alarm. "Stop that! What are you doing?"

Arne turned on him. "What we should have done from the start. It seems to me you didn't stop that pigeon from flying from Male on purpose. Shall I hit him again or are you going to tell me about the trap you've set for us?"

"There's no trap." Ari bravely drew Arne's attention. "Why else would I have questioned your plan?"

Arne got right in his face. "You lie every time you open your mouth. We can't trust anything you say."

"Then use your head and really listen," Ari said reasonably. "Check it out. We all think you'd be better off setting down outside the city and doing some reconnaissance first."

"Send Johnny as a scout," Henri said, even as he shot a worried glance in Thomas's direction. "Or me. Or any of us. None of us are a friend to the King of France. You know that."

Thomas's sole focus was on continuing to breathe, rather than convincing Arne of anything. Maybe that was why he was the first to notice that they were low enough to the ground to be skimming above the treetops.

"Like you'd come back." Arne accompanied his comment with a sneer. "And even if you did, we still couldn't trust anything you said." Then he slid open the helicopter door and with a few thrusts of his foot, kicked out their weapons that had been stacked in a pile.

A moment later, they slowed even further and then stopped, hovering ten feet above the ground. As Marie maintained that position, Jos climbed out of the co-pilot's seat to join Paul and Arne.

With their weapons pointed definitively at Thomas and his companions, Arne next unbuckled their harnesses and pulled them to their feet, albeit without untying their hands. "Out! Now!"

Johnny's eyes were wide. "What are you doing? We need them. We promised my uncle."

"Be grateful we're leaving them alive." Jos made a motion with his gun in Johnny's direction. "You too, while we're at it."

If Thomas had been well and his hands had been free, he might have at least considered fighting back. As it was, he decided to be grateful. This was a gift to them—and likely a mistake on the AZs part. Ever since Henri had declared they must travel with the AZs to Paris, Thomas had been plagued by a vision of Arne tossing their bodies out of the helicopter mid-flight.

They were saved from that, at the very least.

With no help for it, each in turn jumped out the doorway of the hovering helicopter. Since their hands remained bound, it was impossible to catch themselves. Nonetheless, Thomas managed to land on both feet, before falling sideways on the grassy field. Hitting the ground hurt, and he felt like it was all he could do to keep breathing, but they were still alive. God was good.

Then Arne slid the door closed, and the helicopter flew away.

41

28 September 1297

Sam

Having changed horses at every Templar waystation they'd come to since Rouen, Sam and her friends had managed to sleep in the early hours of the morning at the Templar commandery at Soisy, twenty miles outside of Paris. Their determination to finally reach the city had been such that they'd pushed on at first light. The day had dawned clear, which had lifted Sam's spirits. While they'd sailed through a storm, they hadn't had to ride in the rain. They appeared also to have left any pursuit behind.

They'd ridden maybe five miles, with at least fifteen more to go. Because they were still lacking a great earthquake, per Sam's musings, the distance hadn't been shortened just by wishing it. Sam was saddle sore and hoped she wouldn't have to ride anywhere again for at least a few days. Or maybe ever again. She had grown up with horses, as she'd explained to the others, but if she managed to ride once a month since then, she was doing well. She certainly hadn't been expecting to ride hell-for-leather the seventy miles from Rouen to Paris.

"Do you hear that!" Christopher swung around in the saddle, his face tipped towards the sky. "It's here! It's actually here!"

Sam's drowsiness dissipated instantly at the sound of the helicopter. She twisted too, and then the helicopter roared directly overhead, coming from the north and flying low. It scared not only their horses but every creature within hearing distance.

"It's barely fifty feet above the ground!" Robbie pointed upwards, even as a sword, then a knife, and then another sword fell from the sky.

Sam kicked her horse's flanks. "Let's go!" racing to where the first sword had hit the ground. She reined in and dismounted in order to collect it. She then went to the knife, like she was following a trail of breadcrumbs leading to the helicopter.

Robbie was beside her by the time she reached the third item. "It hasn't gone far. I can still hear it."

A moment later, through the trees ahead, she caught a flash of sunlight reflecting off metal.

Robbie took the lead now, urging his horse through a little creek that ran beside the road. There, they found two more knives, and then another sword. Trees lined the bank, which provided enough cover for now, since there were still two fields between the road and the helicopter.

Robbie peered ahead as the helicopter remained hovering in the air, ten feet above the ground.

By then, Christopher and Isabelle had caught up too. Christopher put the binoculars to his eyes, but Sam didn't need them to see the bodies falling from the open door.

"One, two, three, four … five!" Christopher counted them out, at which point Sam and Robbie broke from the trees, hearts pounding in fear at what had happened to their friends.

The helicopter, for its part, was already rising, back on a trajectory towards the City of Paris.

42

28 September 1297

Robbie

"I hate to say it, but so far we're zero for two," Sam said.

"Not at all." Robbie eyed her to hear yet another baseball reference. "We found the helicopter. We've almost made it to Paris. That sounds like two for two to me."

"We aren't in Paris yet, and we lost the helicopter again. Really, from a certain point of view, we're right back where we started. Somehow, nearly six days and four hundred miles later, we've come full circle. The eight of us are back together again."

"Nine," Robbie said. "We've got Johnny now. See, things *have* changed."

Sam's ready laugh was one of the many things he liked about her.

"If you want a happy ending, you might have to continue the story a little longer," Christopher said from behind them. "That's what my mom says."

"Exactly," To Robbie's mind, if things had to go wrong, they couldn't have gone wrong in a better direction. "Our story isn't over yet."

They had only four horses and nine people, so they'd swapped around riders. Ari and Johnny had chosen to walk, as had Robbie and Sam, who had settled into an easy stride beside him. Henri was on Robbie's horse, since he'd twisted his ankle when he'd been shoved out of the helicopter. Huw was a bit bruised from the awkward fall, but only Thomas, on Sam's horse, was in serious pain. Christopher had Isabelle riding pillion behind him.

They were walking their horses down a small road that Isabelle remembered. It would allow them to skirt the main gate into the city in order to come directly at the north entrance of the Paris Temple. To get there, they had to leave the main road from Rouen, which maybe was just as well for maintaining their anonymity. With nine of them, they were definitely more noticeable than when they had been only four.

The route took them close to a village before dropping them straight south to the Templar gate. There, even without Isabelle, they would always be welcomed without question. They had come maybe another mile since they'd rescued Huw and the others, during which time each half of their company had related what had happened to them since they'd last been together in Portsmouth. Huw's group had clearly had a more eventful time than Robbie's, whose experience had been eventful enough!

Then the helicopter appeared in the sky some distance ahead of them. "Get off the road!" Robbie said. "We don't want them to see us."

They were close to a farmer's house, beside which a great tree with widespread branches grew. They hurried towards it. The farmer's wife came out to look at them, her face screwed up unwelcomingly. Robbie had to admit they were a bedraggled bunch, but all the men were armed as they should be again, and the women's dresses, though worse for wear, were still of a fine material.

"My lords, my ladies." Recognizing she had no choice but to be respectful, the woman ducked her head in an attempt at a curtsey. "How may we help you?"

"We just want to stand under your tree a moment." Robbie spoke for all of them.

"And we'd like water for the horses." Christopher reached up to help Isabelle down.

"Of course, my lord—" Then she too craned her neck at the sound of the helicopter getting closer. It was flying higher than it had been when it had passed over them earlier. Then it was gone, beyond the next rise, without giving any indication those inside had seen them.

"That wasn't time to kill the King of France, that's for certain," Christopher said, in English so only their group could understand.

"Are you sure? If that's true, why is it coming back so soon?" Johnny blinked like he'd just woken from a dream. Up until now, through the relating of their various adventures, he had remained almost entirely silent. It was as if he couldn't believe how, after everything they'd been through, the AZs had abandoned him.

Robbie hadn't rubbed Johnny's nose in his mistakes. He had been betrayed now too, just like the rest of them. All that mattered was getting that helicopter back, preferably before the AZs used it to murder the King of France. After hearing of the way the AZs had captured not one but two castles in Flanders, Robbie felt the urgency of their mission flaming in his gut more than ever. Although Christopher's parents were already in the city, they couldn't know what the nine of them knew. They weren't pilots either, nor even soldiers.

"Maybe they decided you and Ari were right," Isabelle said.

"I'm guessing cooler heads have finally prevailed." Ari too had been mostly silent since they'd found him. But while Johnny appeared chastened, Ari's time in Flanders seemed to have increased his confidence, though not in a way that meant he had become more overbearing. Quite the opposite. He was settled in his worth now and didn't feel the need to prove anything to anyone. "I'm guessing they did a brief reconnaissance and thought better of their lack of a plan. Maybe they are out of fuel too. They'll put down some place they deem safe, refuel, and wait until an opportune time to attack. It will be dusk at the earliest."

Robbie nodded. "That means they've given us a reprieve. We need to make the most of it."

"They just gave everyone in the palace warning they were coming," Sam said. "I don't see the sense in that."

"They think it doesn't matter," Ari said to her. "They know a pigeon was sent after Male. Philippe already knew they were coming."

"And they think they are invincible." Thomas hadn't dismounted, which Robbie could understand. Arne's blow must have come like a hammer, and Thomas couldn't disguise the pain he was feeling. That said, he hadn't complained once, like the Templar he was.

"Aren't they?" Johnny said. "They have those weapons—"

"A gun takes a soldier only so far," Ari said. "You're right that it's a massive advantage. You've seen it. The machine gun, in particular, has a rate of fire that's impossible to counter. But if we'd provided Huw with a bow of his own, he could have taken out those men in the barracks at Male as easily, and more quietly, than I did."

Robbie nodded in agreement. "He might have won the archery contest at Carew if it hadn't been superseded by the arrival of the helicopter."

"I definitely could have won." Huw had no trouble with confidence either, also well-earned.

Ari waggled his head. "At the same time, taking those two castles expended many bullets. By my accounting, they've depleted their ammunition considerably. It isn't unlimited, and they are not omnipotent."

"They were confident enough about their chances that they didn't kill us," Henri said. "They let us go. Albeit fifteen miles from Paris, but they let us go."

"They do not believe we can stop them," Ari said.

"They can believe what they like," Robbie said. "It won't change the outcome."

"This is all my fault," Johnny said. "They wouldn't be here at all if not for me. I deserve whatever punishment King David chooses to mete out, even my very life. I'm here now for my aunt. At least let me save her first."

Isabelle put out a hand to Johnny. "Who are we talking about? Is this Philippa?"

Johnny nodded. "King Philippe is keeping her prisoner in one of the towers."

"We know about it," Isabelle said. "Christopher's parents told David about her situation right before we left Carew."

"I can't believe we get to save a princess in a tower." Christopher grinned.

Johnny responded with a frown. "She's not a princess. She's—"

Isabelle cut him off with a motion of her hand. "Don't mind him. He is referring to a story—it's called a *fairy tale* in Avalon—about a girl named Rapunzel."

Johnny was still confused. "Her name is Philippa."

"Yes," Sam said gently. "We do understand that. We'll add freeing her to the list of miracles we intend to perform today."

43

28 September 1297
Christopher

Christopher picked up his mother in a bear hug.

"You made it!" she said.

Isabelle, meanwhile, was engulfed in her father's arms. She hadn't seen Matthew since she'd left Paris with Christopher. Distance and duty being what they were—not to mention politics—Matthew hadn't been able to travel to England for her wedding to Christopher, although of course he had approved of it. Every mile closer to Paris had made Isabelle only that more anxious to see him.

Christopher released his mom, looking around and frowning. "Where's Dad? They said at the commandery he would be here too."

"He is with the king. Didn't they explain what happened?" At the shaken heads all around, Elisa made a face, "You have timed your arrival to coincide with some drama here."

That was for certain. When the nine of them had arrived at the Paris Temple, they'd been told they'd find his parents and Matthew at the palace. In truth, with not much more information to go on, they'd been worried about being admitted.

But once Henri and Thomas had returned to Templar gear, and the rest had spruced themselves up the best they could, they had marched down here like they knew what they were doing. Isabelle was a known quantity anyway, as was Christopher, through his parents. If someone at the palace guard questioned them, the rest could be passed off as retainers and not introduced.

As it was, the guard actually looked relieved to have more soldiers in the palace to help fend off the helicopter.

Elisa related in succinct terms (and ones that had to be leaving out a lot) what the last week had been like for them. And why, to Christopher's point, his father was currently splitting his time between talking to David on the radio and dancing attendance on the king.

"It sounds like you guys came up with a good plan," Christopher said as he walked with his mother into the recesses of the palace. "Next, David is going to make Dad a general."

"Your dad's been in Earth Two a while and, like David, knows a lot of history. He's also seen a lot of movies."

"What are you going to tell the king about us, and why we're here?" Johnny said from behind them. "Me, in particular."

"As little as possible," Elisa said. "Especially in regards to you! Everyone has more important things to think about right now anyway than you young people."

"That's because the helicopter flew over already, right?" Isabelle was walking just ahead of them with her father. "Did the messenger pigeon from Male ever get here?"

"It did," Elisa said. "We still weren't prepared. Up until the actual arrival of the helicopter, most still didn't want to believe it was really a threat, especially those of Philippe's advisers who have a vested interest in him *not* listening to David."

"Like Flote." Isabelle knew him from when she herself had been all but a captive in the palace.

"He's in prison in the Louvre right now, for beating up your father." At Christopher's open-mouthed protest, Elisa put a hand on his arm. "It's being handled. He'll be fine."

"Does he need a doctor?" Christopher said. "A real one?" David had sent eight people out from Carew, each with a range of skills, but none of them was a medic. An oversight.

"He's okay for now." His mother gave Christopher a rueful look. There was obviously more to the story than she wanted to say in front of everyone. "They have been taking us *way* more seriously in the last few hours."

Elisa led them to a large room on the second floor with windows overlooking the inner courtyard of the palace. The main gate was to their right, and they were facing the glorious windows of Sainte-Chapelle. With another wave, she got members of the palace staff moving towards bringing a meal for everyone. They'd eaten at the commandery, but that didn't mean they couldn't eat again.

"What exactly happened here when the helicopter flew overhead?" Henri asked. Both he and Thomas had insisted on coming to the palace with them, even wounded as they were. At Sam's instruction, Henri now sat with one foot up on a chair, and Thomas settled on another chair beside him.

"I heard it, but I didn't get outside quickly enough to see it for myself." Elisa made a motion with her head. "Or rather, Ted prevented me from going outside to see it. Stage one of our plan was to deny them any targets. The whole castle has been buttoned down ever since we heard about the taking of Poeke."

"Another pigeon." Johnny gave a disgusted shake of his head. "We've been behind from the start."

"Our problem has not been a lack of warning." Christopher's mom could have looked grim, but she instead just seemed more determined. "We know they're coming. We probably even know when. We know they want to murder King Philippe. The question has always been what we can do to stop them, both from murdering the king and taking the castle."

"What have you done so far?" Ari said.

"For starters, nobody is allowed on the battlements or the roof without additional cover. We've built barricades in the corridors behind which to fight and to slow them down. We have stockpiled weapons, mostly crossbows. Many of the servants and other residents have either fled the palace or are planning to shelter in the basement of Sainte-Chapelle, once the helicopter returns, that is."

"Why hasn't the king evacuated everyone? That would be the best way to ensure his safety and that of his people," Ari said.

"He refuses to flee. He thinks to do so would make him look weak. He sees this as a defining moment of his kingship."

Ari grimaced. "I suppose he isn't wrong."

"Our job, then, is to save him," Elisa continued, "and, in the interim, to prevent him from doing anything truly stupid. Try, anyway."

"Try not. Do. Or do not. There is no try," Christopher intoned.

"Sure." His mother wrinkled her nose at him. "Let me know when Yoda shows up with his lightsaber. Meanwhile, it's up to us humans to do whatever we can."

44

28 September 1297

Sam

Sam's heart was in her throat. *Again.* When had it not been since she'd come to Earth Two? She had never been to war, so she didn't want to minimize anyone else's suffering, but she felt a certain degree of PTSD every time the roar of the helicopter sounded overhead.

And here it was again, bringing her out of a deep sleep she hadn't meant to enter. At some point in the late afternoon, she had lain down on a couch-like bench her grandmother might have called a *settee*. It had the most comfortable cushions of any chair she'd sat in since she arrived. The instant she'd gone horizontal, she hadn't wanted to get up. Nobody had ever talked about *time travel lag*. Even though Seattle was technically eight time zones earlier than Wales (and nine from France), they had arrived at the same time of day in Wales as they'd left in the Pacific Northwest. She supposed the sleight of hand that warped space to keep the time zones the same was a small matter compared to actually bringing them to an alternate universe.

Elisa had told her to go ahead with sleeping, that they would take turns keeping watch, so Sam had let herself close her eyes. Now, she pushed upright, blinking away whatever horrible dream she'd been having that thankfully was already fading. Everyone else was on their feet, staring up at the ceiling, as if they could somehow track the helicopter through it.

Sam peered through the closed curtains. The only light outside came from a few torches around Sainte-Chapelle. The battlement was completely dark. Maybe too dark, like they'd made the palace a black hole in the middle of the otherwise brightly lit city, and thus impossible to miss.

Then Elisa bustled in, waving her hands. "Get away from the windows. When they find nobody on the top of the wall, they could start shooting at shadows in frustration."

As if brought about by her very words, the *rat-tat* of an automatic weapon sounded like it was right outside their room. Sam leapt for the door.

Elisa, meanwhile, picked up a satchel from a chair and swung it over her shoulder. Then she motioned to Isabelle, Huw, and Johnny. "Come on. If we're going to pull off another heist, now's the time."

"Heist?" Sam looked from one to the other, her mouth slightly open, but they were already headed away, down the corridor. She turned to Robbie, unable to picture Elisa stealing anything from the palace. "What is she talking about? Where are they going?"

"To get Philippa. We made a plan while you were sleeping. Since the king has retired to Sainte-Chapelle to pray for God's deliverance, and most of the court have gone with him, we're getting Philippa out of the palace now, when nobody is looking."

Sam really had missed a lot, though she felt a lot better too. And, to be fair, Sainte-Chapelle, with its bunker-like ground floor, wasn't a terrible place for noncombatants to wait out the attack. The Louvre would undoubtedly have been better, but not if the king refused to go.

Christopher added to Robbie's explanation, "Rescuing Philippa was one of my mom and dad's top priorities even before we came. They've even wondered if Philippe put Dad in the room next to hers so he could."

"If that was the case, why make her a hostage at all?" Sam said.

"For the same reason Philippe is staying in the palace," Robbie said. "Because he thinks he's supposed to."

"Didn't someone say she dies here in Avalon's history?"

"Avalon didn't have David," Christopher said. "My dad thinks this is not the same King Philippe as ruled there, even if it doesn't always look like it. And our family is known for escaping this palace."

"Yeah, with King Philippe's help—" Sam stopped. "Oh. That's what you think he's done again? He wants her free, but can't free her himself without looking weak? He's counting on us to help him save face … again?" When Christopher nodded, Sam shook herself, trying to wake up more fully. "If they're doing that, what are we doing? Other than staying alive, hopefully."

"You're our pilot, so you need to stick with Christopher and me," Robbie said. "We are charged with taking the helicopter if it can be taken. Ari, Thomas, and Henri are going to help defend the palace."

"And provide a steadying influence on the king's defenders," Henri said.

Ari scoffed. "You should know we've agreed to do this, so you can do that. We're the public face, the distraction, if you will." He gestured towards the two Templars, still in their full regalia. "When you have men who look like them in your party, you are less likely to notice who isn't there."

Thus, within a minute, Sam found herself between Robbie and Christopher, hustling back through the palace towards the king's garden, which took up the northwest end of the Île de la Cité. Ultimately, they wound up behind an anonymous hedge on the north side. Although it was pitch black in the shadows, where they were, the garden's central plaza was brightly lit by a wide circle of lanterns set in the grass.

"Whose idea was this?" Sam asked.

"Ari's," Robbie said.

"I should have guessed." And really, Sam herself should have been the one to think of it. She was the helicopter pilot, and the lights were doing a credible job of mimicking the outline of a landing pad. It was meant to be a subliminal cue to Marie that this was where she should set down, if she was going to set down, rather than land the helicopter inside the castle proper.

"Here they come again." Christopher craned his neck to look upwards. "Come on! Have a look, why don't you?"

As if summoned by his plea, the helicopter made its first pass since they'd left the palace, its searchlights sweeping across the battlement.

As it circled, Sam could see Arne sitting in the doorway with a machine gun. "He really is healed up. Yay."

Robbie gave her a side-eyed look, hopefully understanding that was sarcasm. "While you were asleep, Johnny told us it was his blood seeping through the cracks in the floor that showed the AZs where to find the weapon stash. If he hadn't been injured, we wouldn't be here today."

Sam turned her head to look at him, and then past him to Christopher. "That doesn't make sense."

"How so?" Christopher's eyes were on the helicopter. "They obviously found the weapons."

"Yes, but ... remember what I said to David back in Carew? Marie knew about the stash too. She had to have. She was FBI. Are you saying she didn't tell the other AZs?"

"Maybe she didn't know about it," Christopher said. "You and she never discussed it."

"I mean, it's theoretically possible." Then Sam shook her head. "That's an FBI helicopter. It was her job to know."

Christopher spoke slowly as he thought. "If Marie knew and didn't tell the other AZs about it, where does that leave us?"

"Maybe she really isn't on board with everything the other AZs want to do," Sam said.

"It's a nice thought," Christopher said.

"I don't know, guys," Robbie said, sounding very American. "She seems to have gotten on board. She's flown them everywhere they've wanted to go."

"Slowly, though, right?" Sam said, thinking out loud herself. "I thought it was weird when Ari and the others talked about how they'd been traveling, always looking down at the terrain. I shrugged it off at the time since we had so many other things to think about. But really, that helicopter is the fanciest, most state-of-the-art flying machine known to man. And yet, Marie told the other AZs she needed to keep checking below the cloud cover to make sure they were going the right way. I mean. Sure. That's a good idea once in a while, even if the GPS were working, but the helicopter has a computer in it with the entire earth's topography programmed in. It can actually read the terrain and know exactly where on the planet you are. At the very least, you can input any given city, and then where you want to go, and it will take you there. Chad planned on sending this thing to Earth Two from the start. He knew the limitations we'd experience trying to navigate."

Christopher made a helpless gesture as the helicopter circled again, this time with Arne strafing the battlement in a manner that would kill anyone on it. "Maybe like Robbie said, it doesn't matter at this point."

"The good news is he's wasting bullets," Sam said. "I see frustration. This assault isn't going to plan. Killing the King of France isn't as easy as they all thought it was going to be."

"They might be worrying too about where our strategy of emptying the battlements came from," Robbie said, "and wondering if they should have killed Johnny and the others. Throwing them out of the helicopter fifteen miles from Paris must have seemed like a good idea at the time. Really, if they were going to keep them alive, they should have tossed them out a hundred miles earlier."

"Thomas did say the AZs spent the whole flight arguing with each other," Christopher said. "If that fight had to do with them, and what *to do* with them, that would explain why things fell out the way they did."

"And if it was Marie who refused to kill them all …" Sam let her voice trail off.

"When we take the helicopter," Robbie said, "you can ask her."

45

28 September 1297

Isabelle

Isabelle found her mother-in-law intimidating, never more so than when she was being generous and thoughtful. Elisa was a smart and capable woman, but invariably took the time to be genuinely concerned about whether or not everyone had been provided with enough to eat.

Now, as the leader of this mission, she reverted back to the commanding general Isabelle knew her to be. First, she sent Huw and Johnny to scout the corridors to make sure they were clear for when they freed Philippa. The plan had been for small groups of soldiers to defend the doors of the palace, but only up to a point. Because they wanted the helicopter to land, they had left the garden door entirely unguarded.

Then, when they'd gone, she turned to Isabelle. "We came up with this idea in part because of who you are. If the carafe of wine and the sweet smile fails with Philippa's guard, you can be the daughter of the Master of the Paris Temple. Get us past him."

Isabelle wasn't so sure the sweet smile was going to appear genuine with the sound of the helicopter flying above the palace. But with Elisa holding position around the corner so they wouldn't be seen together, Isabelle approached the soldier guarding the door to Philippa's room. They were on the top floor, which only made the sound of the helicopter, and the stutter of its weapon, more unnerving.

Right off, the plan had to be changed because the guard was one she recognized from her time living in the palace, in the days before she'd met Christopher or knew a person such as he could exist. The man's eyes widened to see her too. With that recognition, Isabelle readied her sweet smile.

The guard didn't smile back. "My lady! What are you doing here? You should be in Sainte-Chapelle with everyone else!"

"I have been sent to sit with Philippa." Isabelle wasn't even lying. She had been sent. Just not by the guard's superiors or King Philippe. She indicated the tray she was holding with its carafe and three cups. This part of the plan was the *oldest trick in the book*, according to Elisa. Isabelle thought she understood what she meant by that. "We have wine for ourselves, but there's an extra cup for you."

"I am not permitted to drink wine on duty." He looked towards the ceiling as the helicopter made another pass. "Especially tonight."

"I would think you'd especially need it tonight." Still, Isabelle gave way. "I can leave some for you, for when you are able to enjoy it." Pouring the wine from the carafe into a cup, she set it on one of the tables that decorated the corridor. "I won't tell if you won't." Importantly, the poppy juice intended to put him to sleep was in the cup, not in the carafe.

"You are very kind." The guard opened the door to Philippa's room and then closed it behind her, turning the key to lock her inside. The conversation about the wine had successfully distracted him from the idea that Isabelle had been sent to sit with Philippa in the first place.

The only light in the room came from a lamp on the bedside table. The curtains were open, however, and, as the helicopter circled, its giant lights swept across the walls. The sound of it was louder here than in the corridor too.

Isabelle hesitated a pace inside the room, the closed door at her back. The nearby bed and chair were both unoccupied. "Hello? My name is Isabelle. I am Matthew Norris's daughter."

Philippa stepped out of the shadows in the far corner, near a long ladder to which it seemed she'd been clinging. Her face was very pale in the lantern light. "Help me." She put out a bloodied hand to Isabelle and took a hesitant step forward.

Isabelle ran to catch her. Now that her eyes had adjusted to the dim light, she could see the red stain spreading across other woman's dress. "When did this happen?"

They staggered together towards the bed.

"Just-just now, I think."

"Why were you outside at all?" Isabelle couldn't suppress her anger. She wasn't angry at Philippa, of course, but at the situation.

Count Guy's daughter was the last person at whom Arne should have been shooting.

"I saw that great flying machine overhead this morning. I'd never seen anything like it! When I heard it come back, I went up the ladder. I was only halfway out of the trap door when I felt—" Words failed her.

By now, Isabelle had managed to get Philippa onto the bed and was pressing a pillow hard to the wound. The way the blood was spreading across her torso made it immediately obvious Isabelle could not manage this alone. "Help! Please help us!" And then added, "Elisa!"

Thankfully, the helicopter appeared to have moved away from this side of the palace, so it wasn't drowning out her voice.

Elisa burst into the room, though not through the door to the corridor, but through the door in the wall that led to what had been Ted's room. Pausing for a heartbeat on the threshold, she took in what was happening with one encompassing glance.

Isabella didn't have time to wonder how she'd got past the guard before Elisa moved to the bed, unslinging the satchel on her shoulder as she did so. "You're doing the right thing. Keep up the pressure on the wound."

Elisa had carried the vial of poppy juice in it, prior to emptying it into the guard's cup. She'd also brought a rope, bandages, and a box Elisa called her *first-aid kit*. When she'd shown it to Isabelle earlier, she'd been half-apologetic about bringing something from Avalon to the palace. She'd explained she'd wanted it, *just in case.*

Never had Isabelle been more grateful that her mother-in-law always came prepared.

With Isabelle's help, Elisa turned Philippa enough onto her side to see there was a hole at the back of her dress too, and more blood.

"Even better, the bullet went right through her," Elisa said, still speaking in English. "We don't have to worry about digging it out."

She stuffed a pillow against Philippa there too and told Isabelle to keep pressing. By now, Isabelle was practically sprawled across her.

Philippa blinked sleepily. "Am I going to die?"
Elisa met Isabelle's gaze and then switched to French, "Not on my watch, you're not. We're going to save you, save the king, and steal the helicopter back. It's the whole trifecta we're going for tonight."

46

28 September 1297

Ari

As the others went off to save the world, for a brief moment it was only Ari, Thomas, and Henri left in the room. They were waiting for Matthew to return to give them their orders. Outside, the helicopter roared around another circuit. Ari itched to take a shot at it, but he had no weapon. Huw had left his great bow on the ship, else maybe he could have done some real damage, even shot Arne before Arne could shoot him.

Ari didn't know why the AZs kept circling the palace. His only thought was that, with nobody immediately available to kill, their intent was simply to terrorize. If that was the case, it was working, even on Ari. Any second now, he expected bullets to rip right through the windows and walls.

That fear had him steeling himself to say what needed to be said. What he hadn't had the guts to follow up on six days ago with David. Besides, Henri and Thomas hadn't been at Carew, so they hadn't heard him speak. "We don't have to go along with this, you know."

Henri's eyes narrowed. "Go along with what, exactly?"

"We don't have to protect King Philippe. You know what he did in Avalon to my people and to yours. Who's to say if we leave him alive he won't wipe all of us out tomorrow?"

"You know why we have to." Thomas spoke with some exasperation, as if Ari was being stupid and as if he himself had never questioned an order in his life. Ari knew that not to be true, since it had been Thomas who'd burned down his own uncle's stable to free David and Ieuan all those years ago. "He's the King of France!"

"Is that really an answer, though?" Ari endeavored to keep his voice reasonable.

"You aren't the only one to have asked that question," Henri said. "Master Godfrid spoke of it to David when they conferred before we left London."

That pulled Ari up short. "He did? What did David say?"

"The same thing I believe he said to you: we're saving King Philippe because the consequences of *not* saving him might be so much worse."

"David benefited enormously from King Edward's death. Look how well England has turned out!" When neither man argued with that, Ari pressed home his point. "Think of what changes could be made in France if Philippe dies. He has a son, but he's a child. He can be molded."

"That's the problem, though, isn't it?" Henri said, surprising Ari with an actual counter argument instead of simply going with *because*. "Who do you have in mind to institute those changes? Who gets to mold Philippe's son? France doesn't have a David. Beneath Philippe are dozens of noblemen, rivals, petty magnates—"

"—*lackeys*, more like," Thomas put in.

Henri continued as if Thomas hadn't spoken: "—along the lines of Flote who care most about themselves and their own power. We have our allies—Matthew Norris, Romeyn, the Johns of Brittany. Maybe other nobles who would accept one of them as adviser, but certainly not as regent. And not as king."

"It would be war among them for the throne," Thomas said, "throwing all France into chaos."

"The man with real power to be kingmaker is Artois, since he controls the army. Whom will he choose? Or will he take the throne himself? Regardless, none of them is going to believe in the freedom of religion. His rule isn't going to make any difference to Jews." Henri paused. "And even more than Philippe, any one of them could see the Templars as a source of gold, rather than advice—"

Henri broke off as Matthew opened the door. Ari's moment was gone. And yet, maybe it was better to risk everything than have what he really thought remain unsaid. Matthew didn't have much in the way of power over Ari anyway. "You should think about this. 1307 is coming, whether you like it or not. Maybe one of these other noblemen will be as bad as Philippe, but you know who Philippe is. Ten years from now, he is as likely to look to you to solve his money woes as he did in Avalon."

Matthew hesitated on the threshold at Ari's words. Then he closed the door and behaved as if he'd been there all along. "What are you suggesting? We hand the king over to the AZs and let them do with him as they will?"

"My apologies, Master, for even having this conversation with him," Henri said.

Matthew put up a hand. "You have no need to apologize. Every man may speak his mind in our order, no matter how vile his opinion."

"Thanks for that." Ari's tone couldn't help but be laden with sarcasm.

Matthew's gaze was direct and unapologetic. "And *you* should not take offense either. Nobody should be taking offense. I might object to your ideas, but Templars join our order with our eyes open, some later in life than others. It is a choice, and that means we do not check our thinking minds at the door."

Last Ari had checked, free thinking was not the hallmark of the Templar order he'd read about, but maybe he didn't know as much about them as he thought he did. Gesturing to Henri, Ari said, "He says Master Godfrid voiced my concern directly to David himself."

"And was satisfied with the answer," Henri said.

"Well, I'm not," Ari said.

"Does that mean you're staying here? Why did you come if you were going to refuse to help?"

"I didn't say I wouldn't help."

"Unity of purpose is the important thing," Matthew said. "I would hope, once each man has been given the opportunity to express his opinion, even were the consensus to go against you, you would not then seek to undermine the decision."

Matthew paused, waiting, and Ari realized he expected a reply. "I have followed orders in the past that I did not entirely agree with. Thank you for not condemning me."

It was a partial answer, but Matthew took it to be enough of one to be going on with. "To my mind, there's been too much death already."

"Your people have not been stripped of all your possessions and ejected from France." Ari knew he was beaten, but he couldn't let it go.

Matthew studied him for a long moment. "We have not. The Jewish people have suffered much because others have been consumed with jealousy and greed. You start with nothing and make it into something, and then others freely take what you have when they have the power to do so."

"As I have been saying, the same fate is coming for you at Philippe's hands. The Templar Order was the most powerful institution in Europe, outside of the actual monarchies. And look what happened to you."

"I don't honestly know what happened to us, even with what King David and others have said. I don't doubt your word. Still, Philippe is the sitting King of France. I could never justify helping the AZs murder him."

"Oh, you misunderstand what I was proposing." Ari blinked. His conception had been fully blown to him, so he hadn't realized he had neglected to explain it fully. "I am not asking you to *do* anything. Quite the opposite. Just don't put yourselves between the AZs and the king. We've done enough, don't you think?"

Matthew barked a laugh. "Then, strangely, we are in agreement, since I never intended that to be our task—"

BOOM!

The world shook. The percussive effect of the explosion was so great it blew the window glass inward and knocked everyone off their feet. Ari ended up on the floor, his ears ringing painfully.

The moment the glass settled, he was on his feet again, going from one friend to another. "You okay? Everyone okay?"

Each man basically was, apart from some cuts from the glass fragments. Ari's greatest concern was the possibility a shard had ended up in someone's eye or carotid artery. But Thomas's eyes were wide and staring. "What was that?"

"That, my friend," Ari said, in a tone that couldn't have been more grim, "was a rocket." It wasn't the technical term for the ordinance, but Ari didn't need to confuse Thomas further.

Only then did Ari cast his thoughts back to a few moments before, realizing he'd noted the sound of the rocket's launch but had been too focused on his argument to acknowledge what he'd heard. Not that he could have done anything to prevent it in the allowed space of time. They had known the AZs' arsenal included three rocket launchers. They'd believed it. They just hadn't seen them yet.

"Dear God in His Heaven." Matthew had gone to the window and now stared, horrified, at what remained of Sainte-Chapelle. The chapel had been built in stone throughout, but no medieval mortar could withstand the power of a rocket, which appeared to have entered the building through the central circular window above the altar and exploded in the middle of the nave, blowing out the windows, many supports, and setting anything combustible on fire.

Below them in the courtyard, people were screaming, their hands to their heads as they staggered out of the ground floor doors. Then the helicopter swooped back, and Arne began firing at the survivors.

If Philippe had been within the chapel when the rocket hit, he was dead. As was Ted. As would be dozens of others who'd been directly below him. When under attack, it was common practice to shelter in a church, thinking God could protect people better there. Ari knew the AZs, however, and their reverence for God had always been minimal. Up until now, everyone had thought destroying one of the most holy sites in Christendom was a bridge too far, even for them.

"When bad men combine, the good must associate; else they will fall, one by one, an unpitied sacrifice in a contemptible struggle." Ari turned to look at Matthew. "This is what you meant."

"What was that?" Matthew continued to stare at the wreckage, his hand to his head. It wasn't that they didn't want to help the injured, but rather that all four of them, including Ari, truth be told, were still in shock at what the AZs had just done.

"It's a quote from a man who believed in the wisdom of tradition and experience and preached against radical change because of its unintended consequences."

Matthew pulled in a deep breath. "To act or not act has been taken out of our hands. We will discover now if it is you or your philosopher who is right."

47

28 September 1297

Huw

Huw had left Johnny guarding the garden door. Christopher, Robbie, and Sam had already gone through it and were hiding in the garden, waiting for their chance to take the helicopter. Huw was in a hurry to get back to Philippa's room, but as he hustled down the corridor, a great *boom* shook the palace, rattling the windows, like a great gust of air had just blown through.

He stayed on his feet, hugging the wall for a moment and catching his breath, and then he started to run. When he reached Philippa's room, Elisa was just coming out of the door to the adjacent room.

"What just happened?" he asked before he noticed the blood on her hands.

"I don't know. I can't think about it. I need your help with Philippa."

The man who'd been guarding Philippa's room was slumped on the floor in the hallway. He was awake but, as Huw arrived in the doorway, he looked blearily up at him, his limbs akimbo. He would be of no use, which of course had been the entire point. He'd be asleep in another minute.

"Put him into the room next door to Philippa's. At one time I had a thought to post one of you in his place, for appearances sake, but now I need you to stay with us."

"How much poppy did you give him?" Even as he asked the question, Huw grabbed the guard's upper arms and shoulders and dragged him to where Elisa suggested.

"All of it. I didn't want to kill him, but we couldn't afford to skimp." Then Elisa went through the adjoining door Ted had left unlocked into Philippa's room.

Huw didn't bother to put the guard on the bed, but lay him face-up on the floor. At the last moment, he put a pillow under his head. "Sleep tight."

He closed the door to the hallway as a temporary measure, so nobody passing by would notice anything amiss. Whatever that explosion had been about, their ultimate goal was still the same: to free Philippa without the French knowing who was responsible. Better if it took a while for them to realize she was gone.

Next, he entered Philippa's room to find Elisa and Isabelle caring for a bleeding Philippa. Isabelle was practically wrapped around the girl.

"She was shot?"

"Clean through. I wish now we had some poppy left, because she must be in pain." Elisa waved Huw closer. "I've poured clotting powder in the wound and given her a shot of antibiotics. I'd love to put tea bags in the wound front and back and bandage her with duct tape, but I have none of that, of course. So helpful."

Huw had understood one word in three and accepted his ignorance for now. He gazed down at the young woman. She was lovely, even pale, bleeding, and in pain. "She's alive. That's the important thing."

Elisa waved a hand, introducing them. "This is Huw. He can carry you out of here, but I need to finish binding you up first. I may have to pull tight. Can you handle that?"

"Anything." Philippa was awake, but in shock too, as Huw could imagine he'd be if he'd been shot by a bullet from a helicopter—with both *bullet* and *helicopter* being things she'd never heard of before they'd almost taken her life. Not to mention words Huw himself didn't know, like *clotting powder, tea bag,* and *duct tape.*

On their way through the halls before the explosion, Huw and Johnny had met only two of Philippe's men, both regular soldiers who had passed them by without comment. They had bigger concerns than questioning two knights they didn't recognize who appeared to be going about their duties. The palace was under attack. Practically the whole of Philippe's court had taken shelter in the ground floor of Sainte-Chapelle, which King Philippe considered to be the center of his kingdom and rule. He himself had said he'd be one floor up in the chapel, on his knees before the altar. Enguerrand was to be with him, and Ted, but he'd made clear nobody else was to disturb them.

Huw couldn't worry about the king right now. Or Ted. They needed to make Philippa safe to travel, as well as give Christopher and the others time to take over the helicopter, if that was even going to be possible. He could hear Arne shooting even now, given the *rat-tat* sound coming from outside the walls. Bringing Philippa to the garden too early would mean waiting unprotected with her until the helicopter landed.

If the helicopter landed.

If it didn't, they'd get her in one of the skiffs moored at the little dock. That's how Dafydd and his family had escaped the palace two years ago. Johnny had poked his head outside earlier and informed Huw there were three from which to choose.

For now, Philippa was better off lying on the bed for as long as they could let her.

While Elisa and Isabelle bound her wound, Huw held Philippa's hand. He was pleased to note her grip remained strong. She needed it to be because the look in her eyes told him *by God this hurts.*

"How long have you been imprisoned in this room?" He asked, trying to distract her from what the other women were doing.

"Since just after the Battle of Furnes. It was foolish of me to be captured in the first place. I should have left Male before the French arrived. I wanted to, but my minders didn't think the king's forces could possibly take the castle."

"Minders?" he asked.

Philippa managed to roll her eyes. "I am far too old for a nanny, but my father thinks I'm impulsive, so I have minders now instead. What my father really wants for me is an appropriate husband, but he has been blocked at every turn by King Philippe. If David's sons weren't so young, I'm sure he would have asked for one of them."

"Uniting your two families would encourage Dafydd to intervene on the side of Flanders," Huw said. "What you describe is entirely in keeping with tradition. It just isn't the way Dafydd works."

"Okay." Elisa let out a sharp breath. "I think that can hold for now. Can you lift her?"

Huw scooped Philippa up in his arms. She was thinner than he thought healthy, but a month of inactivity and loneliness probably had suppressed her appetite. Inside, he cursed the king for his inhumanity. Outwardly, he just said, "I got her."

With Elisa in front and Isabelle behind, they made their way through the palace, following the route Huw had scouted after leaving Johnny. Finally, they turned the last corner and saw Johnny just ahead of them, his eyes lighting with joy to see them coming. Johnny's mother was the eldest daughter of Count Guy's first wife. Philippa had been born late to his second. Which was how, by 1297, both Johnny and Philippa were twenty-two years old.

Then Johnny gasped at the way Huw was carrying Philippa, and his face fell. "What happened?"

"It is the day for that question, apparently," Elisa said. "She's been shot. The bullet went all the way through her. We've bandaged her the best we can, but she needs better medical help than I can give her."

Johnny was aghast. "Nobody here can take her to Avalon!"

"So we'll do the next best thing," Huw said. "We take that helicopter. If we do that, we can be in London in an hour and a half."

48

28 September 1297

Christopher

Christopher, Sam, and Robbie had felt the ground shake and seen the subsequent smoke from the other side of the palace. Then they'd watched from the bushes as the helicopter lifted higher in the air so they could see it, and Arne started shooting off his machine gun again. At what or whom they didn't know.

Johnny had put the number of people the AZs had killed, between the two castles they'd taken, in the vicinity of a hundred. If they'd had only three hundred bullets to begin with, which had been David's initial estimate back in Carew, they had to be running out. Christopher had been counting the bullets as they were fired tonight, almost by reflex, praying Arne would find himself empty soon. His supply seemed ridiculously endless.

For that reason, Christopher tried not to let his disdain for the AZs make him underestimate them. They had put together a revolution in six days, coopting the courts of Flanders, Holland, Zeeland, and Brabant in the process—and that was just those he knew about. Count Guy was in the ascendancy. He was well on his way to being able to withstand a renewed assault from the French army, which was in the wrong place right now anyway. The war was on, Philippe or no Philippe.

Behind them, the door to the garden swung open, and Johnny stuck out his head. With the helicopter momentarily hidden on the other side of the palace, Christopher stood up and made a large *come here!* motion, letting him know it was safe to enter the garden.

Huw hustled out after Johnny, carrying a girl in his arms. He was followed by Isabelle. Christopher's heart leapt to see his wife, except Isabelle had blood on her dress. Before Christopher could panic about that, she indicated Philippa with one bloody hand. "I'm okay. It isn't my blood." Then he was able to hold her in his arms and make sure what she said was really true.

Meanwhile, Huw quickly related what had happened and the need for getting Philippa better help.

Philippa coughed weakly. "You can put me down."

"I don't think so," Huw said.

Nobody was going to take that seriously, given the bloody dressing. And the weakness.

Christopher himself was also a bit shocked Philippe had made no provision for Philippa tonight nor even told her the palace was under attack. She should never have been at the top of her tower in the first place.

"Where's Mom?" Christopher asked next.

"She went to find your father." Isabelle's voice was tight. "Last we heard he was with the king."

Christopher had known that and been trying not to think about it. Then the helicopter hove into view again. They ducked below the top of the hedge, holding as still as they could so as not to draw attention to themselves. Philippa moaned, but only under her breath. Certainly nobody but them could hear her. Christopher had his eye on the doorway and saw the moment Arne, who had been sitting half out the doorway, using the machine gun with its endless supply of bullets, pulled back inside.

Seeing that too, Robbie mumbled from his crouch beside Sam. "I can't decide if I should pray that it's leaving or pray that it isn't."

Christopher was entirely sure he would prefer the helicopter landed. He needed to be useful, and so far he didn't feel he had been. They had a job, and a girl to save, and he wanted to do it.

Then Arne returned to his position in the helicopter doorway. Now, however, he crouched instead of sitting, with a tube-like weapon on his shoulder. In the time it took for Christopher to realize what he was looking at, Sam gasped, "No!"

Arne fired.

This second rocket shot out of the launcher towards the front of the palace, same as the first. The ground shook again and the smoke and flames from the explosion reached the sky.

Christopher almost threw up right there on the ground. He didn't know why Arne had fired a second rocket, except to make sure the king was dead. And if the king was dead, so was Christopher's father, along with possibly Ari, Matthew, Thomas, and Henri too.

And maybe his mom, who hadn't come to the garden like they'd planned.

Isabelle wrapped her arms around Christopher from behind, squeezing him tightly and trying for words of comfort. "We don't know what they've hit, and your father might not have been there at all. He could have gone to check on any number of things. He could have gone to meet your mother!"

Christopher grasped his wife's hand as it held his waist, holding on to her and to the thought, even as he knew it wasn't true. It was all he had to sustain him for now. Hope was both necessary and awful, and he gagged on the pain of it.

Then Sam said in a low voice. "Christopher, they're landing. They're using the destruction they've caused as a cover."

It was the same strategy Christopher and his friends had meant to use, except to cover up different things.

The companions ducked further behind their bush, remaining as still as they could be.

Through gaps in the branches, Christopher saw the helicopter touch down. Arne stepped out, the third rocket launcher slung over his shoulder on a harness, since the first two were one-shot only, and the machine gun cradled in his arms. He was followed by Paul and Jos, who gave what sounded like an order. It was in Zeelandic, which Christopher still didn't speak.

Beside him, however, Johnny stiffened. Once the three men loped towards the door to the palace and disappeared inside, he said, "Jos just told the other two to kill anyone they find alive."

49

28 September 1297

Johnny

Nobody had to say *go, go, go!* Robbie, Christopher, and Sam were moving as soon as the garden door closed behind the AZs. Isabelle followed with Huw, still holding Philippa, who seemed to be biting down hard on one edge of Huw's cloak.

Johnny stayed a step behind. He didn't think his presence was necessary nor would exactly warm Marie's heart anyway. Truly, if they had to kill her, Johnny would struggle to do it. He had his sword out, though, and was ready to use it if he had to.

Christopher reached the helicopter first and threw himself through the still open sliding door. He was at the back of the pilot's seat with his knife to Marie's throat before Marie had time to turn around. "Keep your hands where I can see them."

The principle of attack was the same in any world: move at a speed your opponent doesn't expect, fast or slow. And, whatever you do, don't hesitate. Victory was all about commitment.

For her part, Marie obeyed instantly, her hands lifting off the controls. "I suppose we should have seen this coming. How did you get here so fast?"

"Planes, trains, and automobiles."

Johnny didn't understand any of those words, except for maybe *planes*. He knew for a fact that Christopher hadn't ridden in one here, so the reference made no sense at all.

Christopher then reached around the seat and retrieved the gun Marie was wearing on her hip. She was still dressed in Avalonian gear, having given no quarter on that front, same as her male companions. "Get up. Slowly."

Marie obeyed that order too. By now, Huw and Isabelle had settled Philippa in the passenger compartment. Johnny was impressed to see his aunt still awake and lucid. But then, she was strong enough to survive these weeks in captivity too. She could have been thinking her father had abandoned her and despaired.

"There's a first aid kit in the cargo bay," Marie said. "You'll find morphine and antibiotics inside."

Robbie disappeared into the cargo bay, and Sam slipped into the pilot's seat. Immediately, she began flipping switches. Christopher had Marie's weapon pointed at her, even if his hands weren't entirely steady. Johnny stayed on the ground a few feet away from the helicopter, ready to run Marie through with his sword if she attempted to escape.

"Get out." Christopher motioned with the barrel of the gun.

"We aren't taking her with us?" Huw said from behind him.

"I don't want to risk her sabotaging us somehow," Christopher said. "The last thing we need is one of our enemies flying with us."

"I'm not your enemy." By now, Marie was a good two paces from the helicopter, her hands still raised, and she nodded towards the gun. "You should know there's only two bullets left." Then she called through the window that was open next to Sam, "The stick has started twitching a bit to the right. You can probably fix it once you get back to Wales."

Sam glanced out the window, "Just like that? You're helping us now? Why?"

"Would you rather I didn't?" And then, when they were all still waiting for a more complete answer, Marie shook her head. "I hadn't—I hadn't understood about the killing. Franc died and—and then nothing went like I thought or expected. It was all wrong. It had been all wrong for a while but I hadn't been willing to admit it."

Johnny wasn't quite sure he understood, but Sam's expression softened at Marie's words. "What are you going to tell the others? I'm pretty sure they expect the helicopter to be here when they get back."

"I was overwhelmed by your numbers. Seven to one are not good odds." She had included Philippa in the count. "They'll see that."

"They'll say you could have shot us." Christopher's hands were steadier now.

"Not with only two bullets." She motioned towards her former weapon. "You can put that down now."

Christopher didn't necessarily obey, but he did lower the weapon slightly as he spoke to Johnny, "Get in. It's time to go!"

"I think I'll stay." Johnny took a step backwards. "I have accomplished what I set out to do, just like them."

There was a chorus of protest from the passenger compartment. Sam, however, took him at his word. She started the rotors and, a moment later, lifted the helicopter off the ground. Within two breaths, it was ten feet in the air. Johnny tugged Marie back, towards the garden door, unable to take his eyes away from the magnificent machine, though he still wasn't sorry not to be inside.

The helicopter continued to rise, now higher than the palace itself. Then the garden door opened, and the three other AZs rushed out. For once, their guns weren't at the ready. In fact, as they crossed the grass, Arne tossed the machine gun to the ground and kicked it away, like it was a mongrel dog. At long last, they were out of bullets.

Jos, meanwhile, was gaping up at the helicopter, which hadn't flown away like it should have but was hovering above one of the nearby towers upon which two men were standing, one of them waving a torch. "What is happening? Who's flying?"

"Sam." Marie's expression was entirely calm. "She and the others took it." She glanced at Johnny. "We tried to stop them but there were too many of them. There was nothing we could do."

Johnny managed not to gape at her easy incorporation of him back into the group, as if the others, her included, hadn't abandoned him in a field that morning.

Then they all looked at the helicopter again. Sam hadn't turned on the searchlight, but they could see what was happening because of the interior lights shining through the open helicopter door. Someone—Johnny thought it was Robbie—had just thrown down a rope to the two men on the battlement. One caught it and held it for the other to begin to climb, using the knots tied every few feet.

Jos was irate. "You said the helicopter was out of fuel! It had maybe five minutes left!"

"It does. They won't get far."

"You're right. They won't." Arne shrugged out of the case on his back and slid out a long tube, which he put to his shoulder. "I have one rocket left. We'll stop them right here and now."

Pushing Paul aside, Marie planted herself in front of Arne. "You will not shoot them. We killed the king. We're done."

Arne waved a hand angrily. "Get out of my way!"

"If you ever loved me, don't do this."

Arne looked at her with such disdain that Johnny felt his own face flush. Before she could reply, Jos grabbed Marie around the waist and spun her away. Johnny caught her in his arms, staggering backwards at the force of the push.

The man who'd started climbing the rope was halfway up when Arne fired the rocket. It shot upwards, a stream of smoke pouring from the back end. The helicopter couldn't have been more than a hundred feet away, and Arne's aim was true. The rocket couldn't miss. But someone on board must have noticed the activity in the garden because, in the same instant the weapon fired, the helicopter soared skyward, climbing more quickly than Johnny would have thought possible.

The rocket passed harmlessly between the bottom of the helicopter and the man on the rope, who could be seen hanging on for dear life. A moment later, there was a thunderous explosion somewhere on the left bank of Paris.

And then the helicopter flew away.

50

Ari and the others hadn't quite made it to Sainte-Chapelle when the second rocket hit. That was just as well for them, since Arne had fired at the gatehouse, which became a pile of rubble. As a survivor, Ari knew better than to run towards trouble, but he had done it anyway.

Thomas had been in the lead. He had just opened the door into the courtyard when he was blown backwards into Ari. That probably saved Thomas's life, though Ari himself broke a few ribs when the young man hit him and then fell with him to the ground. They both lay without breath and concussed. Somehow, Ari remained conscious. Still, it took more than a minute for him to respond to Henri once he saw him leaning over him, speaking urgently, telling him Thomas and Matthew were still breathing too.

Moaning and holding his ribs, Ari made to sit up.

Relief in his face, Henri tried to make him lie down again, but Ari pushed to a sitting position anyway. The wall was right behind him, and he scooted back to lean against it. That position was actually better for his ribs, and he tipped back his head, trying to draw in easy breaths. "We need to move. You know they have a third rocket."

"You need to stay still. You're wounded. The king is dead. You got what you wanted."

Ari put out his hand and such was Henri's own confusion that he took it and lifted him to his feet anyway. "You stay with Thomas and Matthew. Do what you can for the injured. I'm going after the AZs."

"Surely they're done—"

Ari was reminded again how ingrained chivalry was in Henri's heart and mind. "They aren't done, believe me. I don't hear the helicopter. My guess is they've landed it, just like we hoped. They're going to come through here, killing everyone in their way." He paused before adding softly, "It's what I'd do."

Henri was aghast again. "Why?"

"They have to be sure."

And then he was off, loping awkwardly back down the corridor. He had started out on the opposite side of the palace from the garden door and had made it halfway along a dark corridor when he heard voices speaking Zeelandic. Ari was trained in hand-to-hand combat, but it wouldn't help him against a firearm unless he got very close. He had broken ribs anyway, splinters from which he was loath to drive into his lungs.

The Zeelanders came around a corner, and Ari ducked into one of the rooms on the left side of the corridor. Almost immediately, a man's voice, speaking in French, came from further down the corridor: "You there! We need your help!"

The AZ response was the *rat-tat* of Arne's automatic weapon. This time, however, at long last, the killing was followed by an ineffective *click*.

Arne swore emphatically. "That's the last."

Then came the unmistakable sound of weapon checks. "I have three bullets left," Jos said.

"I'm completely out," Paul said. "The three we killed earlier were it for me."

Through the crack between the frame and the door, Ari saw Jos turn on Paul. "Why didn't you say so then?"

Paul shrugged. "What good would it have done?" He pulled a knife from its sheath in his boot. "Now we're all on the same level."

Jos cat-walked forward, past Ari's door, all the way to the man Arne had shot. "He's still breathing, poor bugger."

Then, farther on, two more French soldiers appeared. Because the palace guard hadn't sheltered on the ground floor of the chapel, they were the only ones in the palace left alive. Jos fired two rounds at one soldier and then a final shot at the second. The first two bullets hit the first man center mass. Jos was used to double taps. But with only one bullet remaining, he'd had to swing his weapon to the left. That last bullet didn't hit as cleanly, taking the soldier in the shoulder. Both Frenchmen were down, but—

"Done." Jos turned on his heel.

Leaving the last soldier to die or survive on his own, the three AZs headed back the way they'd come.

Ari followed, faster than was comfortable for him, but he didn't want to lose them. While he hadn't cared about protecting the king, he was worried about Christopher and the others, who didn't have guns and even now could be taking over the helicopter. Maybe Ari could be of use if the AZs arrived in the garden too soon.

He turned a corner and saw Elisa ducking out of a doorway between him and the AZs, who had run by without seeing her. Her eyes widened. "Are you okay?"

He realized only then that he probably looked a mess, having survived the percussion of two rocket attacks. "I'm fine." He waved her away towards a nearby staircase. "Go. Find Ted."

It was what she wanted to do anyway. And maybe what she had been looking to do. So she went.

Ari reached the garden door and peered through it just as Arne shot off the last rocket at the helicopter. It missed. In a fit of fury, Arne heaved the launcher into the Seine. Johnny was standing well away, and must have caught the movement of the door because his eyes widened at the sight of Ari's head poking out. Ari put his finger to his lips, hoping the message was the same in Earth Two as in Avalon.

Johnny returned his attention to the AZs. "You need to get out of here before anyone comes. You have no modern weapons anymore. You can't fight the whole French army."

"Who was that they picked off the roof?" Arne demanded.

Jos shrugged. "Not our concern." He was already moving towards one of three skiffs moored at the garden dock. Arne and Paul followed. With nobody looking in his direction, Ari slipped through the doorway, keeping himself in the shadows.

Jos motioned to Marie and Johnny, who had trailed after them. "Get in."

The pair stayed where they were, not so much united, Ari thought, as individually making the decision that continued travel with the other AZs could be hazardous to their health.

"I think we'll stay." Johnny was suddenly looking like the Duke of Brabant again. He bore a sword and was better armed than any of the others. He'd freed them from Carew. They were here because of him. He had honor enough to accept the consequences of what he'd done. But he wasn't going to compound those poor choices by riding with them anymore.

Arne glared first at him, and then at Marie. "Get in!"

She took a genuine step back. "No."

Arne made to surge out of the skiff, but Jos and Paul, each with an oar, had already pushed away from the dock.

"Leave them." Jos said when Arne really looked as if he might try to launch himself across the gap. By then it was ten feet. All Arne could do was glare as the gap continued to widen.

Night mist was forming on the river, and the skiff was soon lost to sight. Even so, Ari could still hear the sound of the oars in the water and, above that, the three men arguing in Zeelandic. What about wasn't possible to make out at this distance.

"Are you sure you're okay with letting them loose in Europe unsupervised?" Ari said from behind Marie and Johnny, in a deliberately casual tone.

Marie spun around, having been unaware of his presence before now.

Ari gestured to the dock. "I'm not going to be good for much after that second rocket attack, but there are two skiffs remaining. I'm thinking to follow." And then, without waiting for a reply, he climbed into the skiff he gauged to be the most river-worthy.

Marie immediately climbed in after him, but Johnny still hesitated on the dock. "Why would I get in a boat with her? She tried to kill us."

Marie actually laughed. "I didn't try to kill you. If I'd been trying to kill you, believe me, you'd be dead. Everyone else wanted to throw you out of the helicopter a hundred miles earlier than we did and at a higher elevation. I told them I'd rather crash than do that. We fought about it. I won."

"And now that you got what you wanted," Johnny said, "what's the plan?"

"What I wanted?" Marie scoffed. "You mean Philippe's death? Do you actually think he's dead?"

"Arne shot two rockets—"

"Who do you think was climbing up that rope? Philippe wasn't in Sainte-Chapelle at all."

"She's right," Ari said. "King Philippe and Ted made a plan to use a decoy. Elisa and I were the only ones who knew about it."

Which was, of course, why Elisa wasn't panicked when Ari had met her earlier. Now he made a motion with a few of his fingers, as if to cut through Johnny's hesitation. Any other movement hurt. "Marie threw me out of the helicopter too, but I'm not worried. Wouldn't you feel safer knowing what the others are going to get up to next? And where?"

"It's the least we can do, considering," Marie said. "We could use your help and experience. I also think I could use your help rowing, since, as Ari said, he's not going to be good for much."

Ari chose not to take offense; she was right. "What would your grandfather want you to do?"

Johnny got into the skiff.

51

Christopher

"Take my hand!" Robbie was sprawled belly down on the floor of the passenger compartment, Christopher at his side.

Between the two of them, they pulled the King of France to safety, leaving him trembling and gasping on the floor. The only reason he'd been able to hang onto the rope had been because of the knots tied every foot.

"We thought you were dead!" Robbie collapsed onto one of the seats.

"I saw the wisdom of sending another man to Sainte-Chapelle in my place," King Philippe said between breaths. He was a hereditary king, but that didn't mean he was dumb.

Christopher was still trembling at how close a call that had been. In the second before Arne had fired, Isabelle had shouted a warning, and Sam had shot the helicopter upwards. Her timing couldn't have been more perfect.

It was also Isabelle who'd seen Christopher's father waving at them from the battlement, King Philippe at his side. Both men had been bareheaded and disheveled, but recognizable. Philippe wasn't called *le bel* for nothing.

Huw was still holding Philippa. At least her face was no longer twisted in pain. She'd been given painkillers and more antibiotics from the FBI first aid kit, and was finally able to relax against Huw's chest. That didn't mean her life wasn't still in danger. The wound was patched, not sealed. They needed a real doctor for that.

"Can we fly faster?" Christopher got himself together enough to settle into the co-pilot's seat and put on a headset.

"Top speed is two hundred miles an hour. And that's how fast we're going." She glanced at him out of the corner of her eye. "I would have saved your parents too if I could have. I'm sorry. The AZs are still down there."

"As we pulled Philippe in, I saw Mom come through the door from the nearest tower. Ten minutes ago, I thought they were dead! Worst case, they'll find a room to hide in and bar the door. They'll be okay."

"I'm still sorry we had to leave them to fend for themselves."

Christopher waved off the second apology. "Do we have enough fuel to get to London?"

"Not quite, though they must have refueled this afternoon before they flew back to Paris. We do have enough to get us out of France."

"Are you okay to fly in the dark? Johnny said Marie refused to fly at night."

By way of an answer, Sam turned up the brightness on one of the screens to better reveal a map of real-time terrain. "I thought Marie might have been hiding the helicopter's true capabilities. Now I'm sure of it."

Christopher frowned. "Jos and the others at one time must have known what it could do. She was involved with them back in Avalon, feeding them information."

"I don't doubt it but, in any aircraft, there are a zillion things that can go wrong at any point. Even Chad's engineering can break. She could have said the tech wasn't working correctly—or wouldn't work without contact with satellites. Remember, this is a pre-production craft. Chad was still working out the bugs. I could make up a story just as easily, and you'd never know."

"Is that why the AZs landed in the garden?" Isabelle had found a headset too. "They'd blown up Sainte-Chapelle and the king, or so they thought. What more could they want?"

"To kill everyone," Christopher said. "You heard what Johnny said."

By now, King Philippe had recovered enough to be sitting in one of the seats, though his eyes were on Philippa. Once Robbie helped him with one of the headsets, he said, "How am I going to explain her absence to my advisers?"

Of all the things he could have asked, that was the most likely to raise everyone's hackles. Where was the *thank you?* Instead, he came out with a question that was more like an accusation. Christopher was already sorry they'd saved him.

Because none of his friends looked like they were touching that with a ten-foot pole, Christopher said, "Why do you have to explain anything about her at all?"

King Philippe's eyes narrowed. "Is this really why you came? To abduct her and me?"

"We came to help you." Christopher was trying very hard to keep impatience out of his voice. "We left Carew the day the mercenaries stole the helicopter. We've been tracking them ever since."

"David should have told me."

"He didn't know when we would arrive." As before, Christopher spoke easily, glad he was able so far to just tell the truth. It was so much easier than having to come up with a reasonable lie.

Philippe settled back in his seat. "Take me back to the palace."

Again, nobody else made to answer, so it was up to Christopher to say, in a very even tone, "No."

Even if Christopher's French wasn't excellent these days, the word was essentially the same in French as in English. He hadn't even tried to be diplomatic.

"You must!" Philippe really was recovering from his ordeal. "Everyone will think I died in Sainte-Chapelle!"

"My father knows you're alive, and he'll tell them. Philippa is our priority now. We can't fly all the way to London, so we'll put down in Rouen; Master Amaury will have trained physicians to help her there."

At that moment, Christopher finally realized what was happening. It wasn't random events, chance, or luck that had conspired to put him in a position to reply to the King of France. They'd *planned* for this from the very start, with David, standing outside the prison tent at Carew. They'd come all this way in order to be right here, right now when the AZs overplayed their hand. This was the end game, the moment when everything fell apart for everyone who opposed them.

What's more, Christopher himself had to take advantage of the opportunity he'd been given. That was his job, as David's cousin, as the son of the ambassador to France, and as a member of *Y Ddraig Goch.*

So, even as King Philippe glared at him, Christopher added, "I must tell you that we don't know how soon we'll be able to send you back to Paris. Your general, Artois, and his troops have massed on the border of Normandy. We don't want you to end up like Philippa, caught in the crossfire. Now that we've saved your life, I assure you we intend to be very careful with it moving forward."

52

David

Two months later …

David's first accounting of the adventures in Paris had come over the shortwave radio from Aunt Elisa and Uncle Ted, who continued to act as David's ambassadors to France. Then Christopher had told David his side of the story in person once he and Isabelle got back to London. They hadn't had to sail, to Isabelle's great relief, since Sam had flown them and Robbie across the English Channel.

And then, finally, once he was back in Paris, Philippe himself had renewed his discourse with David. "I take your bishop."

"You can have him." David followed with his move in their mutual chess game. During the medieval period, the rules of chess were slightly different from what had become commonplace in Avalon. For example, in the Middle Ages, queens could move only one space diagonally and bishops only two spaces. Pawns could move just one space per turn. Then, upon reaching the other side of the board, they could be exchanged only for queens.

Otherwise, the game was much the same as when David had been an anchor member of his high school chess club team—for less than a semester—before traveling to Earth Two fifteen years ago.

Philippe, in turn, played a knight, telling David to which square it should go and then adding, "Your cousin has a nose for diplomacy."

"We are incredibly proud of him. We are also very glad he was in the right place at the right time to save your life."

Two things had become obvious in the aftermath of the events in Paris. One, Christopher did indeed have a nose for diplomacy that exceeded what David (or anyone else, barring perhaps Isabelle) had expected. Two, David had been right about the pitfalls of modern weaponry. He had feared they'd soon approach the tipping point into negative consequences. In fact, with these events, they had exceeded it.

Since they were conversing over the radio, David couldn't see the slight tilt to Philippe's head, but he could imagine it. "The loss of Sainte-Chapelle is a constant ache. I feel, however, that my sainted grandfather must have been holding me in the palm of his hand. He couldn't turn aside the evil in the hearts of those Zeelanders, but he could save me, his beloved grandson." He paused for what might have been effect. "Before he sent me your cousin, he sent me your uncle. It was Ambassador Shepherd who suggested the chapel was an obvious target. Seeing the wisdom behind his words, I allowed another man to take my place. He died so I could live."

The fact that Philippe could be grateful stopped David from gagging at Philippe's pious tone—or inserting the actual truth that it was David himself who'd sent Christopher and Uncle Ted to Philippe's side. Not that David was going to argue against the idea that God may have worked through him. He had heard the modern parable about God sending a helicopter to save a man's life long before he'd acquired a helicopter of his own.

David had also known, from the moment he learned of the elevation of Louis to sainthood, that it had a high chance of making Philippe insufferable. That still didn't mean David wanted him dead, nor that David didn't also mourn the loss of Sainte-Chapelle.

It had been a beautiful church. Within weeks of its destruction, even during the negotiations to disband Artois' army and send Philippe back to Paris, the French king had been consulting with masons in Rouen about rebuilding it into something even more grand and ostentatious. David just knew Philippe was going to get himself into debt again. He really hoped the French king wouldn't be looking to the Templars to borrow the necessary money. Regardless, it was up to Jacques de Molay, not David, to decide whether or not to cooperate.

"Any word on your end about the fugitives?" David wouldn't necessarily have brought them up, but since Philippe had already done so, he was happy to continue. He still wasn't referring to them as *the AZs* in Philippe's presence.

"No word." A slapping sound carried across the miles, which David thought was Philippe's fist hitting his thigh. "Those responsible must be found and punished."

"We are looking, too, believe me." David wanted the AZs found as much or more than Philippe did. He was also desperate to find them first. They were *his* responsibility, if anyone's. And, with the destruction of Sainte-Chapelle, followed by the wanton killing of the survivors, they had jettisoned any pretense of being freedom fighters and transformed themselves into genuine murderers.

"They have disappeared, back to Flanders, I presume."

"Your guess is as good as mine." Via the Templar network, David had received an initial message from Ari saying that he, Marie, and Johnny were on the AZs trail. He'd heard nothing since.

Meanwhile, Philippe pulled in a breath, pausing in a way David had learned indicated he had more to say. "Don't think for a moment that I'm done with Count Guy either."

David sat back in his chair, thinking about how to respond. He'd been biding his time for weeks, waiting to broach this subject. "We are of an age, you and I, when we begin to think about our legacy. You have been king for twelve years, nearly the length of your father's entire reign. Your grandfather has been declared a saint by the Church. What will your legacy be? Do you want to be remembered for killing the daughter of the Count of Flanders and expending your wealth in a destructive war? Or would you prefer to be remembered as a king who rose to even greater heights of purity like a phoenix from the ashes?"

Philippe had been breathing a bit heavily into the microphone. He was deservedly still irate about being used as leverage himself against Robert d'Artois. Christopher had refused to reunite the king with his general until his whole army had been disbanded. Of course, it could be called together again, but with winter coming on, the campaign season was over. It was a forced hiatus, but a hiatus nonetheless.

Now, his breathing eased. "You are not wrong."

"Why do you want to rule Flanders anyway?"

"What do you mean?"

"I mean, they aren't your people. You aren't particularly interested in their wellbeing. Why invade the place?"

"I still don't understand the question."

The sad part was Philippe probably didn't.

"I'm asking what you get out of conquering an entire country of rebellious people who don't speak your language and otherwise hate you?"

The hesitation was obvious, as if he was worried David was drawing him into a trap. "More land; more wealth; more power."

If nothing else, that was insightful and the truth, as Philippe knew it.

"Okay, I get that. But still, what does more land/more wealth/more power gain you? I mean, it's hugely expensive to wage war, especially through multiple seasons. Given the cost, I can't see you making much of a profit in the end, not with the unrest over there. Why even start?"

"Says the man who has expanded his territory at the expense of mine."

"It isn't *my* territory," David said immediately, knowing how difficult this would be for Philippe to understand. The man was clever and calculating, but these were ideas that were far beyond the medieval mind and would take some time to absorb. "Each region of the CSB is self-governing. They don't pay taxes to me. They don't tithe. I have no say in their governance beyond the advice the people ask for. I don't have to fight wars. I make more money through trade than through taxation. That's the whole point. In Avalon we call it the *peace dividend*." He actually wasn't sure he was using the term correctly, but it sounded good to him.

And maybe to Philippe, because he was silent for a long while. Or not, since his only reply was to tell David his next move in their game of chess, as if they hadn't just debated the merits of a free market. "Checkmate. I win."

Fine. Don't answer. David had long since decided it was worth the effort to be patient—and to lose a game of chess every now and then. It boggled the mind that anyone could ever think physically going to war was the way to build an empire. He had spent years persuading the members of the CSB that it was far better to war over a board game than over land. Two months ago, he'd said as much to a billion Avalonians all at once. Today, it was just one medieval king he was trying to convince.

And tomorrow? David smiled to himself as he closed the connection to Paris. War changed lines on a map. *Ideas* changed people forever.

David was playing the long game.

And not just on a chessboard with the King of France.

Thank you so much for reading *Renegades in Time!*
It's readers like you who make my job the best in the world.

Acknowledgments

First and foremost, I'd like to thank my lovely readers for encouraging me to continue the *After Cilmeri* series. I have always been passionate about these books, and it's wonderful to be able to share my stories with readers who love them too. Thank you also to all my editors, proof-readers, and beta readers. I am grateful for all the ways each and every one of you make the book better.

Thank you to my husband, without whose love and support I would never have tried to make a living as a writer, and thank to my family who has been nothing but encouraging of my writing, despite the fact that I spend half my life in medieval Wales. I couldn't do this without you.

About the Author

With over two million books sold to date, Sarah Woodbury is the author of more than fifty novels, all set in medieval Wales. Although an anthropologist by training, and then a full-time homeschooling mom for twenty years, she began writing fiction when the stories in her head overflowed and demanded that she let them out. While her ancestry is Welsh, she only visited Wales for the first time at university. She has been in love with the country, language, and people ever since. She even convinced her husband to give all four of their children Welsh names. She makes her home in Oregon.

www.sarahwoodbury.com